THE LUMINARIES

STATIC

S.K. ANTHONY

BOOK TWO

Copyright © 2015 by S.K. Anthony
Cover Design: http://www.maeidesign.com
Copy editing by Lynda Dietz at Easy Reader Editing
Proofreading by Lynda Dietz
Proofreading by Joyce M. Joyce
Book interior design by JT Formatting

www.**skanthony**.com
First Edition: September 2015

Library of Congress Cataloging-in-Publication Data

Anthony, S.K..
    Static (The Luminaries) / S.K. Anthony – 1st ed

ISBN-13: 978-1516946457
ISBN-10: 1516946456

1. Static (The Luminaries) —Fiction. 2. Fiction—Fantasy
3. Fiction—Urban Fantasy

For you, *Brenna!*
There. Now you have to read the whole book
because it's dedicated to *you*.

Always follow your
heart. It knows the
way! :)

Love,
SR Anthony

←⌐THE LUMINARY
└→ORGANIZATION

██████████ Street
Long Island City, NY 11101

Dear ██████████,

I'd like to officially welcome you into The Luminary Organization.

For your protection and ours, names and locations have been blocked. In the event this falls in the hands of the rebellion or the government, your identity will be safe.

As previously discussed, here are some key points to acknowledge and remember:

- You are a Luminary. Your DNA was genetically altered while in the womb and consequently you are now gifted with supernatural powers.
- You may not disclose who or what we are with anyone outside of the Org [The Luminary Organization].
- You will be hypnotized in order to keep all confidential information protected. With or without your consent.
- If you are found to be a traitor, you will be stripped of your memories. Any and all criminal

i

activities on your part will be punishable by law accordingly.

A detailed agreement will be signed in person (with names included) on your start date. The original copy will be filed in a secure location. Please bring this letter with you so we can ensure its destruction.

On behalf of The Luminary Organization and The United States government, I thank you for choosing to use your superpowers to help protect our innocents and keep our streets safe.

Any questions or concerns, you know how to reach me.

Sincerely,

Derek Lake
President of The Luminary Organization

CHAPTER ONE

IT BEGAN.

I took a deep breath as the walls around me turned into rubber bands. They stretched and elongated outward, causing the world to shimmer as if strung with thousands of strands of silver Christmas tinsel. Before I could exhale, they snapped and came back to me in full force. I felt nothing compared to the amount of space I'd just bent. One second I stood in my office; the next, I walked down a street in Manhattan.

Oh, the experience of teleporting. It could be dizzying, but fun.

I made my way into a murky building. The haze rose from the floors as the crowd of people pushed past me from all directions. The intoxicating scent of sweat, alcohol, and pheromones hit me as the deejay pumped the music up.

"Hey, you made it!"

I turned to look at Ryan. "This is where you think I'll

have the time of my life?"

"Are you blind?" she asked, smiling. "Look at all the girls; hit them with a little Kevin dust and they are yours. Take your pick."

"I don't need girls to . . . okay, that one is . . . *hmm*." I slanted my head sideways to follow the waitress in the skimpy outfit walking toward the bar. I pulled off my beanie hat and shoved it in my back pocket. I didn't care about the black mess on my head which was in need of a cut; I hoped the girls would focus on my smile and hazel eyes. That usually did the trick, even in bad lighting like this.

"See? I told you." Ryan smirked. "Oh, here—I got you a beer."

I took the can from her and went right in for a sip.

"Thanks, but I still don't think celebrating my birthday should involve me getting laid while you hang around alone. Unless . . ."—my eyes narrowed—"are you hooking up too?"

"Me? Please, I don't do idiots. This club is filled with idiots." She rolled her eyes.

"Which would include us."

"Well, *you*, maybe." Ryan laughed while looking through the crowd. "But as your best friend I have to say I'm disappointed if you think I brought you here only for girls."

Ryan walked away and motioned for me to follow.

"So what are we doing here?" I asked.

"Well, we're in a club. We might as well bust a

move or two." The baby blue in Ryan's eyes sparkled in the light. "And I'm not talking about the dancing kind. Uh . . . hang on."

I watched as Ryan walked up to a guy sitting alone by the bar. The guy reached into his pocket, gave her a piece of paper, and pointed to their left. I followed his finger and saw a blue door behind the deejay booth.

I walked straight to it and waited for Ryan to catch up with me.

"Let's go." Ryan looked at the paper for the code and entered it on the keypad that unlocked the door for us.

I shook my head. "You know I could have just—"

"Teleported us in here. Yeah, yeah . . . whatever. I'm the one running the show tonight so you'd better do things my way."

Ryan walked in front of me as I threw out my empty beer can in the bin right outside the door. The lighting was minimal but it was enough to follow Ryan's ass as she led the way. "Are we following a lead or something?" I asked as we walked down the tight corridor. We stopped at the end where three different doors greeted us.

"Yep."

"For?"

Ryan gave me a wink and placed her hand on the door directly in front of us. "This one is empty." She then formed a "T" with her body as she reached out both hands to the doors on either side of her, putting her sensing gifts to good use. She beamed and turned to the door on her right. "Ready?"

"Always." I pushed the door open, and raised my right hand. I was ready to stop any bullets that might be coming our way, but all I found was darkness. "What is this?" I asked.

"Not sure yet," she said, and turned the lights on.

I scanned the room. It seemed like a hangout lounge with two large red sofas, a couple tables with nothing on them, and a vending machine. In front of the vending machine we found a man chained to a chair. His arms were pulled straight down, and were tied around his legs individually—forcing him to practically kiss his own knees. All I could manage to say was, "Uh-huh."

The man's head spun as much as his restraints allowed him. He gave me a slight sneer. "You!"

"Hello, Simon. Haven't seen you since you left the Org," I said, recognizing the scrawny-looking man.

"I'm heavily guarded, boy. I'd watch my back if I were you." His body trembled with a nervous twitch.

"That's funny. I didn't see any guards out there. And to be honest I don't think you're capable of trying any of your laser tricks without leaving yourself legless." If memory served me right, his laser beams were as deadly as my brother's. They were able to fire the laser from the palm of their hands and cut into anything or anyone.

"You think so?" he asked right as two guys came from behind us and closed the door.

"Well, hello, boys!" Ryan said, as we both studied the new arrivals.

They were as different as a rainy and a sunny day.

Where one appeared to be in his late teens, tall, and clearly enjoyed a few burgers for breakfast, the other seemed to be in his sixties, short, and anorexic.

"Let's get this over with," the young one said.

The older one nodded as he raised his finger and shot a fireball at Ryan. He was clearly focused on an all-business transaction.

Ryan jumped on top of Simon to avoid the fireball, causing him to scream. While I doubted Ryan's weight could have harmed him, I'm pretty sure her heel did some damage to poor ol' Simon's back. Her jumps were Olympic worthy. She may not have offensive Luminary powers in a fight, but she was a damn good fighter.

Another fireball was thrown her way, and I watched as she dropped to the floor in time. The fireball hit the vending machine and the sound of glass exploding surrounded the room. I went after the bigger guy instead of enjoying the show. The rebels, as they called themselves, sure had a way of going after the Luminaries with their fighting. This particular dummy enjoyed fighting with a big-ass knife.

"Aww, a baby machete. Adorable!" I teased.

He pulled it from his holster and swung at me. I teleported behind him and when he turned I punched his ugly face. He fell but attempted right away to slice my legs off. This I didn't approve of, so I teleported his knife into my hands and held it at his neck as his eyes threatened to jump out of their sockets.

I stooped to his level. "You look shocked! Have you

never encountered a teleporter before?" I didn't give him a chance to answer. I noticed his pupils starting to enlarge and there was no way I'd let him hypnotize me. I grabbed his head and slammed it into the floor hard enough to knock him out.

I turned to see the other guy fighting with Ryan. I'd missed most of what happened, but he sported a bloody nose that made me proud to call her my trainee. I jumped backward and grabbed Simon's chair; the poor guy had been missing out on the fun. I swung him to my left and knocked down fireball-guy.

"Two men, one chair. Boom!" I grinned.

"Really, Kevin?" Ryan asked, annoyed.

"Oh, come on!"

"Just stick to your own guys, and let me have mine. I had him!" She went to the two men on the floor to secure them. I picked up my guy, gave Derek a call, and teleported everyone to the Org.

PAPERWORK WAS DONE, the men were imprisoned, and we were free for the rest of the night. We walked down the stairs to the first floor, which led to the entrance to our parking lot. Ryan had left her car there before being dropped off at the club by Andrew—a sort-of-teleporter—who was nowhere as cool as me 'cause he needed a portal to take people to places.

We didn't have a basement. Instead, we had a whole other Org underground as backup in case we ever had to hide in plain sight. The big boss felt it was more inconspicuous to stay in the same spot—we had used it once before when we thought Annie was in danger from Nick, until we realized he wasn't the real problem—but now we were moved back up to a newly remodeled interior.

Our building was a decent size and it was divided into three large levels. The first floor was split into the gym, cafeteria, and holding cells. The second floor was considered the main floor, and was where most of our offices and cubicles were located. The top level had a few offices for the president of the Org, Derek Lake; his co-runners—my other bosses, Nick and Annie; the small infirmary; and the conference area, which was the biggest room we had. It was perfect for when Derek gave us those special speeches he called meetings. And for close to sixty active Luminaries, we definitely could use the big space.

"I told you it would be fun." Ryan smiled. One of those rare smiles of hers where she didn't hide her teeth. She was very self-conscious about her crooked tooth. Her top right canine had a little twist to it that I found cute and different. Of course, I could never tell her that without being on the receiving end of a flawless eye roll, but whatever.

She'd already wiped off her red lipstick and changed into her usual neutral colors. Her loose blue jeans and gray turtleneck peeked through the knee-length coat as she buttoned it up. Her silky raven hair was still in her signature hairstyle: a bun. So it gave her no trouble when we each pulled out our black beanie hats from our pockets and put them on. I'd gotten us a matching pair a couple years ago for Christmas, and we practically lived in them.

"So." Ryan showed me her watch; it was past midnight. "February 20th is gone officially now. I hope you had a happy birthday! Not bad for a Friday night, huh?" she asked, and gave me a hug.

"That was pretty cool, Ry, but I wouldn't say it was the night of my life."

"Well, you captured some rebels in less than an hour and now you have the rest of the night to go . . . I don't know"—she shrugged—"find yourself some babe to wake up next to after you teach her some loving."

"Dude, I can't complain. This was fun! But don't get it twisted, I'll be teaching sex as a second language, no love in my vocabulary," I said and gave her a fist bump. "I'll catch you later."

"Yeah, what was I thinking?" She gave me one of her cute little snorts and waved good-bye.

CHAPTER TWO

I ROLLED OFF an uncomfortable bed that was definitely not mine. The girl I'd spent the night with snored softly. Her fiery hair spilled across the pillow where her face was half buried. I tried to keep quiet as I looked for my clothes.

Last night was such a blur I hadn't realized she was a redhead until now. After my quick adventure with Ry, I'd met up with our other buddy, Chris, at a local hookah bar and picked up a girl. She'd looked dark-haired like almost all other women there. I swear, those neon lights—in combination with alcohol—were sure made to deceive a man. Not that she wasn't pretty or anything, but she wasn't my usual type.

I retrieved my shoes and teleported home. After taking a shower, I popped to my building's garage straight into my new ride, and drove over to visit Nick, Annie, and the baby. The last time I'd shown up less than presentable, I never heard the end of it from Annie. She swore up and down she could smell girl-stench on me. I told her how ridiculous she sounded, but she insisted pregnancy gave her high sensitivity to smells.

I got there around two thirty, which was right on time since little Jack had just woken up from a nap. I really wished I could be on his nap schedule—sleeping every few hours and waking up for just the basic necessities of life . . . *ahh, the life of a baby!* He was only five months old but he seemed to drain his parents of energy. *Pfft*, and they hadn't been sure if he would be born with any powers since he wasn't genetically altered in the womb, like the rest of us. But clearly they were losing their minds. After all, it took real talent to drain Ms. Kinetic of her never-ending power source. She'd done little more than yawn the past forty minutes or so since I got there.

"What's with him this time?" I heard Annie ask Nick as they joined me in the living room. She cocked her head sideways, and studied me as if I was some strange creature sitting on her couch. She was dressed in her usual mommy getup: black yoga pants and one of Nick's old sweaters.

He shrugged, looking at me. "I don't know. Hung over, I think."

"I'm right here, guys. I can hear you," I said, staring at the drool stain on Nick's white T-shirt.

"Well, you look like you're in a trance," Annie said. She watched me with those almond-colored eyes of hers that seemed to intensify with each passing second.

"Tired, annoyed, headache, hungry, take your pick."
I rubbed the back of my neck. "How long does pasta take
to make, anyway?"

"If you want, you can cook it yourself," Annie said,
and got up to check on the food. She walked past the
dining room table, which was between the living room
and her kitchen. Annie and Nick enjoyed entertaining so
they had a great open concept design. It wasn't a huge
space but it was cozy with beige walls and dark furniture
in contrast. Right now they had a playpen, a swing, a
bouncy chair, and several toys scattered everywhere as
new additions to their décor.

I waited until she was out of earshot. "You'd think
she was making a gourmet meal every time she starts
boiling water, the way she acts."

Nick turned to me. "Tell her that and I'll take the
baby away from you."

"No, but seriously, bro, she gets all 'I'm cooking,
guys, come on over' like we don't all know it's going to
be some sauce and her pasta—and it's not always al
dente, either."

"Why are you messing with Annie? I never hear you
complain when you are chowing down her non-al dente
food."

"Nah, come on. It's cute, look at her." We both
turned to watch Annie drain her pasta and give us a big
smile. Her dark caramel hair sat in a mess on top of her
head. "She is so happy and adorable; why aren't all
women like that?"

11

"She is mine."

"We'll see," I said, teasing Nick.

"So are you going anywhere for the rest of the weekend?"

"Nah, I'll just hang around. This little dude needs his uncle. All this cooing you people give him can't be good for his manhood. You cool with me spending the night?"

"Yep." He nodded, and asked, "You know Chris has me keeping an eye on you, right? The minute you do your own cooing with the baby, he said you lose your bet."

I looked at Jack. "Like I would stoop so low. No worries, little bro, I got your back. I'll talk to you straight, and make no funny faces so when you grow up you'll always recognize me. I'm the cool one."

"Yeah, the cool one." Nick yawned. "Is that what you're teaching my son?"

I held Jack's hand up and gave him a high five. "Damn straight. Hey, is Jenny coming over later?"

"No, I told you already we're not throwing you a party. You're twenty-three now, not a kid. All you get is cake."

"Cake is all I need. Cake should have its own food group, I say."

Nick ignored me. "What do you want with Jenny?"

"I wanted to find out if the boss was still upset with me."

He moved to the edge of his seat, raising an eyebrow. "What'd you do this time?"

"Nothing. It's stupid." I shrugged.

"I doubt that."

I took Jack to his playpen and gave him some toys before returning to the couch. I turned to Nick. *Here we go . . .* "I might have teleported in front of an elderly couple. So what?"

"Kevin!"

"What? They're old anyway. They hardly noticed so I didn't *have* to report it. Chris could have just hypnotized them to forget. It should mean something to Derek that I was taking responsibility for my actions by letting him know about it."

"You can't keep acting like this, Kevin. The only reason he lets you lead your team—"

"Is because you're my brother, yeah yeah. Are you going to preach now? Am I disgracing the family name?"

"Yes, you are."

"Lucky for you we don't actually share the same last name, then." I stood up. "I'll just get going."

"Stay. That's not—"

"—what it's about, I know. Save the talk this time. I'll be careful, yada yada yada." I shoved my hands in my pockets, knowing I was in the wrong. "But if I wasn't hungry I'd be leaving. No need to hurt Annie's feelings. She'd think it was her food."

"I wish you took things more seriously, Kev."

"I will." One look at the disappointment on Nick's face, and I added with a smile, "I promise. I will. This time for real. Look, I'm older and wiser now."

"I'll hold you to it." Nick massaged his temples. "So

tell me about last night. Was it fun?"

"I don't know. I thought it was . . . but thinking back, it was too easy." I frowned. "I think that's why I'm in a bad mood."

"Didn't Ryan set everything up so it was a clean break-in?" Nick asked.

"Yes, she did all the ground work getting the information. She found Simon's location, schedule, and it was great, but I don't know . . . he was already captured. Ryan said she thought he'd just be on a job and we'd bust him, but the rebels had him tied up and in custody. They even tried to stop us from taking him."

Nick's brows creased. "So he was on their radar, too."

I nodded. "I know we needed to be the ones to capture Simon after that robbery at gun point—heaven forbid he lasers out the entire NYPD—but I didn't think the rebels would care. They're the ones creating trouble everywhere. I was surprised to find him tied up."

Nick shrugged. "He's a thug and an addict. Too unreliable if offered drugs. If he's done work for them they wouldn't want him to talk. They were probably going to kill him. It's what they do."

"Probably," I agreed.

A FEW YEARS ago when we discovered what a corrupt system we'd all grown up in at the Org, the boss, Derek Lake, decided he wouldn't use Luminaries the way his father—the former boss—had. Instead, he found all who had been altered and explained to them what The Luminary Organization was about. If they wanted to join us and help the government bring down criminals, they were welcomed. Those who didn't want to join were free to go—no memory modification or power-stripping serum. All Derek asked was for them to contact us if they displayed any special abilities, so we could either train them or weaken it.

Unfortunately, some of those who developed their powers naturally took it upon themselves to join a rebellion group. The rebels used their abilities for personal gain and to try to take us out. Talk about losing some credibility with the government, which didn't help after learning what our former president was up to. They lost trust in all Luminaries. They wanted to shut us down, but realized they needed us to stop the rebel troublemakers.

When we weren't stopping them, though, we worked for the government and helped stop all types of criminals, so the old agreement continued. Derek worked particularly close with the FBI. He had a couple agents there who handled all communication. But we also had some NYPD contacts who took care of civilian arrests and other simpler cases we helped with. They were aware we worked for higher-up ranks in the government and never questioned our involvement. This was handy, especially for those cases with unique situations that required them to cover up for us.

I CHANGED JACK'S diaper early on Sunday morning and let his tired parents sleep in. After giving him his bottle, he went back to la-la-land. I then made coffee and sat outside drinking it while texting Ryan. Our training session had been canceled because Derek wanted to see us at the Org at ten in the morning.

I heard a noise inside and went back through the kitchen door to find my tiny sister-in-law trying to reach coffee mugs from the cabinet above her. She was getting on a small step I'd given her years ago as a present.

"Why do you insist on keeping things so high up when your head is hardly past the counter?" I asked as I reached around her to get the mug and set it down. I should have known better. As soon as I did that, her elbow connected with my rib and had me wincing.

"Stop making fun of me or I'll break a bone next time," Annie said.

"But you are perfect for it, Anniewee. You're already fun-sized," I said, grabbing a cup for her.

"Whatever. It's up there because it's Nick's job. Obviously."

"Go sit down, I'll mix your cup. Where is he?"

"Sleeping. It was his turn for night duty."

"Technically you can fix that by hitting him with some energy." I personally loved when she transferred her energy to me. It was perfect for those all-nighters I was so fond of.

Annie had this ongoing Kinetic energy that could give the rest of us an extra boost to our own powers. It could also give me a certain oomph that kept me energized enough to last me a week or so. Sadly, I no longer got the chance to enjoy the benefits of her powers. I enjoyed Ryan's instead.

I met Ryan in my last year in training. She's a sensor and an amplifier. As a sensor, she could tell Luminaries apart from ordinary people, and because she was in tune with other people's emotions she could tell if they were lying. As an amplifier, she couldn't do much for herself, but she helped expand everyone else's powers, times five.

With Annie, it was different: our energies would last a while and we'd keep going. But with Ryan, it was in the moment. She was a drug to us all. The strange thing was that she and Annie couldn't do anything for each other. They were too evenly powerful in an unbalanced way. It didn't matter, though; they never went on assignments together.

Annie and Nick were now partners with Derek, and they helped run the Org. But their idea of managing was turning Derek down whenever he brought up something they didn't agree with. Before they had the baby, they went on assignments frequently and left Derek to run his own show. Adrenaline junkies was what they were.

I looked at her. "I'm telling you, Annie. You two should stop trying to deal with a baby like normal people."

"No," she said, taking a sip while the cup was still in my hand.

"Well that's stupid; you are Luminaries. Take advantage." I put my empty cup in the sink and smiled. "Speaking of, would you be a doll and charge up my new babe for me?"

She crinkled her nose. "That doesn't sound like something I want to do."

"Relax. As a birthday present to myself, I turned in my Prius for a *Tesla S* . . . *S* for sexy hybrid car. I can't believe I forgot to show you guys. She's like my bride, beautiful in white."

"You and your hybrids. You could have just plugged in your car the whole time you were here. There's a reason you installed a charge port in my garage."

"Come on! Please?"

"If you want to be so environmental you should just teleport everywhere. You know, take advantage of being a Luminary yourself, instead of using me for your shenanigans."

"First, Ryan is the environmental one. I would never hear the end of her yapping away if I didn't get hybrids. Second, I have to keep up appearances that I'm normal for those who don't know our secrets. How would you explain to your nosy neighbors why I was sitting outside if I didn't walk or drive here?"

"Stop going outside where they can see you."

I shook my head. "But I needed fresh air."

"Uh huh, in February?" She raised her eyebrow. "Like I don't know you were checking out their daughter?"

"Look at me. I run on heat. February air does nothing to me. And she just happened to be out there wiping snow off her car, that's all. I even helped."

"How, exactly?" Annie asked, putting both hands on her hips.

"When she wasn't looking, a big chunk suddenly slid off. It was discreet, I promise."

She sighed. "Fine, but this is the last time I charge it. And only because I'm curious to see your new car. Stop smiling."

"You know your special touch will make it last for double the time, right? Your touch, Annie, is the key." I ducked right on time to avoid her punch.

Footsteps behind me alerted me that Nick was up. "My wife's touch is the key to what now? Keep flirting with her and I'll make sure you're unable to wake up next to girls for at least a month."

"Whoa, hey, hey. No harm done," I said, then teleported next to Annie to give her a kiss on the cheek.

"Dunno what's the use of being a teleporter if you're going to be driving around," Nick said.

"I love to drive."

"You love to speed."

"What's the difference?" I asked him.

"Stop it, you two. Let's go charge your car up," Annie said, pulling me toward the front door.

I ARRIVED AT the Org with ten minutes to spare and met Ryan halfway to Derek's office. She was busy trying to pin a strand of her jet-black hair that dared break loose from its place as she walked.

"Hey, we match!" I said, pointing to our black combat boots.

She smiled. "If that's the case, then we always match."

"True." I pulled on her huge beige sweater. "Except for these. My tops need to be tighter."

"Of course. Why would you ever leave your house without showcasing your muscles?"

"I work hard for these babies," I said, flexing.

She rolled her eyes. "So are the Logans coming back to work soon?"

"I don't know; they seem happy at home with the baby. But I can tell by the way Annie elbowed me that she misses kicking ass." I shook my head. "She's too fast to try to hit me these days, so I hope for the sake of my good looks they return to work soon."

"Ugh. Only a cute guy can get away with saying shit like that."

"Damn right, but take it from me: it can be a blessing and a burden to be hot." I grinned.

"Is it? I'll have to ask Chris," she said.

"Now you're being insensitive to my feelings, Ry."

"You have feelings, Mr. I-don't-care-about-love?" I laughed. "Nah, I'm too awesome for that."

"Self-proclamations of being awesome don't make it so, you know." She laughed. "Anyway, I think I'll go visit tonight."

I frowned. "Who? Chris?"

"Annie and her boys."

"Don't piss her off. She's not above hurting girls and she's been holding back for too long," I warned Ryan.

"Oh, before I forget, I got you this." She gave me a box.

"I told you not to—"

"I know. I didn't spend any money on you, I promise."

I looked at the neat and intricately wrapped small box. "How did you fold this tiny piece of paper into a triangle design? Is there a trick to not rip it?"

"Don't worry about the wrap, it's just paper."

"Okay, but don't forget you said that." I opened it and saw a small black flashlight on a keychain. "Oh, cool. Thanks, Ry! Wait, isn't this yours?"

She showed me a blue one in between her keys. "I got myself a new one."

I pulled my keys out and attached it next to my penknife. I liked having these little gadgets and she knew it. "That's cheating."

"Nope. I needed a new flashlight so you get my used one. It's not cheating if I didn't actually buy you something. You'll need to get new batteries, though."

"I shouldn't be surprised you found a way around my wish. Now I won't bother you for yours." I gave her shoulder a light punch as we reached Derek's office.

I knocked and jumped when Jenny opened it at the same time.

"Hey guys," she said. "Kevin, no jokes. He is in a mood."

"So go give your husband a good make-out session before we go in, Jen." I backed away from the look she gave me, but still couldn't help myself. "Go on, we'll wait."

"Don't make him wait!" Jen said, scolding me.

We walked in to find Derek having a heated discussion over the phone. Sitting across from him was Special Agent Robert Pine from the FBI. Ryan and I stopped by the door, unsure if we were to proceed or back out. Derek looked at us and motioned for us to sit.

Pine got up and gave us a nod while Derek was still on the phone. He offered his chair to Ryan and pulled another one from the side, then sat next to me, putting me in the middle. He focused on Derek again, while rubbing his chin. If anyone could pull off a scruffy beard, it was this guy. He looked intimidating and serious, but was actually quite friendly. Combine that with looking like he could be Gerard Butler's brother, and we had ourselves a winner. The women were always happy when he came around, as was proven by Ryan not taking her eyes off him. I turned to look at Derek standing on the other side of his large mahogany desk. His free hand was in a tight fist.

". . . Perfectly clear. But I'll have you know this is a big mistake . . . no, well . . ." He took a deep breath. "I understand. Yes, consider it done," Derek said, slamming the phone down.

"I had the same reaction when I found out," Pine said.

Ryan and I remained quiet. Derek placed both hands on his desk, leaning forward, and looked at Pine. "Do you know who's pulling the strings on this?"

"No," Pine said. "But I'm sure there's good reason." "If they don't want our help with Simon, they can get harmed. He's dangerous."

"I agree." Pine nodded. "The key, I believe, is in finding out who their prisoners are. I'll see what I can find out on my end."

"Good. I appreciate that," Derek said.

"I'll touch base soon." Pine got up. "Ryan, Kevin, stay out of trouble."

AFTER HE LEFT, I asked Derek, "What's up, boss?"

"We have to release Simon into the FBI's custody. And none of us are allowed to assist. If he frees himself he can harm too many of them."

"What? Why?" Ryan frowned.

"Maybe if you did your job right we wouldn't be in this situation. Did it occur to you two to sweep the whole building?" he asked, pacing back and forth behind his desk.

"No," Ryan said. "I made sure there were no cameras and I only sensed those we brought back. The other rooms in the back were empty."

"What about the attic, the basement, their general office, the restrooms, everywhere else?" Derek asked.

"No, but Kevin had nothing to do with it. I was the one running point last night."

"And why is that, Ryan? Have I ever given you orders to lead on a mission?"

"No," Ryan answered, hanging her head.

"Exactly. Because you're not ready."

"Don't be a dick, Derek." I stood up.

Ryan pulled my arm down and said, "Sit down."

"Yes, sit down, Pierce, and show some respect." He took his own seat, too. "Want to tell me what went wrong?"

I hated when he called me by my last name. "Well, first I shouldn't have taken it upon myself to train Ry to—"

"Skip that part. You already know you messed up there."

My shoulders slumped. "Why don't you just tell me?"

"You think you're too good to follow the rules. You think being responsible is above you. You rush your missions . . ." He took a deep breath. "You know better. Before you go on a job and before you leave, unless there's danger, make sure to clear your surroundings."

"It was a club. What did you exp—"

"Yes, Kevin. And did either of you consider the consequences of those innocent bystanders if something had gone wrong? This group doesn't care who they hurt. To escape you, they would kill anyone standing in their way."

"Okay," I said, "that one is my bad, but luckily—"

"Luckily? You realize you haven't yet asked why I'm so mad."

"There's more?" I asked. "Okay, well I guess there's more. What am I missing?"

"The rebels have three civilians as prisoners with them. I don't have the details, but they seem to be important enough that my hand is being forced. We must agree to send Simon with Pine and allow them to do the interrogation in private. What I do know is up until last night, they were being held at the club. And had you followed all protocols you would have been able to bring them in to safety. Instead it's now up to Pine and his people."

"Shit." I ran my hand through my hair. "When Pine mentioned prisoners, I assumed he was talking about the ones we just brought in."

"No, but the pressure is on. We need to finish dealing with the rebels now that the government thinks they can handle them on their own. And they're starting with Simon; they have no idea they're in over their heads."

"Fine, they can have him. But let me knock him around a bit first and see if we can get some information. Ry and I will fix this mistake."

He shook his head. "No. You are not to harm or talk to him. I had Chris modify his memory so he won't share any information about the Org with anyone, in case they attempt that. I was warned against hypnotizing Simon not to use his powers against them, though; that I don't understand."

"Maybe they want to study him," Ryan said.

"That's my concern as well. They're aware of what could happen if they don't take the right precautions. This will not be good."

"So what can we do?" I asked.

"Give them what they want and hope for the best," Derek answered. "I want you both to come to me first next time you have any bright ideas about our missions. Ryan, you're good, but you're not ready."

"I understand," she said.

"Kevin, keep it up and you're going back to basic training."

I frowned. "Hell, no! That's demoralizing. They look up to me there."

"Then I suggest you take more responsibility for your actions. You're free to go."

CHAPTER THREE

C HRIS AND RYAN were part of my team. When I first joined the Org, I ran into a unique situation. Derek had to pull me out of training just three weeks in and send me on the field with Annie and Nick. When that nightmare was over, I went back to the training center for a year so I could undergo the same groundwork as everyone else. But with my experience, and with Nick taking responsibility for me, I convinced Derek he could use me on the field. I went out on many missions with several of our older agents and learned hands-on.

After I proved myself, he assigned my best buddy, Ryan, to me so I could have my own team—and so I could help her perfect her martial arts skills. She needed this training since she was an amplifier and had no extra offensive abilities, although these days she could break a rib with one jab. Shortly after that, Chris, a hypnotizer— and a decent fighter—joined us and we've been at it for close to two years as a team.

I sent Chris a text and asked him to meet us by the cells. He stood by the entrance rubbing a hand over his short hair. He turned to look at us. His brown eyes, several shades darker than his tanned skin, stared intently when he said, "I'm surprised to see you in one piece, Kev."

I opened my mouth to speak, but Ryan beat me to it. "It wasn't his fault."

"Yes, it was, Ry," I said. "I know you're more than capable of handling the situation if necessary, but I should have paid more attention. Guided you better. I was just too eager to let you take charge."

"No excuses on my part." She shook her head. "I've been on missions before. Heck, I'm the one who keeps you organized and makes sure we execute the plans properly. I was so excited to surprise you with this one being ready that I didn't think to make my to-do list to check off."

"You and your lists." I rolled my eyes. "Look, this was your first time leading. Excitement and nerves get in the way. It won't happen again."

"Yeah." She pouted like a sad baby. "Sorry I got you in trouble, though."

I shrugged. "I'm always in trouble. Besides, it was fun to kick those rebels' butts."

Ryan walked a few steps ahead of us and unlocked the gates. Simon's hands were chained to his sides, making him look like a sitting worm. I pulled him up to stand. "Jeez, who wrapped you up so many times?"

"Your ma," he answered, his head twitching as he looked at me.

"You and I are going to have a little chat," I said.

"Ain't telling you shit," Simon said with a splash of saliva.

"We'll see." I turned to Chris. "Be on the lookout and when I'm done you can make him forget this conversation ever happened."

"On it," Chris said and went closer to the stairs.

Ryan stood behind Simon and waited.

"So, Simon," I said, "what were you doing at that club and why were you tied up?"

"Score me some 'H' and I'll tell you what you want."

I lifted him up and slammed his back against the wall. "Listen, you piece of shit, I don't have time for games. What were you doing there and who are you working for?"

He turned to look at Ryan, and said, "Let me have this piece of ass, then, and I'll tell you."

Ryan gagged and I hit him in the gut. He was so frail I didn't have to give him a full-blown punch. "Talk."

Still gasping for breath, he said, "I don't work for no one!"

"What were you doing at the club?"

"Scoring some goods, that's all. Listen, listen," he said, his body still trembling. "Just one hit and I'm sure I'll remember more. Know what I mean?"

I teleported his leather jacket off him and began searching the pockets. He was wearing a dirty T-shirt under it, so I could see the disgusting bruises from the needles on his arms. I searched his pockets and pulled out a few pieces of paper along with car keys. "Are you working for the rebels? Who gives you orders? I need the phone number."

"I'm a free man. I don't work for no one!"

"You have receipts here. If you didn't work for someone you wouldn't have a need to keep these. Who's paying your expenses?"

"I ain't got no expenses."

Blood splattered on his rotted teeth as I punched his jaw. "Talk."

"Okay, okay. How 'bout some water? Then I can talk. I'll tell you where they have the women."

I was about to punch him again when Ryan grabbed my hand. "I'll go bring him the water. We need him alive for answers AND with no bruises for the FBI."

She was right; at least now we knew the prisoners were females. We were getting somewhere. "Tell me what I need to know."

"I'll make you a deal instead," Simon said.

"THIS IS NOT a good idea, Kevin," Ryan said. "Derek told us not to make any moves without talking to him."

"We can fix our mistake and free some innocents. He'll be happy when they're safe. Relax."

She tapped her right foot incessantly. "I don't trust him."

"I hypnotized him. Chill. We're okay," Chris said, grabbing Simon. "He told us all he knows, and I made sure he won't talk about us to anyone. Not even Derek will find out."

"Yes, but still . . . I don't know," she insisted.

I put my hand on Chris's back and turned to Ryan. "Please just trust me, okay? I can't do this without you."

"Fine," she said and held my hand.

A cool wave went through my skin as she amplified my teleporting. This allowed me to take everyone back to the club seamlessly. She'd never know how much I appreciated this—without her amplifying powers I'd have to teleport everyone individually so I didn't lose too much of my strength.

We followed Simon through a secret door in the office at the club and Ryan looked around. "There is no one here," she said.

"No. No, I swear this is where they kept the women." Simon switched the light on. He was rocking back and forth in the corner next to the door. "Look around, look around. There has to be something."

The room was small and filled with repugnant wet dog smell. There were a few chairs and a ripped up

31

blanket on the floor. I think it had been white at some point. I scrunched up my nose and let out a deep breath. Simon had assured us the women would be there. *Dammit.* I needed this to go down as fast as possible. If Derek found out I broke Simon out of there before we returned with the women, hell would break loose.

After a few minutes, Ryan held out her hand. "I sense someone. Let's leave this one here and we'll come back for him."

Before we opened the door, a few rebels dashed into the room, knocking Simon over. He tumbled down and fell next to my feet. I widened my stance and got ready to fight.

"I would do as I'm told if I were you," said a man with a bushy mustache. He held a gun to Chris's head.

I was trying to calculate my best move when a blonde woman grabbed my hand to handcuff me. I chose to play it out and allowed her to finish her task. 'Stache-dude gave me a smirk. Or at least that's what I think he tried to do under that bush.

"Kill him," she said pointing to Simon.

"No, no, no! Wait, I brought them to you. I'm on your side. I'm on your side," Simon begged.

"Let him come," 'Stashe-dude said.

The woman shrugged before using a chain to connect our three handcuffs in front of us and took us to a van out back. They put blindfolds on our eyes and patted down our bodies. Our cell phones—which were the only items we carried—were taken away. Of course they were burner phones; no way we would go on a mission like this and keep our real babies on us. Satisfied with their search, they shoved us into the van. I felt a tug and heard the latches of seatbelts clicking. The engine roared and off we went.

THE BLINDFOLD SOMEHOW intensified the gasoline stench in the van, and combined with the bumps and my hands tied, nausea threatened to hit. It was a little overwhelming but I tried to focus on how long a drive this was. The club was uptown and if I guessed correctly they'd take us out to one of the lovely boroughs of New York. Our captors were whispering to each other but no matter how hard I tried, I couldn't make out one word. Based on the voices though, I knew there were four males keeping the blonde's company. One of them was Simon.

I leaned in to my right and found the familiar scent of coconut shampoo—a miracle really, given how tight Ryan keeps her hair in that bun all the time. She felt me stirring and moved herself closer to Chris. I then rested my head on her shoulder and felt her amplifying Chris. She enhanced his mind-controlling powers, and allowed him to communicate with us unnoticed through telepathy.

"How long are we playing this out?" Chris asked in our heads.

"As long as it takes," I answered. "We'll follow this through and see if we can find out anything about their other prisoners. If we're lucky, they'll lock us up with whoever they are and we can get everyone to safety before the night is over."

"What if they know we teleported?" Chris asked.

"Hmm, I'm going to have to send you back in a few minutes. This way they'll think the teleporter is gone and they won't worry that you'll know their location," I said and yanked the chain connecting our handcuffs. I needed to reach his hand to send him back to the Org. The road was bumpy so no one paid attention to the chain's clinking sound.

Chris pulled away. "Send Ryan instead. I'll stay back so we can communicate."

"No, I still need Ryan. I can't bring the other three back to safety without her. You need to tell Derek what's going on. We'll hopefully be back with the women and Simon soon."

"Okay," he said.

"Which play are we going with, Kev?" Ryan asked.

"Hmm, we'll pull the 'Sister' card. Ready, guys?" I asked and straightened my back against the seat.

They both answered yes and I felt Ryan tugging at both our hands until the three of us touched. Thank goodness her hands were so soft or I would risk sending her instead of him. Her hand wrapped around my wrist and I grabbed the other more rugged hand and teleported him back to the Org.

"Shit! One of them just escaped," I heard one of the men say before I felt a blow at the back of my head. "You try that and the girl dies."

"You think I would be here if I could do that?"

The woman spoke this time. "Don't be a smart-ass. What are your names?"

"I'm Ryan and he is Kevin."

The woman pulled off the blindfolds, and said, "On the count of three I want the both of you to answer at the same time: What are your abilities? One, two, three!"

"Sensor and combater," I said while Ryan said, "Sensor and fighter."

"Combater?" the woman asked.

"Never heard of this one. What is it?" the man in the front passenger seat asked.

The woman was sitting next to me behind 'Stashe-dude who was driving, and Simon was sitting behind us with the other guy. I looked at Blondie. She looked young enough, early thirties probably. Short-cropped blonde hair and a no-nonsense attitude. I didn't think she and I would get along. I turned to the man who'd asked the question. He looked like the male version of her. "What's your talent? Dumbness?"

I felt another blow at the back of my head and turned around to see Simon and his new buddy showing me their guns.

Blondie's eyes focused on Simon. "You brought them to us; what's his power?"

I was already facing forward again so I couldn't see Simon, but I knew he had to be wearing a blank expression.

Blondie shook her head. "Of course you took

precautions. Why did your friend leave?" she asked me. "Let me go and I'll ask him." I smiled. I could also sense Ryan getting annoyed. Not because I shared her sensing powers, but because I knew her and knew exactly what would cause her eyes to roll like a slot machine. She's always said I lack the part of the brain that takes anything seriously. Even when I'm in a situation that— according to her—clearly demands it. Honestly, she's the one who needed to relax. No situation ever required me being serious. I can teleport us out of trouble at any given moment.

"We only need one of you alive and the girl seems like she's less trouble than you. I suggest you answer my questions."

"This one? Please. She is useless." I avoided Ryan's eyes burning into my head. "This is her first assignment and she is under my orders. You need both of us. She's good for trading and I'm the one with the information, but hurt her and my boss will kill me."

Blondie eyed me sideways. "Why would anyone want to trade her?"

"She's Derek Lake's sister."

I looked at Ryan who curled up, hiding her face. She cried out, "Why would you tell them?" I really loved how this girl could play her part well.

Blondie ignored us since 'Stache-dude had chosen that moment to slam on the brake at a stoplight. She kicked the driver's seat. "Can you try to get us there in one piece?"

"No," he answered. "Would you stop the sobbing?" He reached over and pulled Ryan's hair, which just made her squeak louder. The light changed and he let go of her to continue driving. She flashed me a look. I knew she was pissed. If there was something Ry didn't like, it was to have one hair out of place. She was as orderly and proper as they came.

"Let her cry. They'll be dead soon enough. Unless she's really Lake's sister. Then we'll have use for her."

"She looks nothing like him," the man next to Blondie said.

"They don't all look alike. What do you expect? They all have different fathers and whores for mothers."

I would have reminded her they were just like us in that regard—the only difference between them and us was that we worked for the Org and had sense of right and wrong, while they only focused on being money-hungry, stealing and killing—but I got distracted when I saw the fire burn in Ryan's eyes. She concentrated on breathing and continued to pretend she was trembling. Unlike the rest of us, her mother had actually run away when she was pregnant with her and had tried to give her a good life, at least until her mother was killed in a fire. Derek thinks his dad had something to do with her mom's death. Her body was never found.

I can't imagine how Derek felt after learning his dad wasn't the hero everyone thought he was. Of course, I can't imagine what it's like to have a father to begin with, but that must have been tough. Dr. Lake was one of the founders of the Org; he was the first Luminary that came to be. Unfortunately, the greed for power got the best of him and he began experimenting on pregnant prostitutes. The expecting mothers were injected with the Luminary formula so it would genetically alter the babies. Once we were born, they took us and spread us around in different orphanages. And when we were ready, they came to get us and offered us a job where we could use our special abilities. It was all a sham.

I was lucky my brother found me before they did, so I knew exactly what I was walking into when I joined. The good thing was that my sister-in-law, Annie Logan, took care of that asshole years ago, and the Org was now really a good place. Nick, Annie and Derek made sure of that. I came from nothing to having a family. I'm an uncle, I have an awesome sister-in-law who has the delusion of being my mother, and an older brother who looks out for me. We look a little alike; I'm a couple of inches taller than Nick, at 6'1". We both have hazel eyes and dark short hair, except he has some scars on his face.

"Hey, Blondie?" She stared at me in way of response. "What are your plans for us?"

"Interrogation. Then death."

"Sorry to burst your bubble, but we can't tell you our locations or anything else. Everyone's hypnotized to keep all information secret even if tortured."

"Yes, I'm aware. You know what, though? You talk too much." She touched my arm and the seatbelt cut into my neck as I was pitched forward. Oddly enough it wasn't painful, but my body was left buzzing from the red waves she jolted into me. I looked at the spot she touched; lucky for her, it wasn't burnt even though I felt like I had a barbecued arm. *Bitch.*

"Hmm, that's strange. Should have been enough to kill you," she said. "Never mind. I won't hold back next time, but at least you'll be quiet now that you know what awaits."

I bit my tongue and turned to look at Ryan. I gave her a small nod to let her know I was fine.

Blondie stared at me with her brows stuck in a frown position for a few minutes. "It's resistance to pain, isn't it? Your power?" She smiled smugly. "Your lack of reaction when I shocked you gave it away."

I nodded. Let her assume what she wanted. I was just glad my arm wasn't really on fire. Who would even have time to react to that?

After that, we drove in silence for another ten minutes or so before the van came to an abrupt halt. Blondie reached out and loosened our seatbelts. The two guys in the back seat pointed their guns to our heads, and one of them said, "Follow us."

Chris's handcuff was left dangling between Ry and me from when I'd set him free. Ryan caught it and held on to it so it wouldn't swing in front of her the whole way. "Your OCD is going to get you killed one of these days," I whispered.

"Shush it," she hissed.

We parked behind a small white building surrounded

by trees; most of the side fence had terrible graffiti splashed all over it. I couldn't find any signs or landmarks to pinpoint our location, but since the ride hadn't been too long, I guessed we were in Brooklyn. The wind brought the sound of zooming cars to my ears, alerting me to a nearby highway.

We went into the building through the back door and found several guards standing around, talking. "Back into positions," Blondie said.

The men went to various posts. Some went to the windows, the one who'd answered went to join the other two guards by the entrance, and the other two went to the back. We walked into the elevator and Simon stood in front of the numbers so I couldn't tell which floor we were going, I laughed.

"What's so funny?" he asked, since I was looking straight at him when I laughed.

"Nothing." I shook my head and waited. "Ah, we are on the third floor."

"How do you know? Can you see through things? Is that another power?" 'Stache-dude asked.

Everyone was staring at me. "Nah, man, relax. My special power is that I can read." I pointed to the small screen above the opened elevator doors. "Did you forget that the floor number appears there too?"

"Shit, someone block that screen in all of the elevators," he said.

Blondie said, "Idiots. Why does the floor number matter if he doesn't know where he is?"

No one said anything after that.

CHAPTER

FOUR

THEY NUDGED US constantly until we reached the end of the hallway. The place seemed like an old office space. Blondie swiped a card on the wall panel and we went into a big office. There was a middle wall that had been carelessly taken down. The ragged edges of the opening seemed dangerous but it made the gloomy room a little bigger. I peeked through the opening and saw a couple mattresses thrown on the floor. No sheets, no pillows. A door on the right corner opened to a small bathroom.

I turned my attention back to the room I'd been led into. There was a large, beige table. At the end of it, a man sat playing with his phone; he had a gun next to his bottle of water. He didn't look up.

"Sit here," 'Stache-dude said and pointed to chairs on the opposite end from where the man sat. Ryan and I did as he asked. Blondie came to us, pulled our hands backward, and handcuffed us to our individual chairs so we were unable to move too much.

We waited patiently for them to make a move. After what felt like an hour they pulled in three women to the room. Blondie sat them across the table from us with their backs to the large window. There was an older woman who looked to be in her fifties, a teenager, and another girl who I guessed to be around my age. They were handcuffed to their chairs like we were, but each had one hand free, unlike Ry and myself. I was so uncomfortable I actually resented them.

They were in rough shape. The older woman stared me down, while the teenager studied Ryan. The brunette in her twenties had her chin raised up and didn't take her eyes off Blondie.

"Leave them here so they can get to know their new friends," she said. "Two of you guard the door. That one is a trained fighter." She pointed to me. "Or so he says."

They all left, except for the man sitting at the table. He never took his eyes off his phone. After Blondie closed the door behind her, the girl turned to look at Ryan first and then me. Her gray eyes didn't blink once. "Who are you?"

"You tell me who *you* are," I said.

Her teeth clenched. "I asked first."

"Gabriella, that's enough. Forgive my daughter. Sometimes I think I wasted all my time trying to teach her manners," the woman said in a sad tone. Her brown hair had hints of gray and fell on her face in a shapeless bob. The youngest girl seemed to have the same haircut, but shared the same gray eyes as the brunette.

"Are you three related?" I asked.

The young girl nodded. "Yes. I'm Grace, this is my sister, Gabby, and this is our mom," she said, looking sideways at the older woman.

"Hi, Grace. I'm Ryan and this is my friend, Kevin. Nice to meet you, Gabriella, and . . .?" She turned to look at their mom.

"Madelyn," the mom said. "Why are you two here?"

I looked at Ryan to see if she sensed any danger from them. She didn't give me the signal, though. Instead she leaned into me and whispered, "I can't sense anything. But the young girl's wrists are too red and the older girl has some bruises on her face. It should be okay."

I nodded and turned back to the mom. "We are here to rescue you."

"Please," Gabriella said with a snort.

"Stop being so mean, Gabby."

"Grace, come on. They are handcuffed worse than we are."

"We had to get in here somehow, didn't we?" I asked her.

She lifted an eyebrow. "And getting yourself caught was part of the plan?"

"Yes, actually. We had no idea who we were supposed to help free or where you were being kept. So this was the next big plan."

"And how exactly are you getting us out of here?"

"I don't know yet. But I'd like to know who you are and what they want with you."

"We don't have to tell you anything," Gabriella said and turned her head to stare at the gun on the table. The man continued to ignore us.

"I'm Madelyn Ryder. Wife of Marcus Ryder. He works for the government; these are our daughters."

"What sector of the government does your husband work for?" I asked.

"It's classified. I cannot say." She pursed her lips.

"That's fine. You don't have to tell us anything else, but if you want to get out of here, we ask that you trust us."

Gabriella stared. "Again, how exactly do you plan on getting us out of here? Both of you are handcuffed; if anything, you'll need us. And you don't look in distress or have any bruises from fighting, which means you're probably with them. I don't trust you."

"You think yo—"

"Kevin, play nice," Ryan cut in. She turned to Gabriella. "We are not bruised up because we allowed them to do what they wanted. They said stand still, grabbed our hands and handcuffed them, and we let them. I bet from the second they tried to put a finger on you or your sister you've been fighting."

"So?" Gabriella stared her down.

"So, that's why you and your sister were harmed. Your mom here doesn't have a scratch on her because she understands the game. If they wanted any of you dead, you would be. They need you alive for something, but it doesn't mean they can't hurt you."

"I told my daughters not to fight it. They don't listen."

"Whatever. Mom was on medication and sleeping most of the time. That's why she's not bruised." Gabriella rolled her eyes, and turned her chair sideways.

We sat for a few minutes in silence. I was trying to figure out what to do next. Part of me wanted to just free the ladies and have Derek figure out what role they played. But the other part wanted to find out what the rebels were up to. I needed to know what was going on outside this room. If I could do that and get a quick count of them, I could take the girls to safety and return with backup to take down this group of rebels. The teleporting time wasn't the problem. It was having a big enough team to handle all the rebels here. I needed to know their numbers.

I heard some rumblings by the door before it opened. I had my back to it so I had to stretch my neck to see what was going on. Blondie came in with a man I hadn't seen before. A different set of guards trailed behind them.

The man came and stood by my side. He was about Blondie's height, around 5'7" or 5'8" but a little on the chubby side. His dark hair was combed to the side and did a terrible job of covering his bald spot. He was somewhere in his late fifties or early sixties. I could see a stain on his jacket—mustard, maybe—hard to tell with the ancient brown suit he was wearing. "So you two are here to help them get out?" he asked.

"You were listening? Good. I hate having to repeat myself," I said.

"You didn't think we would leave you alone and not listen in, do you? We have cameras in here," Blondie said.

"I know you do. There is one to my back, on the left corner. There is a pen on the floor under the table, which I'm pretty sure is a microphone, and that idiot over there pretending to play a game is actually videotaping us. Oh, right, and there is another camera in that plant right behind the ladies," I said, bobbing my head toward the plant.

"So, Kevin. It seems you are well trained. Now you know we've seen and heard everything. You know we have the building on watch; how were you planning on saving these ladies all by yourself? From what I'm told, this sensor here does little more than cry." He walked over and placed his hands on Ryan's shoulders, making a point to massage them thoroughly. He made my blood boil.

"Well, that's exactly how. Let's make a deal: keep us in here and let the ladies go."

"Why would I do that? I know you've informed us that she is Derek Lake's sister, but I don't have such information in any of my files. You see, I have eyes everywhere."

"You think Lake would allow this type of information out and about where anyone could find it?

Give the man some credit."

Blondie pulled a chair and sat next to me. "So tell me, Kevin, if he tried so hard to keep that information a secret, why are you sharing it now?"

"Because I know you need her alive and if you hurt her you won't get anywhere with Lake."

"Hmm, you know what? I would like to test this. Bring the girl's phone," she said to someone behind me. It took a few minutes before I saw a pink phone being passed down from behind me. Blondie got up and went to stand next to Suit Guy who was still holding Ryan's shoulder. "Let's call dear old brother and see what he has to say, shall we?"

This was the thing I loved from our *playbook*. Nick, who seemed to be the poster child for the Org, was the mastermind behind it. We had a number of plays we'd learned and familiarized ourselves with while in training. They were ingrained in our brains. We could use any of them depending on our situations; the play was determined by the team leader of each mission—me in this case. If the leader wasn't available, the second in command made the call. We had certain keywords and numbers we used for others to follow our leads. We each had roles and we knew inside out what had to be done. I had made the call when I told Ryan we were playing "The Sister Card," so of course she knew exactly how to play it to tip Derek off in case Chris hadn't reached him yet.

One ring, two . . . "Hello."

"Derek!" Ryan started screaming, "Derek, they have me. I'm sorry I've been a brat. Don't let them hurt me, please!"

"Shut up," Blondie said and walked away with Ryan's phone. "We have two of your agents in our possession. Is there any one of them whose life you value above the other?"

"I value all of my crew. What do you want for their safety?"

"I only have room for one more. I already have three other mouths to feed, as you are well aware."

"I can pay you whatever you want; tell me how mu—"

"We don't need your money. Get the girl to me, let him hear as we slice her throat—"

"NO! Do not harm her. She's my—what do you want from me?"

"I've heard enough," Blondie said, and hung up the phone. "The girl seems important enough."

I smiled. "Why didn't you just ask him?" Derek would have said Ryan was his brat sister if he had to.

"Because he would deny all ties." She turned to leave. "Kill the guy."

"No, wait! I have services I can offer. Let me work for you. I have no loyalty to the Org."

"What?" Ryan asked.

"I'm a survivor, Ryan. I come first." I looked up at Blondie. "I can work for you. Use me, or at least get these things off me and I can show you my skills."

"What makes you think we'd believe you?" Blondie rolled her eyes.

"I want to liv—"

"You know what? I do want to see your skills, but it will be with your hands handcuffed. And since you have high tolerance to pain, I'm bringing in some of our best men," she said, freeing me from the chair. She then pulled both hands in front of me and handcuffed them together. "Let's see what you can do. Walk."

"Whatever you say, Blondie." I actually still felt like my bones were humming inside my body from her shock. I followed her to the middle of the room and stood in front of the man-made open space. The man said something to Blondie and left. Three of the guys who were standing by the door came closer to me. They were buffed up and taller than me.

This should be fun.

Here's a fact about my pals and me: we were arrogant when it came to our fighting skills. We trained with the best and loved to get down and dirty. So naturally I was smiling. Admittedly, this is exactly the type of behavior that pissed off my opponents, but I liked it. It meant they were fueled, which in turn added more gasoline to my fire. There's no fun in fighting with pussies.

I raised my hands to my chin, palm up and motioned "come here" with my fingers. Only one of them came forward. We did a little dance until he tried to punch me and I bent just enough to feel the breeze above my right ear. I stepped to my right as if I was going to use my right elbow, but just before he stopped me, I dropped down and extended my left leg to knock him down to the floor. "Nice of you to join me down here," I said as he fell. Then I elbowed him in the throat. It was hard enough that he would stay down, clutching for breath.

I lay on my back, swung my legs toward my head to gain momentum, then jumped forward to stand. The other two were already by my side. "Come to papa!" I said, and grabbed the first one to reach me. I choked him. I maneuvered my handcuff around his neck while twisting his hands upward behind him at the same time. When the second man threw a blow my way, I blocked it with the first man. *There went a tooth.* "Sorry, man," I said, loosening my hold from his neck. I didn't like to kill if it wasn't necessary.

The second guy kicked the first and sent both of us flying. I hit the wall behind me and let the first man drop. I jumped over him and raised my hands in front of me, making circles and shapes in the air.

"What the hell are you doing?" the second guy asked.

"Invoking the gods," I said widening my eyes and catching a glimpse of Ryan rolling her eyes. The guy came back at me.

As I danced around him, he got one good punch into my jaw, which managed to piss me off. I jumped and gave him a kick square in the chest. Right before he went out of my reach I grabbed his shirt and kicked his knee.

The bone screeched loud before he fell in agony. This was one of my signature moves. I turned to find three more guards staring at me. "I told you I was a kick-ass fighter. Use me or lose these," I said, pointing to her guards.

She nodded to one of them who ran at me. As he reached closer, I grabbed him and slammed his body into the rough edge of the wall, right where nails and broken pieces of wood had been sticking out. It wasn't pretty.

"That's enough. I don't need guards to put you down when I have a gun right here," she said, pointing her gun at me.

"Hang on, hang on. You can use me. I told you already I have no loyalty to them. If you pay me, my skills and I are yours," I said, but all she did was bring the gun closer to me. "At least test me out; if I don't work out, then that's that."

"No, thank you," Blondie said.

As I heard her pulling the trigger, I teleported from my spot and stood behind her, disarming her. I had the gun to her head when I decided to teleport all our handcuffs off: mine, Ryan's, and the Ryders'. The oldest girl got up and started fighting one of the guards, and I had to admit she held her own. Ryan jumped over the table and pushed Mrs. Ryder and Grace behind her to protect them. I knocked Blondie unconscious, but a few more men came in with Simon.

I teleported all guns out the window in an attempt to make this a fair fight for Ryan, Gabriella, and myself.

Every time I got a hold of one guard I transported them right out the broken window. I called for Ryan and Gabriella to come to me once I got close to Mrs. Ryder and Grace, but Gabriella got her head locked by one of the men.

I went to free her, but she said, "No! Get Grace!"

I turned and saw Simon with a knife to Grace's head. I called for it and disarmed him. "Glad to see your ugly face. You're coming back with us," I said with a smirk. I really wasn't thinking. While I punched the guard who was holding Gabriella, Simon beamed right through Grace's stomach with his laser.

In my anger, I felt a buzz in my hands. The light bulbs in the room exploded as my body felt like a thousand needles were attacking it. The sunlight shining through the windows helped with the darkness along with the glow now emanating from my hands. I shot out a type of speckled electric spark at Simon. I held it there, not understanding what I was doing. The crackling sound intensified as the needles seemed to dig deeper into my bones. Simon stood there with smoke bursting from his scalp.

I electrocuted him. I think.

In the seconds his body fell to the floor, Ryan's eyes met mine. I didn't have time to question myself or to answer her. I grabbed Gabriella and made a dash to Grace. Ryan ran toward us, pulling Mrs. Ryder with her. We both touched Grace and we got out of there.

I transported us into the infirmary at the Org and

called Derek.

Blood was everywhere.

Jenny came running in with him. "Okay, everyone, move away so I can heal her."

"No," Mrs. Ryder said. "She's already gone."

I couldn't think. I wanted to force Jenny or Derek to heal Grace, regardless of what her mother said. But her limp body painted a haunting image.

I didn't understand. I couldn't. The slow motion pumping of my heart drowned out the cries and screams from Gabriella and her mother.

Gabriella made eye contact with me and I could see her mouth forming the word "you." It was my mistake that cost Grace her life and we both knew it. Only she had no idea just how directly I was involved.

Why did I let Simon loose?

Guilt threatened to break me down. So for the first time in my life I did the cowardly thing and I teleported away from there.

THREE DAYS LATER, I found myself hiding behind a gravestone. I watched as the funeral progressed and saw Grace's sister Gabriella break down while her mother stood with a cold stare. Funny how people had different coping mechanisms.

I jumped when someone said, "Here."

I turned to see Ryan. "What are you doing?"

"I knew you'd come and I figured I could keep you company."

"Go away," I said, but she ignored me. She sat by my side, right on the dust of snow that was still on the ground.

She held out a Dunkin' Donut cup to me. "It's freezing, Kevin. If I know you, you've been here way before they arrived. Just warm up a little."

"Thanks." I took it and took a sip. I couldn't feel my ears anymore so I really was grateful for the little heat in my cup. After everyone left, we walked in silence to where she'd parked.

"I'm going away for a while," I told her, and gave her a good-bye kiss on her forehead.

Ryan nodded and said nothing else. She adjusted the beanie on my head to cover my ears, got in her car, and left.

CHAPTER FIVE

SILENCE. IT SURROUNDED me but what I needed was for it to consume my whole existence. If only my thoughts weren't screaming and echoing in my head, I'm pretty sure I would have found a way to give in. I went to the window and looked outside; the snow painted a beautiful white picture. It seemed so pure. I wished I could say the same about myself. I went to Canada to a cabin Nick owned. I'm not sure why; I guess I hoped the extra cold would numb the pain. It didn't.

I looked at my hand, turning it palm up, and watched as the flakes started falling on it. I teleported the snow inside and watched it melt on the warmth of my skin. I was so lost in thought that I jumped when the phone rang. Nick was calling again. I knew I should answer but I just didn't feel like it. Instead, I started to take a step and my foot came down in my brother's living room.

Nick turned to face me. "You could have just

answered."

I shrugged. "I didn't feel like talking on the phone."

"But in person works for you?" His eyebrow went up.

"Nothing really works for me. I'll just go and be alone some more."

"Don't do that to yourself."

I stared at my feet. "No? So what am I supposed to do now?"

"I don't know, Kevin. How are you holding up?"

"I'll live," I said. "She didn't, but I will."

"You did everything you could," Nick said as he placed his hand on my shoulder.

"Tell that to her. To her family."

"There was too much going on and—"

"She was only fifteen, Nick! I know I did my best but it wasn't enough." I kicked the table in frustration.

He leaned forward. "The scumbag got scared and took it out on a young, innocent girl. There's nothing more you could have done, man. At least you got her mother and her sister out of there before they suffered the same fate."

"If I hadn't gone off on my own with Simon . . ."

"Kevin, your heart was in the right place. You tried to rescue them. Plus, we see death all the time. We can't save them all."

"And that's supposed to make me feel better?" I asked through gritted teeth.

"No, it's not," Nick said. "Ryan and Chris have been

trying to reach you."

"I don't want to talk to anyone."

"That's fine, but you still have to go see Derek. You've been gone for a month. Enough brooding. He's expecting you on Monday morning."

"What if I don't show up?"

"I guess it will mean you're no longer with the Org. So I suggest you think about it over the weekend. I won't pressure you either way," Nick said, holding eye contact. I knew he meant it.

"Whatever. I'm going home."

"Okay, Kev."

I WENT BACK to my apartment in Jackson Heights. I tried resting but when sleep failed to take over, I decided to get wasted. Since Derek had taken over the Org from his father, we didn't take too many side cases, so our salaries weren't extravagant. I lived comfortably, but wouldn't be considered a splurger on any count . . . except for maybe my car. Still, it was a bachelor's place through and through: small, snug, and usually ready for the ladies. It was great that I was on a top floor. I could see the skyline of New York City from here. Girls dug that. Right now it all looked like a snow globe with flakes falling hard. I didn't have to go all the way to Canada after all; the storm—both snow and emotional—followed me anywhere I went.

I'd been gone so long; I didn't have anything to eat. Since I hadn't planned on coming home I didn't think to stop and pick up food. I turned the TV on and got out a bottle of vodka, but there was a soft knock on the door before I could even start on it. I should have known Nick would alert my friends. I opened the door and found Ryan smiling. *Why must she always be smiling?*

I let out a sigh. "Why can't you ever ring the bell?"

"If I do, how will you know it's me?" she asked.

"When I see your face."

Ryan pouted. "No fun. It's a code thing. You know I like code things."

"You like too many things for my taste."

She pushed me aside. "Let me come in. I'm not staying out here."

"You're already in," I said, and went back to get my bottle.

"Chris is on his way with pizza."

"That's good, because I have no food, and I haven't dared opened the refrigerator. God knows what stench will greet me in there."

"I cleaned it and kept it stocked for you," Ryan said, smiling. "The perks of having a key."

My jaw tightened. "I didn't ask you to do that."

"Don't be annoyed. You know I couldn't possibly ignore it."

"God forbid," I said, and took a sip. The burn of alcohol was exactly what I needed.

Ryan looked at the bottle in my hand. "Vodka, straight up. Hmm, you know drinking alone is never healthy. Pour me a shot."

"Get it yourself—or better yet, just leave."

"I thought misery loved company."

"No." I pressed my lips together.

She ignored me and opened the door when the bell rang. "He's in a worse mood than we thought," she said to Chris, who walked in, giving me a small nod. See? That's how you greet an unhappy person, not with a smile.

"Before you two gang up on me, let me warn you: I don't want to be bothered."

"No, bro. Chill," Chris said, handing me a slice. That's one of the reasons I liked Chris. He always had pizza at the ready.

We stayed in the kitchen eating, drinking, and hardly talking. It was the first space when people walked into my apartment. I had an island with stools and that's where we hung out. Behind us was the living room with a small hallway to the bathroom and bedroom. I knew they were here to keep me company and probably to help me deal with things, but something else was up. They kept making eye contact every so often, unspoken questions passing between them. I got aggravated with them. "What exactly did you two come here for tonight?"

"What's going on with your TV?" Ryan's brows

creased.

I turned to look at it and caught the white noise going on in the living room. I hadn't noticed any problems with the cable. They'd come here as soon as I turned the TV on so I hadn't actually paid attention to it—plus I had it muted. It was the least of my problems though. I went to get the remote and turned it off. "It doesn't matter, I'll reboot it later. Why are you two here?"

"We're just here to help plan your next move," Chris answered.

"What next move? I'm thinking of leaving the Org."

"Don't be stupid," Ryan said.

"I'm stupid now, Ry? Because a young girl died under my watch? Because my arrogance got the best of me?"

"Would you just listen for once? You want to leave the Org? That's fine. But not before we catch those who are really responsible for her death. You—*we*—owe her that much."

ON SATURDAY MORNING Ryan drove us to the Ryders' safe house. We usually argued about who would drive anytime we had to go somewhere together. The way

Chris sat in the passenger side like a well-trained puppy, I was sure he'd allowed her to have her way while I was gone. I didn't have it in me to argue or make fun of him so I just slipped onto the back seat and remained quiet the whole ride.

She had parked the car over fifteen minutes ago and was sitting, tapping the wheel with her fingers, but didn't mutter a word. Knowing her, she was counting the seconds until I moved.

After a while Chris said, "I know you're nervous, but anytime now, Kevin."

"All right, all right. Let's go now," I said, getting out of the car.

We walked up the pathway and passed the two guards who were out front. Andrew met us outside and said he was going to visit his wife, Beth, quickly. We promised to call him when we were done, and went inside.

"Hello," Ryan called out, lowering the volume of the radio that was blasting music from a small table by the door. The safe house was a small yellow colonial house in Queens, currently covered in snow even though April was around the corner. Winter had sure been brutal this year. The entrance opened into the living room. There was a large sectional facing an old television set. I had no idea the big chunky kind still existed. To the right was an open eat-in kitchen, and a short hallway that I assumed led to the bedrooms and bathroom.

"What are you doing here?" Gabriella walked into

the small living room backward, staring me down. Her mother came in behind her.

"I came to talk to you and your mother," I answered.

"About?" Mrs. Ryder said.

Ryan walked up to them "Mrs. Ryder, Gabriella, we—"

"It's Gabby."

Ryan looked at her and nodded. "Mrs. Ryder and Gabby, we wanted to extend our condolences in person once again. We can't even imagine how you both must be feeling right now."

"Gracie is gone. A mother should never have to bury her child." She trembled. This was the most I'd seen her show any kind of emotion.

"Mom, sit." Gabby directed her mother to the sofa and sat next to her. "Who's he?" she asked, looking past me.

"I'm Chris," he said, going up to them and shaking their hands. "I'm part of this team." He motioned to Ryan and myself.

"Hello, Chris. Please, have a seat," Mrs. Ryder said. "Gabby, would you offer our guests some refreshments?"

"Are you kidding?" she asked with the energy of a bird. She seemed weak and really worn down.

"Gabriella, I do not enjoy repeating myself, as you very well know."

She rolled her puffy eyes at her mom then let out a long sigh before asking, "What would you guys like to drink? We have water, milk, coffee, tea, and . . . I guess more water."

"We are okay," Ryan said. "Thank you, Gabby."

I went around the sofa and sat at the edge opposite the Ryders. "There was something else I wanted to discuss with you."

"Go ahead, dear," Mrs. Ryder said.

"I—I'm really sorry for what happened," I started.

"Well if you had done your job ri—"

"GABRIELLA! If you can't behave yourself then go to your bedroom."

"That's not my bedroom." At the cold stare given to her by her mother, she amended, "Well, technically it isn't. Fine, I'll try to be quiet." Her shoulders slumped.

"I wish I could have done more," I continued.

"You did enough," Gabby whispered.

I looked at her and repeated, "I wish I could have done more, I do. I am so sorry. I know you blame me for what happened. God knows I do too."

"I told you to get her and leave me alone. Why didn't you listen?"

If only she knew the whole story. I was getting worked up so I decided to stand and gather my thoughts. Gabriella's eyes followed me as I paced around the room. When her mother couldn't see, she flipped me off. The radio went out at the same time and made a loud popping sound. I walked up to it since I was already standing and pressed the power button. It turned on, but I couldn't find a radio station. The screeching sound was almost more annoying than Gabriella, so I turned it back off.

Mrs. Ryder, ignoring the radio, said, "No, dear, we know it wasn't your fault. If it wasn't for you I could have lost both of my daughters. You saved Gabriella, and for that I will forever be grateful."

"I had that asshole!" Gabby said. "If you'd let me fight him I would have finished him off and Grace would have been alive."

Okay, so she really wanted to push this. Man, anger sure brought out her energy. I had nothing to say, though—she was right—so I only looked at her.

"There is no way to know that. Kevin and Ryan did what they thought was right. I know you can handle yourself, but these men were big and armed." Mrs. Ryder reached out and hugged her daughter. "Give him a break. For me."

Gabby made bitter face and pulled away from her mother.

"Thanks," I said awkwardly, taking a seat. "I still want to help, if you'll let me. I know you are still under the Org's protection and we are working on finding whoever did this but I was wondering if you would keep me on your case."

"You have to be kidding me!"

"No, I'm not kidding," I said to Gabriella. "This is very hard. I've never lost anyone before. I've always been good at my job and I know I messed up."

Ryan stepped in. "We want to help. You and your mom are still targets and we wondered if you would allow the three of us to help protect you."

Gabriella stood and looked at me. "You have some nerve. Ryan and Chris can stay. But you? You want to help? Fine, go out there and find them, but don't stay here and add salt to our injuries. Right, Mom? Tell him. Mom?" Gabby checked on Mrs. Ryder. "Figures! Now she sleeps. I gave her that pill about an hour ago; all it did was make her loopy, AND *way* too nice to you."

"Oh, her eyes were glossy but I thought she was just exhausted or something," Chris said, as if realization struck him.

"No, she's been too depressed. I had to increase her medication dosage the past couple days."

I stood up. "I guess we should go, then. Can you please think about what I said?"

"Why would we want you around? We have them"—she pointed to Ry and Chris—"and other super-people who can protect us. We don't need you."

"Umm, Luminaries. Not super-people, and—"

"Bite me!" she said, cutting me off.

"Okay, well yes, there are others, but I would be able to move you to another location in an instant; they can't. It's better for your and your mother's safety."

She seemed lost in thought. Frowning, she asked in a low voice, "So why didn't you do that with Grace?"

My chest was heavy. "It was so fast. You were fighting, Ryan had your mom, and by the time I got you away from them, I heard your sister scream and—look, I couldn't just teleport her out of harm's way. I had to physically touch her. She was too far."

Gabriella nodded and went to sit on the couch. She hugged her knees tightly as tears ran down her cheeks. "All right, I don't want to relive that. I know it wasn't your fault, okay? Deep down I do know it. I'm just so angry at everything," she said between sniffles.

I felt my shoulders drop, and repeated, "I'm sorry."

She sobbed for a while. "I don't know how to live without Grace. They still have my dad. I'm alone. My mom isn't even . . ."—she gave me a slow shrug—"it's fine. She's right, you did save me. You can help."

"Umm . . ." I was shocked. "So it's okay?"

"Yes, but sometimes I get . . ." she wiped her face and drank some water from a bottle on the table. "Look, just know I'm probably going to give you a hard time if I'm having a particularly rough day."

"It's fine, I deserve it."

At that, her expression hardened and she nodded. "Yes. But for today I'm already tired of seeing your face. You can go now."

I walked out with Ry and Chris following behind me. If I had known Gabriella was such a pain in the ass, I probably would have saved the other sister. And I know it's wrong to have this thought, but *"You can go now"*? What does she think I am? I sighed. She looked so defeated, though. I knew my pride wasn't worth it. I would just have to suck it up. If she couldn't have her sister at least she had me to hate. I could do that.

Looking up to the sky, I noticed that rain was on the horizon. Good. At least it would wash away what was left of the snow . . . and with it my feeling of helplessness.

I WALKED INTO Derek's office a little after seven on Monday morning, and found him watching my every move. He sat behind his desk, hardly blinking. It was unnerving.

"What? I'm only a few minutes late."

"Good morning, Kevin. I would ask you how you are doing, but I'm sure you don't want to talk about it."

"No." My jaw tightened.

Derek nodded. "I was informed that you paid the Ryders a visit."

"Yes."

"Do you think it's wise for you to be part of their protection group? I wanted you away from this mission, but I should have known better. You're as hardheaded as your brother."

"Yes," I agreed. "Too bad I'm not as good an agent as him."

"On the contrary. You are an asset to our company."

"You don't have to lie to my face. I know you only keep me around because of Nick."

"I've always been honest with you, Kevin. I never lie to my friends and I would never put my company's reputation under jeopardy to keep your brother happy." He squinted as he studied me. It was distracting.

"Right." I raised an eyebrow.

"I won't say you don't come without challenges. You are sloppy at times, yes, and your ego gets you into trouble, but you are efficient. And neither of those are the reason we lost that young lady."

"I went behind your back."

"You did. But I have to be honest, when Chris came and told me what you'd done, I thought it was an excellent idea. I didn't expect it to backfire, and in reality you saved two of them. The longer someone is kidnapped, the lesser their chances of coming out alive," he assured me.

"I broke the rules because of my arrogance."

"You didn't do anything I wouldn't have done. Believe me, I was fine with that move. And sure, maybe you think you're invincible, but you always get the job done. Even with a death, you saved two innocents. By statistics, this was a successful move."

I clenched my fists. "How can you say that?"

"I can say that because on paper it's true. What happened is nothing any of us are happy about."

"Derek, no one else will die on my watch. I promise you that."

He stared at me. "That I know. Grace is *the one*."

"What is that supposed to mean?" I asked.

"She's the one who will always haunt you. The one who changes how you deal with missions going forward. It's her face you'll see every time you have an innocent to guard."

"You're not helping."

"No, but her memory will. IF you get past this incident and take advantage of the scar it's leaving on you, you'll make damn sure no one else suffers at the hands of the rebels when Kevin Pierce is around. This has changed you. I'm not saying there should be a positive in Grace's death, but she's your turning point. From now on, you'll be the one Luminary they don't want to mess with. I can already see that in your eyes."

"All I want is to not have failed her." I covered my face with my hands.

"And from now on, you won't. You can help us get them. You really want to be in charge of protecting the Ryders?" He leaned back in his chair.

I looked up, fighting the powerless feeling that had taken over me. "Yes. I think it will help me feel like I'm doing something specifically for Grace. Keep her family alive. I can handle it."

"I'm more worried for their emotional state."

I shrugged. "They said it was fine."

"Look, I know this isn't easy for you, and I trust you will do right by them. But I have in my report here"—he showed me a file— "that the daughter is hot-tempered."

"I can deal with her."

"I have no doubt. I'm concerned the tension between you two might cause you to lose focus, and if that happens at the wrong time, well . . ."

I shook my head. "I won't lose focus. Ryan and Chris will be there to help me."

"No, they will not. At least not the whole time. They will take turns when you are not there, but mainly they will be assisting me in tracking down the rebels. And most importantly, in freeing Dr. Ryder."

"Right. Gabriella mentioned they had him."

"Yes, it's imperative we find him. I learned from Madelyn that she and her daughters were kept as incentive for him to work for them."

"What do they want with him?"

"If what I suspect is true, we might be facing bigger problems than the Ryders' well-being. A soon as I get confirmation I'll be sure to fill you in."

"What can possibly be bigger than the life of innocents?" I asked him.

"Good point. It's just some issues that could impact what we do here," Derek said, and left it at that. "Now, on to the other reason I wanted to see you."

"What now?"

He leaned forward, placing his elbow on the desk. "How did you electrocute Simon?"

"I have no idea. I tried doing it again but couldn't. It was some kind of electrostatic."

"Describe it," Derek said.

"I just saw and heard the static-like electricity coming out from me and fed it with rage. That's really all I can say."

"We're going to have to work on that. Train you. Study it. I haven't seen it before, but I imagine it's tied in with teleportation," he said, beaming.

I could feel my veins throbbing in my neck. "I don't care to study it, Derek."

He shook his head. "You being able to control the astral plane, time and space, might be creating friction with electricity and that's why it was unlike a fireball or laser beam."

"Don't push me to study this, Derek," I said, shoving my hand in my pocket and clutching my phone.

"We have to." He stared. "It's part of our growth and . . . quite frankly, it's fascinating!"

I stood up so fast my knees sent the chair flying behind me. "I'm not your lab rat," I yelled, and left his office.

As I slammed his door behind me, the cell phone in my hand grew increasingly hot and began to release smoke. Shit. That's the second one this week. I hadn't thought about it before, but maybe it was my new power that kept interfering with all the devices. It would explain my TV, and the radio acting up when Gabby pissed me off.

CHAPTER
SIX

I WENT TO our gym to punch out the frustration scorching in me. When I felt calm enough, I gave the punching bag a roundhouse kick that knocked it off its hinges. I left the bag on the floor and went to take a quick shower.

I went back to my office and gathered my laptop, along with anything else I thought I'd need while I was at the Ryders' safe house. As much as I loved using teleportation to my advantage, doing something physical helped me focus at the moment. I could have teleported any of these items when I needed them, but I was nervous. Items weren't fragile and didn't have life so I could teleport several in one shot, but people? That was a bit more complicated. Until a few years back, I couldn't handle more than one person to transport along with me without suffering the consequences. I could teleport two people at most, but then I'd feel so weak I would need a few days to rest it off. Lucky for me, I now had Ryan to amplify me when I needed it.

I'D RELAXED ENOUGH after getting everything in my
backpack, and was trying to mentally prepare myself for
what Gabby and her mom might have in store for me. My
office used to be Nick's at one point. And since I'd never
made any changes to it, the simple white walls were
screaming for a paint job. I had even kept his crappy
almond-colored desk and saggy green couch. I ignored
the chipped paint and old furniture and went to stand in
front of the large window.

I stared at the busyness outside: the cars, buses, and
people going in all directions helped to distract me. I
heard my office door open and I turned to see Ryan.

"I saw you went to work out and wasn't sure if you
wanted coffee or water, so I brought you both." She
smiled.

"Thanks." I took the water bottle first and gulped it
down while hustling to grab my gray coat.

"Chris is waiting for us; we should get going," she
said.

I rushed down the stairs behind her toward the
parking lot, and spilled coffee on my new blue sweater.

"Someone looks nervous," Chris said, when we
reached the car.

"Let him be." Ryan opened the car door on the
passenger side. "We have a lot to do and we don't have
all day. Let's go."

"Yeah, like what?" I asked.

Chris answered, "We have to go to check things out—make sure you're settled with them—then Ry and I have to go follow some leads."

"Both of you?" I fidgeted with my seatbelt.

"Yeah, I tried to convince Derek to let me stay with you." Ryan looked over at me. "I didn't want you to be there all day alone with them in case things got heated. But he said if you couldn't handle it on your first day then you had no business being their main guard."

"That's fine," I said, still trying to wipe off the coffee stain. When that didn't help, I teleported the liquid out of the fabric and out the window.

I guess Derek had a point, but I was a little nervous. Mrs. Ryder hadn't exactly been conscious when her daughter consented, but she also hadn't objected after she found out.

"Can you at least try to avoid the potholes?" Ryan said, irritated.

"Oh, I'm sorry, Princess." Chris laughed. "Afraid to ruin your clothes like Kevin just did?"

Ryan reached over and smacked him in the head. "I have dark clothes on. I'm usually with you two all day long. You think I'm stupid enough to wear something that could get dirty so fast? But the coffee is hot, so watch it."

"Whatever pleases you, Princess," Chris said and got a snort in response from Ryan.

It was mid-morning so we didn't have much traffic.

We arrived rather quickly. We got out and I braced myself for what came next. The daughter was one feisty girl. I stared at what would be my post for God knows how long. I hadn't noticed how dull the yellow of the house was last time I was here. The snow had given it life in a way. Heck, even the leafless lone tree looked sad without the white coat.

We didn't need to ring the bell. As soon as we got close enough, Gabby opened the door with a big smile. "Good morning, guys!"

I looked at her, unsure of what to think, so I said, "Hey."

"Well, come on in, you three. Breakfast is ready."

Ryan walked slowly behind us and frowned. "We're good, but thanks."

"Oh, no. You must eat, you crime-fighters." Gabby lowered her voice. "Please eat something and say it's good. Mom's been driving me so crazy, the best I could do to run away was try my hand in the kitchen. I'm not even sure if the eggs are cooked through."

Chris, who ate anything at any time, said, "Yeah, I'll try it."

"Good. Here, sit." Gabby pointed to the tight kitchen nook where her mother sipped some tea and nibbled on a piece of toast.

We squeezed our way in and said our hellos to Mrs. Ryder. She barely acknowledged us before continuing to stare at the ceiling. She looked both sad and bored.

"Are you all right, Mrs. Ryder?" I asked.

"Madelyn, please," she said. "Yes, I am. It's not every day my daughter cooks me a meal. She turned twenty-one last year and I've hardly seen her since. I'm merely enjoying the moments. She's the only daughter I have left, you know." She nodded slowly, looking sideways at Gabby as if this was a secret.

"Right," I grabbed a toast and bit into it. I didn't dare try the eggs. If the cook wasn't sure it was good, I wasn't going to be her guinea pig. Chris, though, was busy stuffing his mouth. And Ryan went to help bring a tray with cups over to the table.

They got back and Gabby rested her hand on her mom's shoulder. It was nice to see some affection pass between them for a change; their usual tension was unnerving. Shortly after that, Mrs. Ryder stood up. "All right, looks like you're all settled. I must go water the plants and take a nap. I'm feeling drowsy."

As her mom left the kitchen, Gabby said, "She took a strong dose of anxiety pills. Before that thing kicked in though, she was a pain in—anyway, I'm sorry, guys, you don't have to eat anymore. I was just desperate. We don't even have plants here, but who's to tell her?"

Chris, who had no intention to stop eating, said, "This tastes good to me."

"Anything you can chew tastes good to you, Chris," Ryan said. "Oh, sorry, Gabby, I didn't mean—"

"No, it's fine," Gabby said, and stared Ryan down.

After a while, Ryan reached for the eggs and tasted it. "Thanks for the food, Gabby. It wasn't too bad. All it needed was some salt and pepper. If I were you, though, I would cook the scrambled eggs a little longer next time. It just depends on what you're going for."

Gabby's eyebrow went up. "And what are you going for with all the baggy clothing? Is it a special undercover style? Would you like to swap unsolicited advice?"

Ryan's eyes widened. "I'm sorry, Gabby. I didn't mean to offend you."

Gabby placed both hands over her face. "No, I'm sorry! I'm on edge with the lack of sleep. I shouldn't get offended if I know I can't cook," she said with a high-pitched laugh. I had no idea what to think of this girl.

"Uh, Gabby," Chris jumped in. "We had some questions for you and your mom. Do you know when she'll be up?"

"It won't be for a few hours, but she's always on medication. It's been like that with her for as long as I can remember. Honestly, she hardly ever knows what goes on around her," she said, looking back at Ryan.

Ryan shifted uncomfortably and checked her phone.

"But she seemed aware and normal before," I said, trying to ease the tension.

"Well," Gabby looked down and played with her watch, "she has her moments. Mental issues are . . . beyond me. But the doctor and Dad think she's a danger to herself and us if she's not on treatment. Which reminds me, I have to ask before it's too late: can one of you pick up her prescription?"

"Sure, Derek will send one of our doctors and they'll

get her what she needs," Ryan said.

"Mom's pills are compounded. She has a specific pharmacy she uses. There should be one ready for pick up, actually. And knowing her, if she doesn't recognize the label she might not take it. Even the rebels got her prescriptions for her while we were in their custody."

"That's fine. I'll pick it up later," I said.

With a sigh of relief, Gabby let go of her watch. "Thanks, I'll give you the address before you leave."

"That's taken care of," Ryan said. "We'll talk to you and your mom tomorrow. Our questions can wait, so Chris and I will get going."

Gabby grabbed Ryan's arm. "I really am sorry, Ryan."

"Oh, yeah—no, it's fine. I know you're stressed," Ryan said with a genuine smile. I'll never understand women. I knew Ryan, and I was sure she would have snapped Gabby's neck if she could just moments before.

"All right, dude, good luck!" Chris slapped me on the back before they left.

Gabby yawned. "Well, make yourself useful and clean up the kitchen while I try to sleep."

"Not getting enough rest?"

"You tell me. My sister just died." She stared at me.

I held her gaze for a few seconds before looking away. She didn't move immediately, I could feel the hatred oozing from her and spiking up my neck. Maybe I just imagined it, though. Guilt was getting to me.

When I finished in the kitchen, I walked around the

outside premises and took pictures with my phone. I always liked to have something to fall back on in case things looked out of place in the future. I went back into the living room and turned on my laptop. Derek had been waiting for my reports of that night long enough.

"WHY ARE YOU still here?" Gabby asked, slumping down on the couch across from me later that day.

"Because you agreed I could have the job?" I asked.

"It was stupid. I don't want you here. Go switch with one of the guys outside."

"Sorry. I'm the one you're stuck with in here." I took a good look at her. "Did you even sleep?"

"No. I tried. I just can't shut my brain off," she said, resting her head back on the couch.

"Not that I like to encourage it, but I can bring you something to help you sleep for tonight if you want."

She shook her head. "I don't want to be dependent on drugs like mom."

"It's just one night, Gabriella. It would do you good to rest a little bit."

"Maybe. I don't know. I don't want anything from you." She got up and walked toward her bedroom before turning back. "Ugh! There is nothing to do in there. I'm going to watch TV. Can you go to the kitchen where I don't have to see your face?"

I did, but not before the television screen blanked out and the cable box powered off. *Oops.* I smiled and went into the kitchen like she asked me to. I understood her anger but her behavior was getting to me. She was such a brat. I closed my eyes and counted to ten like Derek taught me. The last thing I wanted was to short-circuit my laptop because she pissed me off *again*. By the time I reached number eight I heard the voices from the news show coming back on.

I couldn't deny it anymore. I was definitely behind these electrical charges. I seriously had to figure out what this new thing was and how to control it soon. The problem was it reminded me of what I did to Simon, and in turn what he did to Grace. The fact that she died because of my carelessness made me resent my own powers. Under different circumstances, I would have been excited to start exploiting my cool new trick. Life really could mess with you sometimes.

RYAN AND CHRIS'S lead hadn't been helpful. So while they waited for instructions from Derek, they were with me at the safe house for a few days. Luckily the girls played nice and even Mrs. Ryder had been in a good mood since I brought her special compounded meds. Ry and Chris kept Gabby occupied and I didn't have to deal with her attitude. This was especially good news for all the appliances in the house, considering by the end of my first day I'd had to request a new microwave oven.

Around five o' clock on Thursday I texted Beth—our resident Luminary whose speed rivaled a cheetah's—to see if she could come by a bit earlier. I wanted to ask her to bring some sleeping aids for Gabby to take. I was going solo once again on Friday and didn't want to deal with cranky Gabby. Derek had decided Ry and Chris could be of more use to him at the Org.

THAT MORNING, RYAN called Andrew ahead of time to tell Gabby we were bringing food, and not to cook. We were all tired of her disastrous attempts. The last thing we needed was finding out how many ways there were to screw up eggs. But she was so bored and upset we didn't have the heart to tell her to stop trying. It kept her busy and distracted, and that was better than dealing with her when she was frustrated. Because no matter how cute she was or how guilty I felt, if she kept going with the ugly attitude, I'd end up committing murder.

We made a stop to get some breakfast wraps to take back to the safe house, and got there a little before nine. I would have popped over but I figured it would be a long day; the least I could do was start with better company than that pain-in-the-ass girl. And apparently they needed to discuss something with her before going on about their business of abandoning me.

Gabby greeted us when we got there. "Hey, guys."

"Where's your mom? Is she okay?" I asked. It was the first morning Mrs. Ryder wasn't in the kitchen nibbling on her breakfast with us.

"As usual, locked in her room. She's fine. I took some tea for her not long ago."

"You look rested," Ryan said, and lifted the bag in her hand with a smile. "Hungry?"

"Very," Gabby said, and went to the kitchen. Chris and Ryan followed her.

I stayed back to talk to Andrew. "Hey man, I know you're anxious to go home, but did everything go all right last night?"

He smiled. "Of course. Why?"

"She hates having me here and we're alone today. I rather she not be too irritated."

"Nope. Both she and her mom were in their rooms and were quiet through the night."

"All right, man. Thanks," I said to Andrew and went to meet the guys. I walked into the kitchen and they all stopped what they were doing to look at me. I frowned. "What's up?"

"Kevin, have fun today. We have to get going," Chris said, and pulled Ryan with him. "Thanks for answering the questions, Gabby."

Gabby nodded and waved after she stuffed her mouth with more food.

"Later, dude," Ryan said, and they left.

"You guys had a chance to talk?" I asked Gabby.

"Yeah. Hey want coffee? I don't understand why

you like it, but I made some."

My eyes widened. "Coffee is life!"

She scrunched her face. "I don't like it."

No wonder we don't get along. I shrugged. "More for me."

"Here you go," she said, handing me one of the wraps. "It's really good. Much better than what I made yesterday. I can't believe I made you guys eat charred toast."

I tilted my head to study her. "You're in a great mood."

"I slept. Good call on that sleeping pill. Beth talked me into it and told me you'd asked her to give it to me. Thanks." She smiled.

"Are you actually nice when you sleep?"

"I'm not being nice, I'm just tolerating you. If we have to spend time together and you're here to help save my life, it's in my interest not to piss you off." She winked.

"Really?" Hard to believe that she'd be so playful now, given her usual coldness toward me.

"Yes." She took a sip of her tea. "Besides, your girlfriend made it clear I had to lay off you."

"She's not my girlfriend."

"Could have fooled me the past couple days. I mean, she even protects you like she is."

I smiled. "That's just Ry. Now, you do have to tell me what you discussed with them."

"Nope. She told me I couldn't."

"I don't have time for this," I said, taking my cell phone out of my pocket and started dialing.

"Oh yeah, she said not to call or you'll blow her spot."

I ignored her and put the phone to my ear. No spot to blow up if they just left anyway. It went straight to voicemail. "Dammit."

"Told ya." She grinned.

I looked at her. "Seriously, you're not gonna tell me?"

"Relax, I'm just messing with you. They only asked if my dad ever mentioned another scientist named Lumin."

"Lumin? Did he? Your dad—I mean. He knew him?"

"Yes," she said, stretching. Her arms went up and the top she wore followed them. She had a pierced belly button. *Nice.* She was talking and I had no idea what she was saying. ". . . they worked together for a while. Dad had an internship with him. They kept in touch for a few years and then Dr. Lumin stopped returning Dad's calls. He was pretty bummed out about it. All we knew was that he was killed by some asshole. Nick something, I think, my dad told us."

My brows creased. "Nick's not an asshole."

"How would you know? This was years ago," she said.

"I know because Nick is my brother, and he wasn't the one who killed Dr. Lumin."

She rolled her eyes. "Right, because you wouldn't defend your brother."

"Don't talk about business you know nothing about. I was there. I know."

"So who killed Dad's mentor?"

"That's classified information." I crossed my arms over my chest.

"Bull"—she fake-coughed—"shit."

"Stop while you're ahead," I warned.

She stood and came closer to stare me in the eyes. At 5'6" though, she had to tippy toe. "Or what? You're gonna send me off to the big bad wolf, Nick?"

"You're annoying. You know that?"

She came closer. "Why? Because I tell you like it is?"

Gabby tilted her head upward a couple inches from my face. I felt her hot breath and noticed the specks of lights swirling in her gray eyes. She had no makeup on. Her dark under-eye circles weren't gone completely, and yet I couldn't look away. I was entranced. This one was more trouble than I'd thought. All I said was, "No, you're just a brat."

"Whatever," she said, and backed away quickly. I swore her cheeks got some pink in them all of a sudden. I smiled.

She spent the rest of the morning clicking away at the remote. I emailed Derek to ask for recent reports to look through, then texted Nick and begged for a new picture of little Jack. Around midday, Gabby went to make chicken sandwiches for lunch. She took the first bite, and immediately knocked my sandwich out of my hand—the chicken was undercooked. She laughed all the way to the kitchen and brought one of the morning wraps for us to share.

I definitely liked rested Gabby better.

Mrs. Ryder came out a few minutes past three and demanded an apple from Gabby. If she slept all day and ate like an ant, I could see how she kept her corpse-like figure. Her daughter wasn't like that, thank goodness. She was pretty, Gabriella. Lean with some curves, choppy shoulder-length brown hair framing her gray eyes, and lips that defied the color of sangria. Not that it mattered, I told myself. I only noticed because she'd stood so close to me when she was messing around earlier.

"Kevin, dear. How are you?" Mrs. Ryder asked, sitting on the couch far away from me. Her hair looked greasy, like she hadn't washed it in days, and her face looked run down. Not surprising, given all she'd been through.

"I'm okay, thanks. Is there anything you would like? That might make it easier for you while you're staying here?"

She smiled as Gabby came back with an apple and a bottle of water. "Can you get my husband?" she asked.

"Sorry, Mrs. Ryder. I'm not in charge of that part of the mission. I'm here to protect you and Gabby. But if you need anything else . . . books? Movies? Anything else. Please let me know."

"That's all right then, I'm fine."

"Mom?" Gabby said. "It looks like this has something to do with Dr. Lumin."

Mrs. Ryder's eyes widened. "What makes you say such a thing, Gabriella?" She turned to me. "He's just an old acquaintance who passed away years ago."

"He already knows, Mom. His brother was the one who killed Dr. Lumin."

"No," I said through gritted teeth, "my brother was originally accused of killing him, but that was a lie. In fact, my brother saved his life and tried to protect him but—"

Mrs. Ryder's tapped her fingers on the couch. "Does it run in the family to get people killed?"

"Mom!"

"I apologize." Mrs. Ryder got up abruptly to leave, then stopped and turned around. "I think it's time for my medication. I do appreciate you going out of your way to get them for me. I wonder, could I ask one more favor?"

"Sure, Mrs. Ryder. What can I do for you?" I asked, keeping in mind I had to play customer service rep of the year.

"I'd like to go see Mr. Lake at his office to discuss our arrangement. I cannot be expected to live under these conditions for long."

"I will call him right now. He might be able to stop by and speak with you soon."

"No, I will go to his office. I expect to be treated

with the respect I deserve. Are we clear or are you not capable of understanding a simple request?"

I tensed, gripping the remote tightly. The poor thing was already feeling rubbery hot in my hands. "I will make it happen, Mrs. Ryder."

"Good. Now excuse me. I need to freshen up," she said and walked away.

"Kevin, I'm sorry about that."

"Seriously? You are worse than her. You're like a team of bad cop/worse cop. I think I'm the only good one around here."

She played with her hair. "Have I been that rude today?"

"Well, not really, but you're still pretty annoying."

Gabby shook her head. "Like I said before, I know it wasn't your fault. When I get angry I can't always control my attitude and I tend to go overboard."

"Yeah, I can tell," I said, laughing.

"Anyway, my dad was the one who got us in this mess, I know that."

"What makes you say that? He's just another kidnapped victim."

"No. He was trying to find a better way to treat Mom, and contacted the wrong people. He got in over his head."

I frowned. "Why? Was her treatment not working?"

"It was, but he wanted to get access to some private facility where he could alter her—uh . . . sorry, I'm . . . I don't really know. I just assumed he was a crazy scientist and all that." She laughed and played with her watch. Exactly as she had the last time she was nervous.

We spent the rest of the day being polite to each other, and I made a mental note to mention to Derek what she'd said.

I WENT TO the safe house that Saturday also. It was a slow day. Ryan texted me a few times while on a stakeout waiting for movement. She was bored. Gabby was nice again, and didn't try to give me food poisoning with her cooking this time. She sent one of the outside guards to get food for us. She wore jeans, T-shirt, and flip-flops this time.

"So, where did you learn to fight?" I asked, thinking of how well she had defended herself that dreadful day.

"Oh, I'm a black belt. I took karate when I was younger and enjoyed it so much that I teach it now."

"Guys must love having you teach them," I blurted out.

She smiled. "No, I teach young kids. Well, I also have a self-defense class for women. My assistant is a guy and he actually has a problem with me ordering him around. He wanted to be the one to teach it, but our boss said women were more comfortable with a female instructor. And it's true, they are."

"Cool. So that's what you do," I said, shoving my hands in my jean pockets.

"I'm in college. That's just the job I have to keep my sanity intact."

"What are you taking?"

"Honestly, I had a hard time deciding. I took two years off after high school," she said. "Dad was pissed. Then I started last year, just taking general stuff. I didn't want to commit to a major so I didn't declare any."

"So you're not interested in anything specific?" I asked.

"For a while I thought of becoming a dermatologist."

"I like skin."

"I bet." She looked up through her lashes, smiling. "But when I go back, I might try psychology or psychiatry."

"Because of your mom?"

"No, Grace. She was bipolar."

"I'm sorry."

"Let's see if I can actually make a difference to others dealing with family members like my own." She sighed.

"You will. You seem too stubborn not to give it your best shot."

"Now, that's true." She nodded.

"You're so much prettier when you smile," I said without thinking.

Her cheeks turned red. "Thanks. Lately it's been

hard. I thought you would make it impossible for me to relax, but you've been a welcome distraction."

"Why? Am I so funny looking that it's distracting?"

What the hell was I asking? I seemed to have forgotten how to talk to girls.

"I wish," she whispered, and cleared her throat. "You're just not the asshole I thought you were."

"Wow, an asshole. And this based on being kidnapped together?"

"No, based on anger because you didn't . . . *couldn't* act in time to save her."

"Right," I looked away. "Hey, you want me to make dinner one of these nights?"

"Can you cook?"

"You look surprised," I said, and put my hand over my chest. "How insulting!"

"Ah, get over it. Yes, make us dinner. Let me see what magic you can do in the kitchen."

I raised my eyebrow and thought better than to say what came to mind. "Oh, I'll blow your brain up. Just you wait."

She had no clue how badly I sucked in the kitchen. But I had to admit I was probably better than she was. She was a disaster in the kitchen. I was joking about her trying to poison me with raw chicken during yesterday's cooking experiment when the doorbell rang. We were still laughing when I opened the door to find Andrew and Beth looking at us. They'd come to take over watch for the night.

"I brought takeout," Beth said, smiling.

"You are my new hero!" Gabby said. "I'm so glad it's you two again. How is your daughter?"

"Well she's not really—"

"Elisa is great," Andrew said, putting his arm around his wife. "She's staying over at Kevin's old house."

Beth and Andrew had adopted Elisa after her mother—Beth's sister, Lisa—died years ago.

"Oh," Gabby looked at me.

"My brother's place," I clarified.

She smiled. "Oh my! Better watch out for that one. I heard he was a murderer."

"What?" Beth asked, taking a step back.

"I'm kidding, I'm messing with Kevin. Do you mind checking on Mom, Beth?"

"Sure." Beth looked at Gabby and me with a wicked glint in her eyes. She shot me a wink and said, "Andrew why don't you take the food to the kitchen?"

Andrew nodded and they both walked out of the living room.

Gabby looked down at her feet. "Thanks for today. You're not half bad company."

I smiled. "You are."

"Funny!" she said and punched my right shoulder. "Good night."

"'Bye," I said, and teleported myself home.

LATER THAT NIGHT I met with Chris and Ryan at a bar for an update. We were nowhere closer to finding Gabby's dad or the rebels' location. We agreed I should join them soon for some fun out in the field.

"Wow, did you notice her legs, man?" Chris snapped me out from my thoughts. "That Gabby is hot, the way that little dress fit her the other day."

"A pain in the ass is what she is," I said. "But yeah, she's hot."

Chris and I smiled and Ryan rolled her eyes. "Of course you two would go for beauty over brains."

"She doesn't seem dumb to me," I said. "Immature when vengeful, maybe, but not dumb."

"No, I guess not. But it's typical of you two to drool over any girl who shows some skin."

"If they don't grab our attention, Ry, how are we supposed to give them any of our time?" I asked.

"Especially time to find out how smart they might be under their clothes?" Chris laughed and gave me a fist bump.

"So that's how a girl gets attention? That's what makes you two care who they are as a person?"

Chris and I nodded. "Pretty much, yeah," I said, still laughing.

"Jerks," Ryan said, and narrowed her eyes.

"I think Kevin here will find out just what she has going on in her brain and other parts soon though," Chris said.

"Me? Nah. She can't stand me."

"You said yourself she's being nice."

Ryan got up. "I'm heading home. You two stop plotting to sleep with Gabby. She's under our protection. No messing around."

"You're too hung up on rules, Ry. Go out and live a little," Chris said, smiling. He then turned to me. "And you, just kiss her and shut her up next time she starts bitching."

I watched Ryan leave, then nodded to Chris. "If she goes without sleeping for a while again and I get desperate, I just might."

CHAPTER SEVEN

A T THE END of the second week of watching over Gabby and her mom, it was time to meet Derek at the Org. He'd canceled on me last Friday and decided two weeks' worth of work made for better catching up anyway. I told him our routines and mentioned what she'd said about her father wanting to "fix" Mrs. Ryder, but other than that I had no more news.

On his end, Derek didn't really fill me in on what was happening. He never even mentioned the conversation between him and Mrs. Ryder after she came to talk to him at the Org. All he said was that things were progressing slower than they wanted, which made me upset. The longer nothing happened, the longer Gabby and her mom were in danger.

"Kevin, look at me. I need you to relax."

I stood up, and turned to Derek. "I'm fine. It's just infuriating that the rebels have the upper hand. It's unacceptable how—"

"I understand, but don't blow out my lights," Derek said, staring at his ceiling.

I looked up and felt the tingling in my hands ease as the flickering stopped. "Sorry, man."

"Look, I know you're frustrated. We all are. Why don't you let me help you with this new power development? It might take both our minds off things. It might even help us think clearly about our next move."

"We're busy enough to keep our minds occupied. You just want to study me."

"As your friend, I'm more worried about you than I am about your power. We don't have to work on it if you don't want to. I understand how you feel about it."

"No, you don't."

He picked up a pen and twirled it between his fingers. "You don't connect it to Grace's death?"

I sat down and slumped my shoulders. "I can't see it as a good thing. No matter how much I try."

"Like I said, I understand. I am here for you. We can talk it out; maybe I'll help you keep calm enough so you don't explode. We can put it off for as long as you need."

"What if I never want to work on it?"

"That's your call. I would never push you. But let me suggest meditation so you can be more aware of yourself. You've had minor incidents with appliances but if you get too worked up, someone can get hurt."

"Meditation again? You're just obsessed with breathing."

Derek put the pen down. "It's helpful. Once you feel

more centered, I suggest you at least practice on your own or with Ryan. You do *not* have to tell me your progress. But work on it for yourself at least."

"I'll think about it."

"It's all I ask." His phone rang at that moment. "That's all for now. Go drop off these reports to Pine for me. He'll be at his usual café waiting for you."

"Yep." I got up and left.

THE FIRST SATURDAY of every month the whole gang got together for dinner. Growing up, none of us really had any family, so Annie thought it was important for us to start a tradition for ourselves. It was a way to stay close. And it was just a little something so we could all have that feeling of belonging somewhere—to know that we belonged to each other as family. It was great. So the following evening, I found myself hanging with my favorite people.

"Where's my li'l buddy?" I asked Annie as I saw everyone in the living room listening to Derek share a story.

Jenny walked down the stairs with Jack in her hands, and came straight to me. "Here. Go to your uncle, pumpkin."

"Pumpkin? Man him up, Jen! That's no proper nickname," I said as I gave him a kiss on his forehead. He was the cutest baby on Earth. "I swear I have a bro-crush! Yes, I do. *Yes, I do!* He's more than a pumpkin. He's an apple pie. A yummy bread pudding.*"*

"You think you'll man him up by calling him any of that?" Chris asked, laughing. "By the way, you just straight up 'baby talked' him, bro. That, my man, is another bet lost."

"Shit."

"Yep. Go teleport yourself home and get it. Come back in gear; you know what to do," Chris teased.

I did as he asked and returned to the family.

Annie's eyes were bulging out of their sockets. "Oh my God!"

"Shut up," I told her.

"I need a picture of this," Nick said from behind her.

"No way!" I heard and turned to see Ryan walking in from the kitchen with her mouth hanging open.

When I turned back to Annie, she was busy snapping pictures. Here I was in her living room shirtless, my black beanie hat on, and . . . in a kilt.

"This is epic, man!" Chris said.

"I'll get you back, you little piece of—"

"Hate the game, bro. You lost fair and square. You said you would never fall into the baby-talking trap and there you were, calling Jack bread pudding."

I looked down at my dark green kilt. "I'm changing."

"One hour, then you can change. That's the rule!"

Ryan backed Chris up, and took a picture of me flipping her the finger. "Ahh, new profile pic," she said, laughing.

I looked at her. "When did you get here?"

"Not long ago," she said, handing me a blue gift bag. "Here. I figured you forgot to buy this for li'l bro."

"What's this?" I asked.

"I think you froze your brain in this skimpy getup," she joked. "I remembered you said you wanted to get him a little Yankees outfit. I saw this one and I thought you'd like it." She snatched the gift bag from me and took out a blanket, a little Yankees hat, a couple outfits and a mini T-shirt that said "Rookie of the Year."

"That's perfect! Here, little man. See what Uncle Kevin got for you? I'm the best uncle, don't you forget it." I looked at Ryan. "Thanks, dude. You so know me."

"Don't thank me yet. You haven't seen the receipt. You're the one who owes me," she said. "Believe it or not, little people's clothing is expensive."

"Tell me about it!" Annie said, taking the baby away from me. "He has to eat."

"Why does he always have to eat as soon as I hold him?"

Annie laughed. "It's not personal. He has his uncle's appetite."

"Oh, well, that I understand."

"Hey, Kevin, what's under that kilt?" Nick asked.

The teasing continued the whole night as would be expected. We hung out and as always had an awesome time. I changed back into my clothes as soon as I knew the hour was up. I couldn't really complain. I once made Chris wear hot pink shorts at the beach on a dare. Any other time I would think that was worse than a kilt, except he got quite a few numbers that day. He played the victim with girls and scored big. Right now, though, he was busy following Ryan's every move with his eyes.

And apparently I was busy watching him watching her. I noticed his eyes travel from the kitchen where Ryan was leaving Beth to come to where I was sitting, bouncing little Elisa on my knees. Our eyes met and Chris nodded, looking away. I turned to Ryan.

She sat next to me, and asked, "Kev, we're on for tomorrow?"

"What?"

Her eyes widened. "Don't tell me you forgot again!"

"I don't want to swear in front of Elisa, but what the bleep are you talking about?"

"We have a training session. It's Sunday. Remember? We do this every week, and you already left me hanging last week, Kev."

"Sorry, I didn't even realize. Man, time is slipping away from me." I gave her a smile. "I'll meet you at the Org."

"You're not picking me up to teleport?" Ryan asked as she tucked Elisa's red hair behind her ears.

"I'm going over tonight to see Gabby for a bit. Then I'll probably sleep in for as long as possible. I'll meet you there."

"Okay. I'll take your gym bag from my car then, so

you won't have to worry about that."

"You are the best, you know that?"

"Of course I know," she said, smiling. "Hey, have you had any more incidents?" She was aware of all my electronic adventures.

"Nope. Nothing else has happened."

"Okay."

"I know I have to deal with it soon. Wanna help?" I asked.

The corner of her lips turned up. "You know it, dude. Let me know when you're ready."

Chris joined us. "Kev, I wanted to run something by you."

"What's up?"

"Ryan and I have been staking out the club, but no luck. I tried hypnotizing a few of the men for information—the ones who are always moving equipment in and out of the club, but they know nothing. They say their bosses are always quiet around them."

"Hmm, who else goes to the club? Drink vendors, cleaners, waitresses?"

"Yeah, we tried them too. I mean, anyone we could think of. Derek should just grab the few rebels who run the place and be done with it."

"No, that could put Dr. Ryder in danger." I looked around the room and noticed the one thing everyone needed. "What about food?"

Ryan's brows creased. "You're hungry again?"

"No, I mean what do they do for food? They go out

to eat during their workdays? Or they order in?"

"Oh my God, Kevin, you're a genius!" Ryan said. "They seem to only order from one place and always have the same two delivery guys."

Chris looked at her. "Yes, that's true. I can hypnotize them for information, but they're in and out so fast, how much help can they really be?"

"That's where patience comes in. Make them gather everything they hear for us. Could be a day, could be a few weeks, could be nothing, but what else do we have?" I said.

"Can we make one of them bug the club?" Chris asked.

"You can try, but they're only dropping food off. Make them listen. If you get nothing after a couple weeks, then drop the bug."

"I can just do that now so we don't waste time."

I put Elisa down and gave her a doll to play with. "I know, Chris, but they might pay attention to what the delivery guys do. We don't want to lose our only in too quickly."

"Okay, we'll run it by Derek," Ryan said. "This should work out for us one way or another."

I MET WITH Ryan to train the next day. It had been over a month, but even so, I didn't appreciate waking up at the crack of dawn. I hated that she insisted on training so early every week. I mean, it was really nine o' clock in the morning, but on a Sunday it was almost the same thing. I always had a great time, though. Nothing better than blowing off some steam fighting and training with Ryan; she always made it challenging.

I HEARD A knock at my door when I got out of the shower on Monday morning. I ran my fingers through my wet hair as I opened the door for Ryan. I knew it'd be her. She was the only one who refused to ever use the darn bell.

"Good morn—" Ryan looked at me. Her mouth hung open.

"What?"

"Put some clothes on," she said, and ran to sit on my couch.

I followed her. I had to, since my bedroom was right off the living room. I stood by my door and enjoyed seeing her blush. "Oh, sorry. I didn't mean to hurt your innocent eyes. It's not like I expected you to surprise me this early."

My skin was still dripping water and I saw her staring at my chest. After a few seconds, her eyes traveled to the towel wrapped around my waist. I grabbed it and pretended I was going to take it off.

"What are you doing?" Her blue eyes were popping.

"Messing with you," I said, laughing. "The last thing we want is for me to be the first guy you see naked."

"I've seen naked guys," she said, avoiding eye contact.

"Uh-huh." I smiled and went to get dressed.

We had a while before either of us had to start our working day, so she had come to hang out a bit.

"I hope this is presentable enough for you, Little Miss Prissy," I said, sitting next to her. I wore a black T-shirt and a pair of jeans.

"Your feet are out."

"Oh, you got jokes?" I put my feet up on the coffee table and wiggled my toes.

She laughed. "I probably should call next time. I had that one coming."

"Please, like I care. You know everything else about me. Why not see me naked? Actually that would be unfair to your future boyfriends, their poor litt—"

"Stop it!" She punched me.

I laughed. "I forgot you were waiting for true love and all that shit."

"Just because you're scared of anything to do with love doesn't mean it's not worth it."

"I'm not scared. I just don't believe in it *for me.* I'm not letting anyone have that kind of power over me."

"Bullshit." She pointed her finger at me. "I've heard you tell Jack you love him. If love equals power then he sure has it over you."

"It's not the same. I'd give my life for him," I said. "No one else gets to hear that from me."

"Yeah, we'll see. Someday you'll find that one girl and you'll have to say it."

"Nope. Not doing it."

"It's not control. It's—"

"Being stupid?" I asked.

"Kevin! I swear that's how you get all the new trainees running after you. You're a jerk but still adorable enough for them to think they can change you."

"Dude, it's not my fault they're up to the challenge, even if it's futile."

Ryan laughed but gave up on the topic. She didn't have much to tell me on her investigation and I told her about my new, improved relationship with Gabby. She thought it was great we weren't at each other's throats anymore.

Chris was coming to meet Ry at my place so they could leave together, but called to say he was running late. While we waited, she walked around the apartment rearranging my things. I had some fitness and car magazines on the coffee table that were now neatly stacked on top of each other—by category and date of issue. I was pretty sure some of them had been on the floor.

When she finished those, she grabbed my loose DVDs and put them back in their cases, then proceeded to put them in a Ryan-worthy order.

"You only have five out of hundreds of my DVD

collection in your hand," I said. "Are you really going to alphabetize those?"

"Yes. It will bug me all day if I don't," she said, bending over to put them away.

I followed her movements, which then forced me to take a good look at her. She had come in with a gray hoodie, the one she'd stolen from me the first time she beat the crap out of me in a fight. In my defense, I wasn't able to really hit her because she was a girl. I learned soon after that how wrong I was; she was tougher than most guys I knew. She boggled my mind for so many reasons. Right now, though, she wore it over a black short skirt, tights, and boots with three-inch heels. A belt with a big, diamond square buckle hugged her waist. How she made it look stylish, I had no clue.

"Does that really go together?" I asked, pointing at her outfit.

"Not really, but it's cold." She smiled, and proceeded to open the belt and take off the hoodie. Underneath it, I found out what an hourglass figure truly looked like. She wasn't too skinny; she had meat on her, but it was in pretty good proportions. Her black, very tight, long-sleeved top was immediately adorned with the belt she'd taken off, accenting her tiny waist. And her hair? Well, she even had it loose. It was long and silky. I'd always thought of her as my sister, but this chick didn't look like she should be anyone's sister. She sat down next to me.

"What'd you do to your hair? And are you wearing

makeup?"

Her brows creased. "Don't make fun of me."

"Well, it looks funny. You—" I stopped at the look of murder that crept in her eyes. "It looks nice, it's just different. I didn't think you liked being girly."

"I'm a girl. How can I not be girly?"

"You know what I mean; you are more of a tomboy."

"That was because I was still trying to learn how to be out in the field and use my powers. Now that I know how, I think it's perfectly fine to dress up if I want to."

"Right. Come on, you only dress up for missions if you have to. Like at the club," I said, laughing. "Even in training you were always more boyish."

"I was not." She frowned.

"Yes, you were. How did you even learn to put on makeup? You probably practiced all weekend—" I saw her fist coming at my face and teleported right on time. Unfortunately, Ryan fell over. I went to pick her up but she stopped me. Shit. I'd pissed her off real bad. If I was not mistaken, her blue eyes were a bit teary.

"You are an ass."

"Dude, I'm sorry. I was just kidding. I'm not used to seeing you as a girl," I said, and dashed to the door. Man, that was perfect timing on Chris's part to ring the bell.

"Well, get used to it. And stop making fun of me or I'll give your face some scars to match your brother's."

"That's harsh. Jeez," I said, rubbing my face.

Chris walked in at the same time, and said, "Hey,

you look pretty, Ry."

"Don't be a prick," she said and got up. "We have to go."

"I'm not," he said frowning. "What's up with her?" he asked me in a whisper as we followed her.

"It's not you. I made fun of her before, so now she is all defensive, like it's our fault she suddenly decided to be a girl."

"She looks nice as a girl," Chris said, checking her out walking down the hallway.

I shrugged. "I guess. But she's the one who always made fun of them and now she's all dressed up. Look at her skirt, too tight for her own good—what are you doing? Stop staring at her. She's going to melt your eyes if you don't stop."

"I'll make her forget," he said with a grin.

"You and your hypnosis. Do you ever confront anything head on, or do you always modify your way out?"

"Modify my way out. Why deal with crap if I don't have to?" He shrugged.

"Good thing you'd never do that to me," I said to Chris. "Wait, what was that look? Dude, that would be very un-bro-like!"

"It would be." Chris smiled, and hurried out behind Ryan.

THEY LEFT AND I made a quick stop at the store

before popping over to the safe house. The Org provided a fair amount of grocery, but nothing great, so I wanted to stock up the fridge and pantry with better stuff. I was twenty minutes late, but Andrew was okay with it, especially after I told him he could spend an extra couple hours with Beth before coming over later. He was on guard alone tonight.

I also brought my old iPod so Gabby could listen to music. I offered to add any specific songs she wanted, but after going through it she said our playlist was pretty similar in taste. She spent most of the day with her mom who was having a tough time, so I hoped we wouldn't have any issues during dinner.

Late afternoon, I made my usual inspections around the premise and went back to set the table. My palms were sweating like crazy as I waited for Gabby to meet me. She'd gone to take a shower before my "special meal" which I had avoided making until now. I swore she took forever; what was it with women?

"Okay, where is my food?" she asked as she walked in, one slow step at a time. She wore a pair of shorts and some kind of camisole.

"Are you in summer?" I asked while I stared at her legs.

"No, but they keep the heat cranked up in this place. Especially at night." She took a seat.

I went to get our plates. "Okay, brace yourself for the goodness of—wait for it—hot dogs!"

"Hot dogs?" She eyed the plate. "And chips?"

"Yes, what do you want? I have all the toppings on the table so you can pick your favorite. And if you hate what I have, chips are always good backup." I grinned.

"You said you could cook!"

"No." I shook my head. "You asked and I changed the subject. Sort of."

"Well, you were right though," she said, rolling her eyes. "You blew my mind! But I'm not sure in a good way."

We were laughing and having a good time when I noticed Ryan looking at us from the living room. "Hey, when'd you get here?"

Gabby turned around to see who I was talking to. "Ryan, hi! Come here and have some dinner with us. Kevin cooked."

"Hi guys." Ryan frowned. "Kevin cooked? You're kidding, right?"

I smiled. "Yes, she is. All I made was hot dogs."

"Ah, well that explains it. How's everything here?"

"Good. Kevin's awesome," Gabby said, getting up and taking the dirty dishes to the kitchen sink.

"Yeah, I am." I laughed but noticed Ryan was serious. "You okay?"

"Fine." Her eyes went from Gabby to me. "Andrew said you were staying here later than planned and I just wanted to make sure things were running smoothly."

"Silky smooth. You know me," I said, smiling.

Gabby gave a loud *pfft*, and Ryan said, "Well, that's good, then."

I saw her shoving something in her purse, and asked, "What's that?"

"Nothing. Did you want a ride or should I just go?"

"Hang out a bit, Ry; what's the rush? What's in your bag? That's not . . ." I teleported her purse to me and took out the paper bag. I would recognize the logo from my favorite bakery anywhere. "Cupcakes!"

"That's my purse. Give it back," Ryan said, frowning.

"Aww, you are so sweet! You got me red velvet cupcakes." I took one out and handed it to Gabby and took one big bite out of the other one. "Lucky thing you started carrying these huge stylish purses or you would have crushed my dessert." I finished my cupcake and noticed both girls staring at me. "What?"

"Could you've eaten that any faster?" Ryan said with a loud laugh, which sounded unlike her.

"Nah, it's too good," I said licking off a bit of frosting from my fingers. "Try it, Gabby. Tell me it's not good."

Ryan said, "Yes, take a bite. You'll love it."

"Okay." Gabby turned to Ryan with a half-smile. "Sure?"

"Of course, enjoy it." Ryan got her purse from me and pulled her beanie hat from inside it. I was shocked that she still used it with her new looks, but it was cute the way her dark hair fell and framed her face from under it. I swear her baby blues seemed to intensify more than when she carried it in a bun. She finished adjusting it on her head and said, "Well, I'll leave you two to it. Good night."

"G'night! I'll text you later, Ry." She waved and walked out of the kitchen. A few seconds later I heard the sound of the front door closing.

"Are you sure that you two . . ." Gabby paused. "Umm . . ."

"Nah, Ryan's my buddy. She's cool. Wait 'til you get to know her better. You'll love her," I said.

Gabby stared toward the door. "It was nice of her to bring cupcakes, but I'm not sure it was for—"

"Yeah, she does that kinda stuff all the time."

"That's nice. Hey, can I ask for a favor?"

"Sure, what's up?"

"Andrew is cool, but he's intimidating and doesn't talk much. He moves from window to window and patrols the outside constantly. I get bored. I have a TV in my bedroom but no cable."

"I don't think they'll run a second cable box."

She played with her watch and her voice lowered as she asked, "Okay, but can you get me a laptop with Netflix?"

"Sorry, you can't have Wi-Fi here. But I can get you one of their extra DVD players with some movies. Do you want me to bring it back later?"

"No, I have your iPod to keep me company tonight. I don't know how much longer we'll be here, so I figured I ask. The weekend is coming and you're not on as babysitter. I'll need something to entertain me all day long."

"I'll hook you up tomorrow," I said.

She let go of her watch to hold my hand. "Thank you. And if you'd like to hang out with me and watch them instead of working in the kitchen it would be nice."

The warmth of her fingers felt great. "I just might."

LATER THAT NIGHT, I found myself thinking about her before falling asleep.

Jesus! Why did I dream of her? As much as I tried, I couldn't stop thinking about it. She was so happy in the dream, laughing with her hair flying in the wind and those gray eyes staring into mine.

All I thought about was how her lips would taste. I made it a point to never get involved with anyone I worked with *or* for. Okay, so I did spend a few nights with some of the girls from missions, but those were quick jobs and they were meaningless. This one, though . . . I would be protecting her until we got her father into safety and probably send them all off with new identities, far away. Maybe once this job was done . . . no, I couldn't. Her sister had just died because of me. What was I even thinking?

Dammit.

I went straight there, since I didn't have to go to the Org until the end of the week. It wasn't like I had anything new to report on my end, anyway. The guys were off doing their thing and I knew I wouldn't see them for a few days. It sucked. I needed to know how fast this was all progressing.

The rest of my days were spent watching movies with Gabby and listening to music. It was nice to make a new friend. And the fact that she was a hot new friend made me even more invested in her. I could see Ryan wanting to smack me if I told her that, though, so I kept that to myself. Actually I could see Gabby smacking me over that, too. Women. They're not even here and I'm busy filtering my thoughts in fear of what they'd think of me.

CHAPTER EIGHT

FRIDAY AFTERNOON I stopped by the Org to check in with Derek, but he wasn't in so I went to my office to catch up on some work.

"Hey, stranger," Ryan said, waiting for me.

"Stranger?" I asked.

She placed her hands on her hips. "I'm still waiting for that text or for you to return my calls from the past few days."

I slapped my forehead. "Crap! Sorry, Ry. I was going to call you today. I got busy."

She smiled and said softly, "I know."

"Where's Derek? We were supposed to have a meeting right now."

"I don't know. Pine came here and they left in a hurry."

"I wonder what that's about." I frowned. "He didn't even call to cancel."

Ryan shrugged. "Who even knows which side

required them to go running off, Pine's or ours? I can't keep up with those two."

"Any news on your investigation?"

"Oh yeah, something's about to happen. Derek said we should take the weekend off and relax because he's going to make a move on Monday. Things should start getting interesting."

"Finally!" I rubbed my hands together.

"Yeah. Hey, wanna go to the movies? We're behind on new releases," she asked.

"Nah, I'm all movied-out." I saw her frowning. "What? It gets boring and it gives Gabby and me something to do."

"Nothing, I just really wanted to go see—"

"Call Chris, maybe he can take you," I suggested.

"I can ask him; he's meeting us in a few. It's just . . . you had said we would—never mind. I got in my cooking mood last night—I made lasagna and still have leftovers if you want some."

"Hell, yeah, I want some."

"Shocking," she said, flipping her hair.

That action made me study this new Ryan. She'd been dressing weird lately, more womanly. I wasn't used to it. Skinny jeans, dresses, high heels . . . she was clearly feeling stifled, being paired with us boys for too long. And we were such man whores, I really couldn't blame her. Any chance we got, we left her to go enjoy the company of some real girls. Her baggy slacks were gone, her hair bun was gone, and she was wearing makeup every day.

Today she wore fitted jeans with a red see-through blouse. She at least had the decency of wearing a camisole under, though. "What happened to your wardrobe and all your neutral colors? I never thought I'd see you in red."

"I like red." She shrugged.

"What's going on with you?" I asked as I heard my office door opening. "And don't get mad again. Seriously, why are you suddenly a fashionista?"

She laughed. "Beth finally got to me. Between her and Annie, I had to give in. But I like it. Unless . . . do I look bad? I look like a clown, don't I?"

"Oh, hell, no!" Chris said, coming in. "I'm scared of clowns. And I can tell you, that would not be the case if clowns looked like you."

"Hi, Chris. I can count on you to always say the right thing."

"The right thing, the true thing, whatever the thing is, he's feeling it," I said, noticing how he looked at her.

"Damn right," Chris said, still admiring Ryan's appearance.

"Okay, hate to ruin the fun but we have to get going. I'm starving," I said, looking at them and shaking my head at their image.

Ryan was the same height as Chris, at 5'10", but in heels she was eye to eye with me. And since he hated that I was taller than he, I could only guess Ryan's new height was pretty much a slap to his face. But my team and I made one tall, intimidating group together, and that was awesome for our line of work.

Ryan drove us to her place. She lived ten minutes away from me so I wouldn't have to teleport home if I didn't want to. The weather was finally nice enough to enjoy a good walk. She had a small apartment; her best space was her large bedroom, which she'd recently redecorated. From the entrance, you walked straight into her living room, and then her kitchen was in the opposite end. She had no dining room space but had a large island, which served as a decent eating area.

Ryan had an interesting mix of dark shades throughout the apartment. And she was so particular about her choices she'd really made it difficult to surprise her when I wanted to buy her stools for the kitchen island. Who knew there were so many shades of black and gray? Still, when she lit all her candles that she loved so much, the whole place looked amazing.

Chris left us right after dinner. We were chatting away when I got an idea. "What are you doing tomorrow?"

"Not much. Why?"

I tilted my head. "Wanna go shopping?"

"Yes! That would be nice. What are we buying?"

"Clothes."

"Cool," she said, beaming.

"You're really into this girly thing, huh?"

"Not really. I've got Beth for that. I'm just excited to finally hang out some more."

"Oh, I'm not going. I was hoping you could pick up some new clothes for Gabby. She doesn't have much with her and hates doing laundry."

Ryan gasped. "You like her!"

"Why the accusatory tone? Yes, okay. She's so different. We like the same music, the same movies, almost everything, AND she kicks butt fighting. I can talk to her all day long and never get bored . . . unless she's in one of her moods." I laughed. "But, I mean, I've never had that before with any girl."

Ryan blinked. "*Never*?"

"Never."

She stood up suddenly, grabbing her head. "Not one girl?"

"Nope. She's the coolest one I know. You okay?"

"Headache." Ryan walked toward the kitchen. "I need Advil or something. You know, maybe you should pop in and visit her now, then. It sounds like you miss her."

I followed her. "Yeah, you know what? I'm gonna. You just made my night." I gave her a kiss on her forehead. "I'm going to stop by the bakery. She liked the cupcake the other day." I went to put my jacket on. "Don't forget to buy her some stuff tomorrow."

"I won't," Ryan said and sat back down on the couch. "Have fun. I'll bring the things to you on Sunday at the Org."

"The Org? Oh, for training, yes. But I wanted to get the stuff to her tomorrow night. I'll call you in the afternoon to pick it up from you."

"Okay."

I TELEPORTED STRAIGHT into Gabby's bedroom. The pastel blue colors were pale in comparison to her and the way she looked in her flowery pajamas.

"Holy shit! You scared me," she said when she saw me.

I laughed. "Sorry, I didn't want to deal with Andrew."

"It's okay." She sat up. She'd been lying on the bed watching a movie when I got there.

"I brought more cupcakes," I said, raising the bag up to show her.

"Oooh!"

We ate them and she went to get us something to drink while checking to see what Andrew was up to. I stood by the window, but began to think that was awkward so I sat at the edge of her bed.

"Not that I'm complaining, but how come you are here?" she asked.

I raised an eyebrow. "Want me to leave?"

"No, just wondering."

I shrugged. "I figured you'd be bored, and I had

nothing to do."

"I'm glad you came." She smiled.

We looked at each other for a few seconds longer than normal. "Uh, I haven't seen your mom lately. Is she okay?"

"Mom is Mom. Not much different from life at home, to tell you the truth. She's locked up in her bedroom, all drugged up. She's either asleep or writing away in her notebooks."

"And she's always like this?"

"Yes, she's obsessed with writing and rewriting her life. She doesn't want to forget, she says. But honestly, what life does she have if all she does is record her past over and over?"

"I can't imagine how hard that is," I said.

"You are lucky. You don't have to deal with a crazy mother." She shook her head.

I looked down at the floor. "You think so?"

"Yes, family is just luggage. Well, my family, anyway. They suck. I thought so many times of running away, but I had Grace to look out for."

"Come on, they can't be so bad."

"Yes, they are. I would be so much better if I was alone. Look where I am now because of them."

"I don't know about that. Family matters," I said.

"They do, I guess. I just hate mine; wanna switch?" She laughed.

I tucked my hands in my pockets. "I'm an orphan."

Gabby looked at me for a while. "I'm sorry. I'm so

insensitive . . . I didn't know."

"It's all right."

"No, it's not. Here I am complaining about something you probably would give anything to have."

I nodded. "Yes, but I understand where you're coming from."

"So it's just you and your brother?" She moved closer to me and held my hand. "Tell me about you."

Her warmth felt nice. "Him, my sister-in-law, and nephew. Nick is my half-brother. I hate living in his shadow at work, but I'm lucky he found me. Don't tell him I said that if you ever meet him."

She nodded. "So the four of you?"

"The four of us and our friends, we are each other's family. Always have been, always will be."

"All super-people?"

I smiled. "We're all Luminaries, yes."

"Do you want a family? Of your own?"

"I don't know if I'm cut out for my own family. Most of the time I think I'm not, but sometimes I look at my nephew and think it would be nice. I'm too young to give it any serious thought, though," I said. "You?"

"I would. I'm just nervous about kids and my . . . umm, family's history with mental disorder."

"You can always adopt."

"I've thought about that. So, you"—she played with her watch—"would you adopt?"

"Definitely. I wish someone had adopted me but I wasn't that lucky."

"Hopefully your future wife wants that too," she said, letting go of her watch to hold my hand.

"Hopefully." I smiled. Telling her I wasn't really into the idea of marriage didn't seem natural at the moment. In fact, with her hand in mine, it didn't seem that scary a thought.

"You're gonna make sure I'm safe, right?" she asked, changing the subject.

"Of course."

I could feel the heat rising as she looked down at our hands. "Good. I think my future just got a little brighter."

"It did, didn't it?" I asked as I leaned in to kiss her.

I was one breath away from her lips when I stopped. We sat there and stared at each other for a few seconds. Gabby then slowly moved back. "Sorry, I thought you were going to . . ."

"I was. I am."

"Are you nervous? I won't judge too harshly," she joked.

"No, I'm a good kisser." I smiled and tucked a piece of hair behind her ear.

"Everyone thinks they're a good kisser."

"I have references." I smiled again.

"So why not, then?"

"Well, we only get to have our first kiss once. I want to remember every detail of it."

"Oh."

"Yeah, the best part of the first kiss is the lead up to it. The moment just before, you know?" I pulled her closer to me and caressed her face with the back of my hand. Our eyes locked in place. Then ever so gently our lips met.

"YOU DOG!" CHRIS said the next day when I told him. He'd gone to see Ryan to discuss some details for their assignment on Monday, and since he was coming over to me next, he brought the clothes that Ryan had gotten for Gabby. "So?"

"So what?"

"That's all? You didn't . . .?"

"No! What's wrong with you? She's in my care. We can't get involved right now."

"But you already kissed and that's never stopped you before," he pointed out.

"Yes, but we won't again. We'll wait for all this to be over before attempting a relationship. Derek was upset enough that one time. If I do it again he'll pull me from Gabby's post."

"Nice. Finally a girl to tie you down. Bro, you might as well give me your little black book."

"I don't have a black book, dude."

"What kind of a player are you, then?"

"Whoever said I was a player?"

"Oh, come on, player is your default setting." He laughed. "Wait until we tell Ryan; she's gonna flip."

"Why would she flip?"

Chris shrugged. "She called it. I owe her twenty bucks. I thought you would keep on living the life, but she was sure you were hooked on Gabrrrrriellllahhh."

"Okay, okay, that's enough."

AFTER CHRIS LEFT, I went to visit Gabby and we hung out 'til the morning. We were so good and innocent that we didn't even kiss once. But we did hold hands while listening to music. I wasn't sure what it was about her, but she made me feel so high that time passed in the blink of an eye when we were together. When the guard shifts changed, I decided it was good time to go home and rest. I'd received a text from Derek telling me he needed me on Monday with the team, so I wasn't going to see Gabby until that was all over.

I left her and went to check out the premises as I usually did. I noticed the year-round green hedges right below the fence seemed a bit off. Someone had climbed down, I was sure of it. I looked around and alerted the other guards. We found nothing. In case I'd lost my mind, I double-checked the pictures I'd taken a few weeks back and confirmed one seemed lower. It had been trimmed to even out the spot where someone must have fallen on top. Thank goodness for cloud storage technology; with my recent phone issues I'd have lost it all. A quick call to Derek and he had Andrew and me relocate Gabby and her mom.

I made sure they were settled in the training center before going home. Derek wanted them to stay there until he could figure out how we'd been breached at the safe house. I went to bed around eight in the morning and when I woke up from my deep sleep, it was already starting to get dark outside. I got up and ordered some Chinese takeout while I forced myself to do some laundry. Gabriella was right on that one—she had said laundry was the work of the devil.

RYAN WOULD BE proud: my alarm went off at seven o' clock on Monday morning. I'd set it so I could squeeze in a run before reporting to duty. I usually had to be at work by nine and I got up at the last possible minute. Teleporting my way around made my life so much easier. After I was ready, I stopped by the coffee shop to pick up some liquid sanity for the guys and me.

"Good morning!" I said, meeting Chris and Ryan in their shared office. Since they were newer to fieldwork and Ryan was training Chris, they were stuck together. Their office was larger than mine, but had three desks, each facing the middle of the room. Ryan's desk was across from the door and was by far the tidiest. Chris had a collection of signed basketballs in the office: two on his desk and three on the unoccupied desk opposite him.

"Here you go." I handed each of them their cups.

"You're in a good mood," Chris said.

"Why wouldn't I be? This thing is finally starting to make some progress." I took a sip of my own coffee. "Any of you know what Derek has planned?"

Ryan kept working on her computer and still hadn't said a word. "No idea, man." Chris answered.

"Who else is on the team for this?" I asked.

Chris shrugged. "Just us, as far as I know."

"Ry, do you not want coffee?" I noticed the cup sitting at the edge of her desk where I left it.

"I had some already this morning."

"I don't know if you've ever turned down coffee before, but I'll take it," Chris said, and picked up the cup. "I'll be right back. I'm gonna give this to the new chick Jenny's training."

He left and Ryan continued staring at her screen. I frowned. "What are you concentrating on so hard there?"

She looked up. "It's called work, Kevin. You should try it sometime."

"I do plenty." I laughed.

"Sure you do," she said without looking. "What did you do yesterday?"

Okay, so she wasn't joking around. "First, I helped Gabby and her mom relocate Saturday night. Yesterday I slept all day, then washed some clothes when I got up."

"Bum."

"What did you do?"

"Oh . . ." She got up and went around her desk to sit on it, and faced me. "Glad you asked. I came to the gym here and waited about an hour for you. I tried calling but it went to voicemail. You didn't show up, but Annie did. We trained together."

"Shit! I'm sorry! I was so tired. I got home past eight in the morning and turned my phone off so I could sleep. I forgot we were supposed to meet."

"In two years you've left me hanging a lot recently. I mean, I figured you were tired, but I expected a text or call at least." She got up. "It's okay though, Annie is way better at fighting than you are."

"Better?" I lifted an eyebrow.

"Yes, and tougher. Man, I'm in pain! Annie is hardcore."

"Trust me, I know." I nodded. "See? I did you a favor. You got to train with the best."

"If that wasn't true, I'd be really pissed."

I finished the last of my coffee right when Chris came back. "How did it go?"

He grinned. "Good. She blushed when I gave her the coffee and agreed to go out to dinner sometime."

I gave him a fist bump. "Nice, dude!"

"Well if you two are done with your compliments on getting girls, we should head up to see Derek," Ryan said, walking out.

We followed her, and I asked, "No heels today, Ryan? Tired of pretending to be a girl?"

She stopped and turned with a hard look on her face. "I don't have to pretend to be anything. We're in the field today and I expect some good action. Excuse me for dressing for the occasion," she finished saying through gritted teeth.

I raised my hand in defeat. "Okay, okay. Jeez."

I still wondered what the hell had gotten into her. She was pretty and didn't need to pretend, playing dress up. It just wasn't our Ryan. But now she was in the "I'm woman, watch me roar" phase and I didn't know what I was supposed to do with that. She was walking in front of us swaying her behind in those tight jeans. Her wavy hair reached down to her waist. I didn't even know it was that long before she decided to be a girl. Then again, that was a pretty girly thing . . . to even have hair that long—but why the makeover?

CHRIS AND RYAN were my bros. And now she'd gone and messed that whole thing up; the way Chris stared at her you would think he'd never met her. "Did you know her eyes were so bright and blue?" he asked me.

"Have you not seen her before?"

"Yes, but her lashes are extra long."

"I think they call that mascara. It's not like it's natural."

He kept staring at Ryan. "And the way her hair falls—"

"Don't mess with her."

"Are you calling dibs?"

"What? No, she's like my little sister. And hello—Gabby? I just don't want to be in a triangle thing with my friends."

"I don't like her that way, don't worry. It's just new; I have to look."

"Good."

"I get it, she's one of us. It's just I didn't know she was hiding that kind of ass and did you see her cleav— uh, nothing." He looked away.

Ryan turned around to talk to me. "Was your girlfriend happy with the clothes?"

"Yes, she liked it. Thanks. I scored major points," I said, and Chris gave me a knowing look. "No, not like that. I told you, we're not getting into anything until this is all over."

"If you say so," Chris said as Ryan's steps picked up in speed.

"Wait for us, Ry," I said and turned to Chris. "See? No heels. That's proof that girly-ness holds Ryan back from her full potential."

AFTER RECEIVING INSTRUCTIONS from Derek, we went to a residential address and waited in the car for any sign of movement. Chris and Ryan were able to retrieve pieces of information from the food delivery guys who always took lunch to the club rebels. Not paying attention to them was stupid on their part, but having such a strict routine was just amateur. Patterns were our friends when trying to gather intel of any kind.

They talked freely in front of the guys, but since

their visits were short, Chris hypnotized them to look out for when they were especially agitated or excited. In gluing the bits and pieces together we knew something was about to happen soon, so Derek ordered Chris to plant the bug.

As expected, a small U-Haul truck pulled out from the back of a colonial house that reminded me of Superman with its deep blue exterior and bright red door. We followed the truck closely. They were to transport an important cargo to some secure location. We'd hoped this new location would give us some new answers. We drove for a while until the truck made a stop in the middle of an almost-isolated street. We weren't too far behind, so we kept going to avoid any suspicions in case they had anyone looking. I teleported out of the car and went on top of the roof of one of the houses with a clear view of the truck.

The driver spoke on his phone and after a few minutes, a second man joined him. He got in the truck and they made a U-turn to drive away in the opposite direction. Crap. I called Chris to let him know what I was going to do next.

I hung up the phone and the next second I found myself in the dark small space of the moving truck. This was a tight space; I could hardly move. "Who's there?" I heard behind me.

I got the small flashlight on my keychain Ryan had given me and clicked it on. I turned to find a man sitting on a box in the truck. He was handcuffed to a makeshift bar above his head. Since I'd seen his picture, I recognized the bald man. "Dr. Ryder?"

"Yes. Who are you?"

"I'm here to get you back to your family," I said and grabbed him. We appeared at the Org right in Derek's office.

Derek jumped out of his seat. "What—"

"He was the shipment," I cut him off. "We would have been caught if we continued tailing them so we had to move on to plan B. I got inside the truck."

"Dr. Ryder, please have a seat." Derek pointed to a chair, after getting over the shock. "Are you okay? Can we get you anything?"

"I am fine. I'm fine! They take good care of you when they need you to do work for them," Dr. Ryder said, shaking his head.

Derek insisted, "Are you sure? We can—"

"Ah-ha! Indeed, indeed, a teleporter. Yes, yes. Makes sense now." Dr. Ryder stared at me, and nodded excitedly. Even though he was wearing a big lab coat, it was easy to see he was a thin man. His head was bald, but had bushy eyebrows above those gray eyes that were the exact shade as Gabby's.

"Kevin, would you get his handcuffs off?" Derek asked.

"Uh . . . okay." I got the handcuffs off and tried ignoring the man's eyes burying into my skull.

Derek placed a hand on my shoulder to get my attention. "Now go share the news with his wife and daughter and bring them back here."

I did as asked. When I walked out of the office, I called Chris. He put me on speakerphone and I filled them in on what happened and told them to meet me at our training center.

CHAPTER NINE

"**Y**OU REALLY FOUND Daddy?" Gabby jumped into my arms and hugged me. "We are free now!"

I stood in the small room next to two bunk beds at the training center. Gabby was hanging on to me while her mom pursed her lips. Chris and Ryan waited by the doorway.

"Behave yourself, Gabriella. I'm sure our safety is still of some concern. Am I correct, Kevin?" Mrs. Ryder asked.

"I think so. I'm sure there will be a protection detail, but you should be able to resume your regular life soon."

Ryan went and put a hand on Mrs. Ryder's shoulder. "It might be a while, though. We still haven't caught those responsible for the kidnapping. Depending on how much your husband knows, we'll take them down soon enough."

"Okay, so we shouldn't pack our things yet. Is that

what you're saying?" Gabby asked, distancing herself from me.

"It would be best to remain here. But let's just go for now; I'm sure Derek will share his plan with you," Ryan answered.

We took Gabby and her mom back to the Org and left them in Jenny's care. It was only noon and Derek had given us the rest of the day off, so the guys and I decided to go hang out. Ryan had driven, so I told them I would meet up with them at her place.

"WHERE'D YOU GO?" Chris asked when they walked into Ryan's apartment half an hour after me. I loved the speed of teleporting. It gave me the upper hand when I needed it.

"To leave a note for Gabby."

Ryan walked over to me and pushed my feet off her coffee table. "Could you've taken off your shoes at least? And why is it you two always want to hang out here? You constantly end up leaving my place a mess."

I laughed. "Because your place is clean and we get to see exactly how much fun we had before we leave. If we went to my place or Chris's, we'd never know the difference."

"Didn't know we measured fun according to how messy we are now." She rolled her eyes. "What is that sound?" Her head spun.

"I got you something." I stood and walked to the

opposite end of her apartment. "Follow me."

"Oh my God!" Ryan yelled.

I stood in the kitchen, smiling. "I know you probably would've preferred a puppy, but with our job . . ."

"No, oh my gosh. Awww!" She picked up the tiny kitten from the bed I'd brought with him. "You are perfect, aren't you?" She hugged him. He was white with gray spots and a few inches long.

"You like him?"

"Yes. Thanks so much, Kevin," she said, beaming.

"Aww, it's a him."

"Yeah."

"Someone's feeling guilty," Chris said, slapping my back.

I laughed. "My neighbor's cat just gave birth. I'd told her a while back that I was going to take one for my buddy. But yes, I do feel bad for leaving you hanging yesterday," I told Ryan.

"Yesterday, and?" Ryan tilted her head, staring at me expectantly.

"And all the other times I left you hanging recently."

"Aww, it's okay. I'll name him Milo." She laughed. "Smart, this one, huh, Milo?" She pointed at me. "Now I can never stay mad at him for too long. I'll just look at your cute face and forgive his douchebaggery."

"So we're good?" I asked.

"Yes, I didn't think you cared. You didn't say much about it."

I tucked my hands in my pockets. "Do I look dumb

to you? The wrong time to admit to that or remind a woman of something is when she's pissed."

"Well played, bro." Chris gave me a fist bump.

I picked up some bags from the kitchen floor and put them on the counter. "I got you everything you need for him, Ry."

"Thanks," she said, looking at me. "I love him already."

It was nice to see her smiling, crooked tooth and all.

"Good. We like it when you're happy. Right, Chris?"

"I'm just glad you busted her rut, man. If she isn't happy we pay for it." He turned to look at Ryan. "If he hadn't, I would have stayed away from you no matter how hot you look now."

She gave us one of her cute little snorts. "Men."

WE HAD AN early meeting the next day for Derek to fill the rest of the Luminaries in and explain what we were expected to do about the rebels. I walked into the conference and saw that Nick and Annie had returned to work.

The huge room had windows alongside the internal wall, so we could see most of the third floor when the blinds were up. It gave a much needed open feeling. Toward the entrance there was a medium-sized brown table. It was used for smaller conferences, and could seat ten people. Derek usually sat on the edge of the table or paced in front of it when he held full-sized meetings. The rest of the room was a wide area that was currently occupied with fifty or so chairs facing the table.

The rest of the Luminaries hustled in, taking a seat, and I stooped between Annie and Nick, who sat at that table facing everyone else. I smiled, knowing they hated that type of attention.

"Who's watching the baby?" I asked.

"A babysitter. Who else?" Annie answered.

I frowned. "Do you know this person?"

She laughed. "He's in good hands. I promise."

"Better be."

"Gabby is a lovely girl," Annie said. "She was a bit intimidated by Nick, though."

My eyes narrowed. "You met her?"

"Yesterday. We came to work and you played hooky on our first day, the nerve." Annie shook her head in disappointment.

"She still has it in her head that Nick killed Dr. Lumin," I said.

"Ah, well that explains it," Nick said. "She likes to stare."

"She probably was wondering how we can be brothers when you look like that and I'm all hot and stuff."

He whispered, "I doubt it. She said she digs my scar."

I frowned. "That's 'cause you look like me."

"Stop it, you two," Annie said. "I liked her. But Kevin?"

Oh crap, she was about to mommy me. "Yes?"

"Don't take your friends for granted."

"That was only a couple times," I said. "And I made up for it, anyway."

"I heard. Still, just keep that in mind. You never know how fragile your friends might be."

"My friends? There's nothing fragile about them." I stood and went to take a seat as I saw Derek walking in.

He closed the door behind him and went straight to business.

I LEFT THE conference room and went to my office. I realized Derek had been vague with the information he shared. In fact, now that I thought about it, Derek had hardly mentioned anything during the meeting. He welcomed the Logans back, and gave a general account of all that had happened the past weeks with the Ryders. Then he ran off to attend some business. I was thinking how unusual that was for him when I ran into Ryan in the hallway.

"Hey, how was the meeting? Bummer I had to miss it," she said.

I frowned, seeing the cat food in her hand. "You brought Milo to work?"

"He's a baby! I can't leave him alone."

"Yeah, tell that to Annie and Nick. They left Jack with a stranger," I complained.

She raised an eyebrow. "It's not like his uncle volunteered to babysit or anything. Besides, he's with Elisa and her babysitter."

I rubbed my neck. "Umm, which one's that?"

"Oh, I think you know just the one." She grinned. "So if you wanted to go check on the li'l dude and li'l dudette, be my guest. I mean, it's not like you didn't call her back after your night together, right?"

"Shut up." I punched her in the arm. "You have a kitten to go feed."

"Yes, I do. Hey, can you go with me later to get a new car?"

I pulled her to stand by the side of the wall. The rest of the Luminaries were leaving the meeting and rushing to get back to work. The hallway was spacious, but we were walking too slowly for our coworkers. "What's wrong with yours?" I asked.

"Lease is coming up."

"Any ideas on what kind you want?"

She shook her head. "Not sure yet. Maybe you could just give me yours since you hardly use it."

"Nope."

"Ass," she said, sticking her tongue out.

I spent the next couple hours or so browsing the Internet for cars and ordering consumer reports before I was interrupted. Derek was always paranoid that we would have a setback if something distracted us or if something went unexpectedly wrong, so he scheduled routine checkups on anything and everything that needed to be kept up and running. From light bulbs to electronics. My laptop and computer were being updated, rebooted, getting new spyware, and whatever else the guy explained.

He mentioned something about a new chip anyone of us could enable by holding down "esc + d" to fry all our motherboards if it came down to it. I didn't really listen; no one could find our location. The only way would be if they broke into Worldsafe. It's the only place we had storage of all paperwork related to Luminaries, including assignments and personnel files. Worldsafe was considered the most secure location in the world to store belongings. Not everyone knew it existed nor was the location disclosed. Those who knew about it kept it quiet because they had just as much to lose as everyone else.

Ry had come to my office at the same time maintenance started. "Hey, Kev. I got your email. You need me to be home for a delivery a couple Saturdays from now? Could you've been more vague?"

We sat on the file cabinet by the window and just looked out at the streets as we played with Milo between us.

I smiled. "I wanted it to be a surprise, but it's best you know. I ordered a shoe organizer for you. Did you know they have hundreds of designs? It took me forever. I just went with a custom design to save myself a headache."

She gasped. "You did what?"

"Well, now you're sporting so many different shoes I thought you'd like a nice organizer. I got one customized to fit in that corner in your room where you have that hideous bean bag chair."

"Hey! I like that chair."

"Didn't you say Milo ripped a couple spots?" I asked. "Now you can get rid of it and you'll be able to organize by color or occasions, whatever system you come up with."

"I wish you'd involved me in this decision. I would have loved to—"

"Match your new headboard? Close your mouth. Yes, I know how much you love your new furniture and that board is awesome. Really nice gothic wallpaper. It goes well with your plum accents."

She had a string in her hand and was dangling it for Milo to play with. "You didn't find that wallpaper!"

"I did. You make it easy, Ry. You file and organize everything. I looked into your files. I pulled out the folders titled *Décor*, then the subfolder titled *Bedroom*. Then the sub-subfolder titled *Colors*. How do you find the time, woman?"

"Don't complain. If it hadn't been for that, you wouldn't have found it. And how did you know that would be my choice? I could have wanted the espresso color of my vanity."

"Nah." I shook my head. "I stared at your room long

enough to know you'd like it to go with the headboard; the opposite corner where your mirror is hanging has the wallpaper as background. This makes the perfect triangle design. And if you don't like it, paint the damn thing yourself."

She smiled. "You put a lot of thought into it."

"Of course. I wouldn't mess with your decoration style just for the hell of it." I pulled out my phone. "Look, here's a picture of the design."

Her jaw dropped. "Wow!"

"It's floor to ceiling and fits in the corner. Open the door and the inside rotates. You have twelve shelves so you should be able to fit about sixty pairs of shoes." I smiled.

"I don't have enough shoes for it," she said, taking my phone and staring at the picture.

"Get shopping. Oh, and look—the last two shelves have more space in between for your boots. Both your girly and your combat ones."

"Kevin, that's perfect. Thank you!"

I shrugged. I just liked seeing her happy. "I emailed you the delivery time, so just make sure you're home."

We were still busy playing with Milo when Chris walked in around five with a big smile on his face. "'Sup?"

"'Sup with you?" Ryan asked, "Oh, no. Please tell me you weren't trying to corrupt that poor nurse."

"Okay, I won't tell you, then." Chris laughed. "I'm here to get you guys. Jenny said Derek is back and wants to see us."

WE SAT AROUND the table in the conference room and waited for Derek to talk. There were two empty disposable cups of coffee and one energy drink on the far side next to his files. As he read through the papers, he was gulping down a bottle of water. When he finished it, he placed it next to the others, and made some notes. Without looking up, he said, "One more minute."

I turned to look at Ryan and I could see her twitching to clear the trash out of the way. "Suck it up," I whispered.

"Shush it!" she said, reaching out and gathering the napkins that were also left scattered in between papers and pens.

I put Ryan out of her misery and teleported all the waste into the trashcan.

"Thank you," she said, before Derek started talking.

"Here's what we know," he said. "Marcus was Dr. Lumin's apprentice and he knows everything there's to know about Luminaries, our powers, and our formulas. He was captured by the rebels because they needed him to enhance the power they already have."

"Figures," Chris said, shaking his head.

Derek leaned back in his chair. "Marcus assumes since the rebels never received the booster shot we give everyone when they join the Org, that their powers haven't grown much. He didn't mention the particular formula to them, so we don't have to worry about that issue."

"Wait, I thought your dad lied about the booster shot," I said, recalling what happened years ago. Nick had found out that Lake Senior was dangerous and left the Org in order to get answers and to help bring him down.

Derek nodded. "He did . . . and he didn't. In Dad's files, we found that he'd given the booster shot to everyone when they first joined the Org, and actually we still use it. It's the only sure way to wake up powers in those who have it. Many Luminaries display powers on their own, but even they need the shot to help at first."

"But didn't he also lie about us *needing* monthly booster shots?" I frowned.

"Yes, the monthly shots were a way for him to control us. Dad gave that shot to weaker Luminaries to keep their powers active as he claimed, so that was partly true. But he also gave a different weakening shot to those who were strong and he felt were a threat to his . . . *greatness*. He didn't like competition." Derek rubbed his temple. "But he lied and told everyone they were getting booster shots every month. Only he and his team knew who received what shot."

"Got it. So Marcus thinks they're not as powerful as

we are," I said, getting the conversation back to our current situation.

"Right. And that brings us to the next problem." Derek let out a long sigh. That action brought my attention to the dark circle under his eyes.

He continued, "The rebels have hired regular people to do the dirty work for them. Marcus only met with three of them, but is convinced the group is quite large."

Chris leaned forward and placed his elbows on the table. "If they have the numbers and some power, why are they using regular people?"

I knew why. "Because we don't kill them or anyone innocent. We just bring them in, and they go to jail for their misdemeanors. And they can hire more people without losing their numbers. It explains why hardly any of them displayed abilities when Ryan and I fought them during the rescue."

"Exactly," Derek said nodding. "They're not putting themselves at risk with us until they have their full powers. Marcus believes their goal is to wipe our powers out. So not only were they intent on getting stronger, they also wanted a formula to take away our abilities."

"We already have that, though," Ryan said.

"Yes, but it's only a weakening agent. That, along with a strong hypnosis therapy, have helped us keep those who don't make it into the Org at bay. In their cases, their powers were already weak to begin with, so we never had to worry about them."

"But you've taken powers from others who've left,

right?" she asked.

"No, it's just a tactic my father used to keep everyone in line, but no one had really gone rogue before Nick five years ago. Anyway, we've done the same thing to the others. Weakened them, and hypnotize them on a regular basis not to remember their powers or to stop them from reacting. As per their request, that is. However, that's only been two people, and they both have a happy, normal life."

"So what's going to happen?" I asked.

"The Ryders are still in danger because the rebels still need Marcus's expertise. They're staying in our training facility for now. Marcus wanted access to a lab to see if he could work on a counteracting serum fo—"

"A what?" Chris cut him off.

"A counteracting serum to prevent the power stripping formula working on us," Derek explained. "Since Marcus wasn't the only apprentice Dr. Lumin had, nor was Dr. Lumin the only scientist who worked on our formulas, they might still succeed in developing that formula."

Ryan frowned. "Can we trust Dr. Ryder?"

"Yes, both Jenny and Nick agree on that. The wife, they're not so sure, though—but she's always on meds so it's difficult for them to get a proper read on her."

"Did he share anything else?" she asked.

Derek nodded. "As you know, when we raided Dad's secret lab five years ago, some of those scientists fled and became rebels. Marcus said the lab definitely had advanced serums even back then."

"If they have those scientists, why do they need Dr. Ryder?" Chris asked.

"Marcus says the reason he's so valuable is because he had many more formulas they'd love to get their hands on. Dad had funded Marcus's research as long as he agreed to use that facility so they were aware of his work. Either way, we have to find the rebels and their labs without destroying everything. We might benefit from the work they've done already."

"Any plans on how to do that?" Ryan asked as Derek's phone buzzed.

"I have some leads—hang on." He read his message and started gathering his files. "We'll continue this tomorrow; I have to go. Kevin, walk me to my office."

"Sure," I said, getting up and grabbing some of the files to help him carry them.

We left with both our hands full of folders. I wanted to offer to teleport them, but he seemed to be lost in his own train of thought. I followed his pace, hurrying to his office, but didn't say a word.

As he opened his door, he turned to me. "The girl, Gabriella, isn't in much danger since we have her father. Beth got her hands on her, and changed her appearance so she is free to go out on a date."

I took a step back. "How did you . . .?"

"She asked if she would be allowed to date you," he said, putting on his coat.

"And you are okay with me taking her out?"

Derek smiled. "She'll be safe with you. No one will know who she is, and you can teleport her away if needed."

"Right. Uh, thanks?"

"No problem, but really, thank Jenny. She's the one who talked me into it, then Beth and Annie joined in trying to convince me."

"So they all ganged up on you?"

"Pretty much. But I know she will be in good hands or I wouldn't have given in. Go and have fun."

"Okay, thanks." I placed the files on his desk and noticed him typing quickly on his phone, shaking his head. *Rough day for the poor guy.*

I left and went to the training center.

CHAPTER
TEN

THE TRAINING CENTER was an old high school that was less than fifteen minutes from the Org. They'd turned the basement into the main laboratory, the two middle floors were the training rooms, and the two top floors were the boys' and girls' bedrooms.

I went to the basement where Gabby and her parents were staying. The whole training center was secured, but Derek had a couple Luminaries guarding them at all times in case anything happened. The basement was divided in two sections. One side had the laboratories, the other had dormitories for when they needed to supervise experiments through the night.

The three of them shared one room that had four twin-sized beds. Derek had offered to push two of the beds together for Dr. and Mrs. Ryder, but they both politely refused. Gabby said it was better this way, and that her parents were happy being independent.

"Wow," I said when I saw her.

"You like it?" Gabby asked while blinking fast. She stood wearing one of the lacy tops Ryan had bought her. Her hair was the biggest difference: it was straightened out, cut shorter, and dyed blonde. Her gray eyes were looking at me expectantly. I thought her dark hair was cuter but no way I'd tell her that.

"Your hair looks beautiful."

"I'm glad you like it. I love it!" she said, beaming.

"Let's get outta here."

I took her around the city. We hung out in Times Square, visited Madame Tussaud's Museum, and then to a get a quick bite. Derek wanted me to bring her back by nine o' clock at the latest. At our age, a curfew was funny but we had no choice.

"This is where we're eating?" she asked when we walked into the small space.

"What? I love Gray's Papaya. Ryan and I eat here all the time!"

"Ryan . . . as in dates?" She frowned.

I shook my head. "I told you. We are just friends."

"Are you sure she feels the same way?"

"Of course."

"What about Chris? He stares at her all the time. You think he likes her?"

"Who knows?" I shrugged. "He's having too much fun playing the field for now."

She tilted her head to look at me. "And you are not?"

"Playing the field?" She nodded in response. "Nah. I

mean, sure, that's what I did. But this feels different."

She smiled and seemed a bit nervous. She finished her hot dog and said, "This is good. I can't believe I've never actually eaten here before."

"You come to Manhattan a lot?"

"Not really, but it's pretty popular. And I've driven by here often enough that I probably should've made a stop at least once."

"Oh well, you know New Yorkers. Always too busy to live in the moment."

"Except I'm from New Jersey, but . . ." She stared at me, unblinking. "Listen, if you want to hang out again, maybe next time take me out somewhere you've never taken any girls before."

"Umm . . . sure."

She finally blinked and gave me a big smile. "It's not a big deal, but next time."

Seemed like a big deal to me . . . staring like a deer in headlights, but whatever, she was all smiley again. "I didn't have enough of a notice to plan this, you know. I was told I could take you out so I jumped at the opportunity and didn't ask any questions."

"Thanks. We should get going, I guess. It's getting late."

"It is, but first, come a little closer." I placed my hand on her waist, pulled her to me, and leaned in one breath at a time. She raised her head to meet me halfway and I felt her lip tremble as I caressed it with my thumb. I took in her scent and her warmth. I kissed her, losing myself in the moment and in the burn she ignited in me.

As much as I hated it, I ended the kiss and teleported us to the training center. I dropped her off with her father, who was busy looking through a magnifying glass over several petri dishes. He barely looked up to make sure I brought back the right girl. I shook my head. Apart from being sisters, with her kind of parents I could see why she and Grace were so close. They truly only had each other. And now she was alone. Well, no; now she had me. I couldn't give her Grace back, but I could be there for her.

"Bye, Kev," she whispered, holding my hand. She was always so warm.

I don't know what it was about Gabby, but I craved her soothing warmth. Maybe it's like Ryan always said: if I invested my time in actual talking and getting to know a girl, I might be surprised.

I found myself more interested in Gabby than I ever thought could be possible. It felt almost addictive. I guess maybe I was too young before to see the positive side of being in a relationship. Girls are always too jealous or fighting or demanding. I'd seen Chris go through that, and what a hassle that ended up being for him.

But Gabby? I did get to know her better. I knew I was in trouble when I even forgot about Ryan because I was busy thinking about Gabby. We enjoyed each other's company, and her lips . . . *man, I could still taste her*. She wasn't one to just hang out with and leave hanging. She was more of a keeper.

I didn't have to go in to work until the following

afternoon to hash out the rest of the plan with the guys, so I stayed up thinking of her and watching some zombie show on TV.

I JUMPED UP, ready to fight, when someone shook me out of my sleep. I squinted and found Ryan sitting at the edge of my bed next to me.

"What are you doing?" I yawned. "I'm not too sure you value your life."

"Of course I do." She smiled. "That's why I brought you coffee."

I rubbed my eyes. "What time is it?"

"It's quarter to eight, you sleepyhead!"

"Can't you give me another hour?" I asked, yawning again.

"Oh, okay. Umm, I'll go outside and clean up your coffee table while I wait."

One look at the disappointment on her face and I sat up. "No. No, Ry. I'll get up. Give me that coffee. I swear only you can manipulate me to get up this early."

"I know." She grinned. "What time did you get in?"

"Oh, not late but I stayed up watching TV."

"All right, well, drink up and go get dressed." She stood and picked up some dirty clothes off the floor. She then put them in the laundry hamper she'd given me for Christmas. Only she would think a triple sorter hamper was an exciting present.

She turned to look at me. "Do you ever use this?"

"Uh . . . sure. I love it . . . SO much. I can separate whites, darks, stripes, socks, ankle socks, long sleeve, short sleev—"

"Shut up!" She laughed and walked toward the living room. "I'm still going to deal with that mess on your table."

I followed her. "Where are we going?"

Ryan placed her hands on her hips. "We have to see some cars."

Her tight yellow top paired with skinny jeans helped wake me up a bit . . . it was so bright. "Shit! I left you hanging last night."

"Yes, you did. But you can make up for it now," she said.

"I didn't read through the consumer reports yet. I didn't get a chance to research more."

"So?"

"So, we're going in blind, dude." I took another sip of my coffee.

"I think we can at least do some test drives, don't you?" she said, winking at me.

"Wicked, Ryan. I'm liking where this is going. Give me a few minutes." Thank God, she didn't seem too mad about last night. Milo must still be working his purring magic.

"Yeah, and we start with your new baby. I walked here so you could drive me around. I bet it's been a while."

I nodded and went to shower. I really had been teleporting a lot more lately, and Ryan understood me so well, she knew I'd appreciate this. We were very much alike . . . well, sort of. If we weren't so different in our ways, me with my messy life and player habits, and her with her orderly disorder and prudish personality, I'd say we were practically the same person. She calls it two sides of the same coin.

We went out, drove a handful of cars and sped like crazy. None were hybrid, though, so the speed was better than I was used to. It almost made me reconsider changing to a regular car. Almost. We were bad and loved every minute of it. When we were done with that, we still had a couple hours before having to report back to work at two o'clock so we decided to go to our old junkyard spot. We've been going there on and off over the years when we wanted to get down with hardcore training.

Ryan popped my car's trunk open and took out a duffel bag. "I've had this backup just for this occasion."

"You knew we'd come here?" I asked, confused.

"No, silly. I knew you'd give in and be up to practicing soon. I was just prepared, is all."

I raised an eyebrow. "What if we'd taken your car?"

"I would have figured out something. It's not like I don't know a teleporter or anything." She laughed, opening the bag and pulling out a battery-operated radio, a solar-powered light, and her old MP3 player.

"What am I supposed to do?"

"King of training, you said you were always upset when you noticed the electric spurts. So I don't know. Get yourself worked up or try to focus."

"Oh yeah, 'cause it's that easy."

She gave me the MP3 player to hold. "See if you can melt this like the phones, and listen to me. Umm . . . how great is it to have Nick as a brother? The best Luminary, in Derek's eyes. He's so . . . *strategic* . . . never fails to deliver . . ." She walked side to side in front of me. "It must be tough living in Nick's shadow. Here you are, the total opposite . . . *always* making mistakes." She shook her head. "If it wasn't for being his brother you wouldn't even have a job as a Luminary. He feels so bad he even gave you his old offic—"

The MP3 player in my left hand was okay, and the radio started making a crackling sound, but that wasn't what stopped her. It wasn't what shocked me either. The white sparks coming from my right hand and melting through the hood of the car? That's what did it. It didn't last long though. I pulled my hand and jumped off as soon as I saw what I was doing.

The radio stopped and nothing even happened to the MP3 player. But when Ry tried to turn both on, neither would work. I picked up a rock and banged the spot I had melted on the hood so the hole was irregular. I doubted anyone really would pay attention to a piece of junk, but the perfect cutout of my hand and fingers would definitely stand out if anyone was to inspect it.

Ryan was still trying to fix the radio. "Nothing seems burnt, and the battery was new." She took out a pack of new batteries from the duffle bag and switched them for the old ones. She pressed power and music came on. "I think you're draining it."

I frowned. "That doesn't explain how I electrocuted Simon."

"Doesn't it?" She turned to look at me, "Kevin, the lights went out when that happened. I think you're pulling the power and then projecting it back out."

"The only other person I've seen with the electric thing is Jessica, Derek's crazy scientist aunt. But from what I can recall, she didn't pull from anywhere. Too bad she's dead now; I'd love to question her."

"She's not the only one," Ryan said. "Remember when we were captured? That woman had some electric power too."

"Blondie, yes. That bitch shocked me. I felt like my bones were humming for days."

Ryan's eyes widened. "Kevin, that's it! Maybe she woke up this power in you. Like we get booster shots, but a booster shock?"

I laughed. "A booster shock."

"Well, it makes sense. She said she had expected you to be dead after that. Instead you were able to electrocute Simon. And you'd never done anything like it before. She kickstarted you."

"We couldn't see it physically affect the lights or power, so it's still not the same."

"I don't know about her, but we all work differently. It's the same as you and Andrew, I guess."

"But . . . how come I didn't burn this like I did Simon?" I asked pointing to the car.

"Probably because batteries aren't as powerful as full-on electricity. Plus you jumped off the hood as soon as you noticed what was happening. Maybe all that energy transfer and pulling you did with Annie made you learn how to do it with electricity?"

"You and your scientific theories. I don't know why you didn't continue studying that," I said, trying to change the conversation.

She shook her head, taking the hint. "Are you kidding? I wouldn't miss kicking ass out on the field for anything."

"Hey, umm, about Nick . . ."

"We don't have to talk about it, Kevin."

I took a step back. "Ugh. You throw me off when you call me by my name. It sounds too serious."

She smiled. "I am serious."

"How'd you know?"

"I know, just like you know exactly how I like my coffee. Okay, don't make that face; I know it's not the same but we get each other on all levels. I accept you're careless—"

"Hey!"

She laughed. "I do, and you accept that I'm an insane

OCD. But also don't forget I'm a sensor."

"Right, you do have an upper hand." I frowned. "I do keep messing up, though. What must Nick and Derek think?"

"Nick couldn't be more proud to have you as his brother, and Derek respects you. All your little mistakes have proven to pay off with big results one way or another."

"You must think I'm terrible for feeling that way about Nick."

"Never. You're more sensitive than you care to admit. And you love Nick. Being in the shadow of one of the most respected Luminaries is not an easy thing. Especially after being called out so often in training on being Nick's brother—who never made mistakes. It would mess with anyone. We all know it's why you act up."

I stared at the floor. "You're only saying that."

"Would I really?" Her serious blue eyes pierced me deep down.

No. She really wouldn't.

"Let's go back to work." I held her hand and pulled her in silence back to my car.

While I drove, Ryan asked how my date was.

"We straight up acted like tourists of the Big Apple, it was fun. Then I took her to GP to try it out."

Her head spun to look at me. "You took her to Gray's Papaya? Our spot?"

"Yes, what's the big deal? It's one of my favorites,

and nothing says it's ours."

"Come on! We call it GP. We shortened the damn name; obviously it's *our* spot. We don't even take Chris there with us."

"Well, I took Gabby. It's a public place." I didn't mean to be rude but then it hit me what Gabby had asked. Did Ryan not see our relationship the same way I did? *Nah, I'm just overreacting.* I brushed it off. "She's obviously special enough for me to share GP with her. And, I don't know, I have a soft spot for Gabby. She pretends everything's okay but I know she's lonely. You should have seen the disappointment in her eyes when I took her back and her dad didn't even acknowledge her."

"That's sad."

"I'm not sure what's worse: being an orphan and being unwanted, or having a family who is supposed to care for you, but make you feel unloved instead."

Ryan nodded. "She's been through a lot. It's a good thing you're showing her someone cares."

"Yeah, well she makes it easy . . . she's really hot," I said, trying to lighten the mood.

"Of course . . . without that, how could you possibly connect so deeply with her?" Ryan sighed, then giggled in a non-Ryan way. Taking the new look and girly-ness to a new level.

"Laugh it up. I want to see what you would do if I threw a fireball at you."

"You need Nick around for that or you can't do it." She stuck her tongue out.

"Keep it up, I'll muster up my own new sparks," I said, waving my fingers in the air.

She ignored that and got lost in her thoughts. "You have to try teaching me that transfer thing again, you know. I would love to throw some fireballs when I'm fighting. My powers are so different from yours; you can't even pull from me to amplify yourself." She looked at me. "And you said Jenny was able to do it and learn fast because of the sensor in her. Right?"

We were at a stoplight, so I turned to look at her. "Yes, but we never tried real hard with the transferring. We can—"

"You tried to teach me for a whole week during our road trip last year. I would say that's trying real hard."

"I'm not sure how to explain the channeling, except we focus on the vibe or energy a person gives off. I told you, if we ask Jenny she would help us. I think she was the key when we were all learning."

"It's frustrating!" She grabbed her hair and tied it up in a bun. After a couple seconds, she caught her reflection in the mirror and quickly let it loose again.

She let out a deep breath. "I should work similar to Annie, though."

"Not really. Annie makes us, the person, go longer and with more energy so we don't tire out. But you expand the actual power way above its limit. It's not the same but still very impressive, Ry. Believe me."

She smiled. "If only I could use it for myself in sensing or something. Amplifying my amplifying powers is well . . . how would I know if it even works?"

"No idea, dude. But you're still learning to control it, and now I have to learn to deal with my stuff, too."

"You're going to have to let Derek help sooner or later."

I pulled into my parking space at the Org and turned the car off. "Yeah, I'll go for later. It's not top priority right now."

"Mmm hmm. With you, nothing ever is."

WE'D BARELY MADE it into the building when our phones buzzed. Derek was ready to continue the meeting we'd left off yesterday. I sent Ryan up and went to get some coffee for all of us so we could at least stay awake while he yapped away.

When I walked into the conference room, I noticed Derek's under-eye circles were even darker than before. I quickly handed everyone their cups, gave Chris a fist bump, and sat down to listen.

Derek stood up. "I don't have much time so we'll just get straight to it: as you've noticed, I've been busy with Agent Pine. He's convinced we have a plant in the Org and possibly even with his higher ups."

I put my coffee down. "Nah, that can't be."

"I felt the same way at first, but I'm afraid I have to agree. It's not a coincidence the rebels found the safe house. Plus, there are things I'm being forced to do. The FBI is now asking for all our personnel files."

Chris shook his head. "I thought we had an agreement that our identities would remain secret in exchange for our services."

"Yes, Chris," Derek said, nodding. "But when we failed to deliver Simon to them and with me refusing the files, they're hinting at us being in league with the rebels. They want more control."

I snorted. "Like we haven't been trying? Do they think this is a piece of cake? If we could have controlled the rebels we wouldn't be here."

"No, Kevin. They want more control of *us*. They're trying to make me give up my seat and have us become their direct agents. Work for them."

"That doesn't sound too bad. Even if you gave up your seat, it's not about being in charge for you," I said.

"It isn't. For me, it's about protecting my people and doing good. But they want to study us and see how far they can push our powers. And we do have our limits. Which they won't understand until there's a pile of Luminary bodies to dispose of."

"Ah, come on, they wouldn't be that reckless," Chris said.

"Perhaps, but I'm not willing to sacrifice my people. I've earned your trust and I do my best by you. Even to those who have done harm. We take care of our own problems. They misbehave and can't be responsible with their powers? We hypnotize them, give them the weakening shot, and send them to have normal lives. Unless they've killed, and then they would go to jail afterward."

"What makes you think they would change the way we work? Just because they're calling the shots on the jobs we take doesn't mean we can't run our operations the same way," I asked.

"When the FBI asks me to send them the worst Luminaries we have—those I *'wouldn't mind losing'*—for the government to study, a red flag goes up. And if Pine thinks something else is up, I believe him."

"So you think they turned one of us to give them information? I mean, we can't, anyway. I don't get it," I said.

"That is the other thing. As far as who might be in the FBI, I think it's the rebels, but in the Org, Marcus confirmed we do have a spy."

Ryan, who'd been quiet the whole time, asked, "How would he know?"

"Marcus said the rebels were waiting for the right moment to use that person. You're all hypnotized to prevent you from sharing anything about what we do with others, but we still have free will." Derek took a sip of his coffee and walked back and forth. "If that person were to attack us and use his or her knowledge to harm us from within we have no way of stopping them."

"Then let's hypnotize everyone to stop that from happening," Chris suggested.

"That doesn't solve the actual problem. We still need to find the person, so I'm going to need your and Ryan's help. We're going to have to interrogate everyone and see if we can find them."

"Feels wrong," Ryan said. "These are our people."

"I know, but Nick agreed this was a good move on their part. You know he's all about strategic moves." Derek shrugged.

Nick was always good at making and carrying out plans, especially those long-term plans that were sure to benefit any operation. It was the best way of finding the root of the problems and gave the upper hand when it all went down.

Ryan seemed sad. "Well, I guess we have to do it," she said.

CHAPTER ELEVEN

M Y FUN MORNING with Ryan had me in a good mood the whole day. After work, I wanted to keep the happy feeling going so I went to visit my li'l bro.

I parked my car and teleported into the Logans' living room. At my sudden appearance, Annie almost dropped the container she'd been carrying.

"Hey guys." I grinned. I loved catching her off guard.

Nick didn't even flinch when I popped in. He was sitting at the table with Jack. He just looked up and said, "I'm going to walk around my house naked from now on. Go ahead and keep showing up here unannounced if you're up for the view."

"Don't be gross, bro." I frowned.

"Hi, Kevin." Annie ignored us. "Is that your car keys?"

"Yeah, I drove here." I smiled, tucking them into my

pockets.

"But you teleported in?"

"Annie, bells weren't made for me."

"And you complain about Ryan not using it either." She raised an eyebrow. "Anyway, you're right on time for dinner. Grab a plate."

I sat on the other side of Jack and gave him a kiss on his forehead. "Hey, little man!"

"Don't pick him up until we're done eating," Annie said.

I shook my head. "You run a tight ship."

"She does," Nick said, feeding Jack some smashed-up looking orange paste.

"What in the world is that?"

"Carrot puree," he answered, looking at me. "What's new, man?"

"I wanted to ask: can you share your report of the lab raid from during your honeymoon?"

He wiped Jack's face. "Yeah, why? Something going on?"

"What's going on is that I wouldn't have to beg for that report if you guys had allowed me to come with you on that mission," I said.

Annie sat down facing us. She scooped up some macaroni and cheese and put some on her and Nick's plates. She handed me the serving spoon. "You were too young and needed to keep training."

"I was eighteen!"

"But you had to finish your training. Just because we

had you helping before didn't mean you had graduated. You hardly knew anything about the Org."

Nick turned to me. "How come you want to know now? You didn't care for the details before."

"Well, now it's connected and I need all my facts straight," I said, taking in the cheesy scent. Bacon was in the mix. *Yum.*

He nodded. "I'll get it for you when we go in tomorrow. Eat your food before Annie kicks your ass. Did you have any specific questions, though? We can answer some now."

"Tell me what you remember off the top of your head," I said, taking a bite of the mac and cheese. "Hey! You didn't make this."

Annie laughed. "Nope. Ryan said she was cooking last night and I asked for leftovers. But you know her, she made me a full pan."

I nodded, stuffing my mouth. I took my food seriously and this was too good to waste time talking.

"So you know that we left the Bahamas right after our wedding night and went to Chicago," Nick started. "Jessica gave us the location and even the security codes. Unfortunately that specific code alerted her group here of what we were up to and they activated her kill chip. We believe that was the beginning of the rebellion group as we know them."

"Right," Annie cut in. "When we got there it was an almost empty facility. We did find some scientist interns and Luminaries whose experiments had gone wrong. But mostly, there were women. Some pregnant and some new mothers of Luminary babies. Lake Senior had been busy creating more of us," she said, clenching her fists.

"Where are they now?" I asked.

"They're well taken care of. Those kids have their mothers and those mothers were given a second chance." She let out a deep breath. "They're now in charge of running daycares and babysitting the rest of the Luminary babies. They know how to care for them."

"Yeah, I bet they're useful since your generation is busy procreating." I thought about it, and asked, "Li'l bro's babysitter . . . was she one of them?"

Nick nodded. "She was experimented on but nothing too impressive happened. She took the weakening agent and stayed on with us so she could have a job. It's easier this way. If the kids ever display powers, there's no need to explain anything to the babysitters or to modify their memories. You know how Annie hates having to do that to anyone."

"Right. Umm, but what interesting things did you learn? Apart from them having a separate lab and doing much of what we do at the Org?"

"Not much, really. The research papers were destroyed. The scientists we found were severely hypnotized; they hardly knew who they were. Nothing I did helped." He shook his head. "And I'm damn good at helping people gain back their memories."

I looked up. "Anyone I know?"

Nick took a bite and was chewing, so Annie

answered. "Yeah, Dr. David Carson from quality control was the main one, I think. There were two other scientists, but only David was able to recall his name. Not too much of what he did, but he remembered enough of his work to get a job in our labs."

Nick nodded. "The other two were beyond my help, so I ended up giving them new identities and they all work for us."

I frowned. "But aren't they all rebels or criminals? Why did we employ them?"

"We didn't know enough to charge them with any criminal offense." Nick shrugged.

"Plus, it wouldn't have been fair in their state of mind," Annie said. "And Derek agreed with me that we could use them and still help them out. So we gave them all jobs. It has worked out."

"Hmm, those scientists . . . I wonder . . . if we get Ryan to amplify you"—I looked at Nick—"if it would help to snap their memories back into place?"

"Oh that's—I have to say that's worth a try, I think. Nick?" Annie asked.

"I'm not sure, but yes we can try it. I'll talk to Derek about it," he said, and continued eating.

"All right, Kevin. Not just a pretty face, huh?" Annie teased. "Speaking of pretty faces, how was your date?"

I grinned. "It was really cool. Ry—I mean, Gabby and I went to the city and I took her to Gray's Papaya."

"To Gray's? But isn't that—" Annie stopped talking at Nick's stare.

"It's a public place! What's with women? The three of you already said the same shit. Whatever. The first meal I cooked for her was hot dogs and she wasn't amazed so I took her there to impress her with good ones."

"And cheap."

"Annie, come on. I didn't get a chance to plan it out. I thought I was pretty slick pulling that one off at the last minute. Anyway, we had a great time. I have to thank Beth; I think Gabby looks good. She loves her makeover."

"I'm glad she does. The color is pretty on her." Annie took a sip of her water. "And how did it go with Ryan and car shopping?"

"Incredible! We sped down the highway as you would expect us to. She almost got caught by the cops, but she sensed them in time to slow down. We test-drove the fast cars first then finally checked out the Prius and the CR-Z. She hasn't decided which one she wants. They're both fun to drive."

Annie leaned across the table to give Jack a set of toy keys. "Good. I thought it was thoughtful of you to get her a replacement for your friendship."

"What?"

"Milo." Annie raised an eyebrow. "It's like, now that you're busy and consumed with Gabby, you got Ryan a 'Kevin replacement.'"

"Please." I snorted. "No one can replace me."

She nodded and got up to take dishes to the kitchen,

but turned and said, "Exactly. Don't forget that."

"What's that about?" I asked Nick.

He raised his hands. "I'm not getting involved."

"Bro?"

"She thinks you are being insensitive to Ryan. You stood her up a couple of times because of Gabby. Annie thinks you're forgetting all about your friends."

"Come on! When she started dating you, she didn't spend all her time with Beth, did she?"

"Well, to Annie, friends are important. Beth has always been like her sister, and she made sure we both knew we were important. Or at least let one or the other know if she had to cancel."

"It doesn't even count, dude. You guys were in the training facility at the same time, and the two of them were roomies." I wiped some drool off Jack's chin. "Besides, Beth had Andrew, too."

"True, so maybe Ryan just needs to . . ." Nick paused to look at me. ". . . get a boyfriend herself?"

I took a sip of water. "She should. There aren't enough good guys our age, though; we're all players."

"Chris I think likes her, and I think he would treat her nice."

I laughed, and scooped a second round of mac and cheese. "Please. He's after Jen's new nurse."

Nick got up, and took Jack out of his intricate baby seat. "Doesn't mean he can't be interested in Ryan."

"Exactly," Annie said, agreeing with Nick as she returned.

I crossed my arms. "Nah, Chris hasn't said anything to me."

"If you would pull your head out of your ass once in a while, you would notice more. The world doesn't revolve around you, Kevin. Open your eyes and be there for your friends. Chris wasn't—"

Nick cut her off. "Annie, let him be."

"No, I want to know," I said.

"He was never too sure if you liked Ryan, like *liked* her."

I laughed. "She's like my sister. He can have her!"

"Can he?" Annie's head cocked to the side.

I raised my chin. "Yes—I mean, if he treats her right, obviously. But I don't know. Chris isn't the relationship type."

Annie squinted. "Chris is like you."

"Like how?" I asked.

"He enjoys having a good time with girls. But maybe *like you*, he might calm down and try to be serious with Ryan as you are trying to be with Gabby."

I shrugged. "I guess. I only know *my* intentions."

"And you think he would risk your and Ryan's friendship for just a good time?" Nick asked.

"Who knows? Maybe it's because Ryan is dressing differently now. Why didn't he notice her before?" My jaw tightened. "He probably just wants to get in her pants."

"Who said he didn't notice her before?" Annie asked.

"He would have told me."

Her eyes narrowed. "Not if he wasn't sure about you and her."

"Come on, everyone knows that Ryan and I are like brother and sister. It would never even cross our minds. He can have her. In fact, that's good. We can double date." I dropped my fork on the plate. "I'll set it up."

"Pull the brakes, Kev. We might want to ask for Ryan's opinion. Maybe she doesn't feel the same way toward Chris," Annie said.

"Why wouldn't she? Chicks dig him. They like them dark, mysterious bad boys, don't they?"

"I don't know. My guy has a scar, and at one point he was even a one-eyed hero." Annie laughed.

"Please, you know my right eye is a big turn-on; that's why I made sure it was the left—"

"Umm, guys, yeah." I shook my head. "I'm still here."

"What? Back to Kevin Central?" she asked.

"All right, Annie. I think you've picked on me enough for tonight. I'm going now. I want to spend some time with Gabby before her dad has to close up the lab at midnight."

"Tell her we said hi."

"You got it," I said, giving Jack a quick kiss on his forehead.

I DROVE BACK to the training center. Once there, I went straight to the basement, and found Chris and Ryan chatting up Gabby. They were sitting on some folding chairs out in the hallway close to her bedroom.

I smiled. "Hey guys."

"Kevin, you came!" Gabby grinned and walked up to me for a kiss. She smelled so good.

"Of course I came. I told you I would. I went to discuss something with Annie and Nick, and figured I'd have dinner with them." I looked at the guys. "What are you two doing here?"

"We thought you were here," Chris said.

"Yes, we wanted to hang out." Ryan looked at Gabby. "I was going to invite you guys over for burgers at my place."

"It's late now, though." Gabby held on to my arm. "We already went to the cafeteria and ate there."

"Right. Well, we're gonna get going. You two have fun. We can plan something for another time," Ryan said and gave Gabby a good-bye hug.

"I never did understand that," Chris said. "Why do women like to hug and kiss every time they see each other?"

"Right?" I nodded. "Like, you just saw each other yesterday, *chill*."

Gabby shook her head, laughing.

Ryan just rolled her eyes and said, "Add it to the list of mysteries we women like to keep. Have fun, lovebirds!"

I waved 'bye and pulled Gabby in for a kiss.

I smiled afterward and asked, "How did your day go?"

"Gosh! Boring-ish?"

"How so?"

She tilted her head. "Well, for one, I didn't go test-driving cars with a hot chick."

I shook my head. "Neither did I."

"Right! Ryan told me you two had fun. I hope it wasn't *too* much fun."

"Yes." I shrugged. "We did what we always do."

"I know, I can see that from your end. It's just on her end . . . I don't know." Her lips tightened. "Anyway, I guess part of me is sad, knowing you and I might never have that special connection you share with Ryan."

"Oh, but you and I can connect in so many other ways." I grinned. "Hey, I'm not supposed to take you out of this building this late, but wanna go with me to one of the training rooms?"

"Sure. What's in there?" She pointed to the backpack over my shoulder.

"Laptop. I thought I'd show you some pictures and videos of Jack, and squeeze in a make out session . . . if you're up for it."

"Yeah, I'm up for it!" She blushed. "You're not tired of me yet?"

"Why would I be?"

"I don't know. We've spent so much time together the past few weeks." She bit her lip. "I guess I get nervous you'll get tired of me, since, you know, you're not the relationship type."

"*Was* not. Besides, I'm more and more intrigued by you every day," I said. "Aren't you getting tired of me?"

"Nope."

"Good. I do wonder, though, when we'll have some time to be completely alone. Did you want to come over my place next time?"

She smiled. "That would be nice."

I rubbed my sweaty hands on my jeans. I hadn't even realized it made me nervous to ask that. I'm normally more confident, but this girl made me freak out. As we walked into the empty training room, I turned the light on and saw her yawning.

"Are you tired?" I asked, raising an eyebrow.

"Not really tired. Just haven't been sleeping."

We pulled up a couple chairs and sat by the desk. "If you're worn out—"

"Yeahhhh . . . it takes a lot to sit and read books all day long." She rolled her eyes.

"You don't like reading?"

"Oh, yes, but I have to be in the mood. I think I'm just feeling forced to read, or something. You like to read?" she asked, moving her chair closer to me.

I placed the laptop on the desk and hit the power button. "I'd rather fight."

"Of course you do. Grace was a reader," Gabby said and laced her fingers together.

"Right. How have you been holding up with that? I

know I don't ask you, but I figured you're alone a lot with time to think . . . and I'd rather take your mind off anything bad when we are together."

She smiled. "Don't worry about that; I think only good things when you're with me. But yes, it's hard. I miss her so much. You know? As she got older, she kept pushing me to date and go out more. I'm glad I didn't listen to her. I would have been regretting the time away from her now."

"Did your mom not spend time with her?"

"No, Mom has her own issues as you can tell, and Dad lives in the lab, hoping to find a cure for her."

"Your dad really thinks he can help your mother?"

"Fix her, you mean? That's what he calls it. He keeps saying it as if she's broken."

I leaned back. "Do you know how he plans to help her?"

"I thought if he could help Mom then there was a chance he could also help Grace, so I did ask. But he didn't really share much beyond 'I'll fix her' so I don't know."

"Hmm, I'll be shocked if you don't have your own ideas," I said.

"It has something to do with the Luminary thingy you guys take."

I frowned. "We don't take anything."

"Well, I don't know what or how it works but it's something to do with that formula. Wasn't it from out in space? How do they even still have enough of it to keep experimenting?"

"Oh, Dr. Lumin was a mastermind. Since he figured out the composition of the formula, he also came up with . . . how do I explain this? You know how a vaccination works? If someone is immune to a certain disease, his or her blood can be used to formulate a vaccine? Well, like that. Existing Luminaries are contributing with their own blood or DNA thingamajiggy to make more of the formula."

"Wow. You know a lot about chemistry, psychics, and thingamajiggys?" she asked me, laughing.

"Nope, I'm just repeating Ryan's words. She loves to learn all these Luminary power theories."

"Ha! You had me believing you *kind of* understood how it all works."

"My head can't handle that. Are you kidding me? I just memorized certain points so when she talks I can repeat and she thinks I'm listening."

"Give yourself more credit. You can fit more of it in that head of yours if you wanted to," she said, ignoring my joke.

"I could, but then I'd have to give you up if I wanted to make space. And I'm sure I would need all my brain cells to understand any of that lab thing."

Gabby's head tilted. "Is that your way of saying that currently I occup—"

"Hang on a second." I closed the laptop without even showing her any pictures. I tapped my fingers on the desk. "I thought you didn't know about Luminaries before we saved you."

"I didn't." She shrugged and played with her watch.

"So how did you come up your theory on our formula?"

"Well, I didn't know what formula he was working on, but I can put two and two together now."

"And who filled you in on our history?" I asked as she snatched my hand tightly.

"Daddy told me a little last night. He's lost in his work these days so he was in his robotic state. I didn't understand half of what he said." She leaned in to hug me. "I don't know much, really . . . but you can teach me. Right?"

"If you're curious about anything else, you can ask me, but save that for another time," I said and pulled her closer. I suddenly felt desperate for that make out session we had pending.

I IGNORED GABBY'S odd behavior and spent the night smiling and thinking of how much fun I'd had with Ryan. My mind also wandered to what Annie had said about Chris maybe liking her. I'd noticed but I tried burying it deep down.

I knew I was in denial . . . I mean, I didn't want our trio ruined by hormones after all. But I came to the conclusion that it was okay, so I fell asleep pretty satisfied knowing I'd support whatever my friends decided . . . as long as Chris understood I didn't care that he was my buddy—if he disrespected Ryan, he'd have me to deal with.

"GET UP, SLEEPY head."

I opened my eyes to find Ryan sitting next to me, pulling off my blanket. "Umm, everything okay?" I asked, trying to wake up my senses.

"Everything's fine," she said with a smirk.

I sat up and noticed a few candles spread around the room. "Uh, yeah . . . what are you doing here?"

Ryan twirled a strand of her hair, and in her smoky voice said, "I came to . . . give you a gift."

"Tonight? Couldn't it wait for tom—"

Ryan placed a finger on my lips and said, "*Shhhh.*"

She went to the edge of the bed, facing me, and let her dress fall to the floor, leaving her in a spectacular set of white lacey underwear. "It—it . . . it's cold, wh-uh-why are you wearing a dress in this weather? You're gonna get sick . . . umm . . . or something," I said, swallowing hard.

"*Was.*" She smiled. "I'm no longer wearing it."

I concentrated on the shiny rhinestone in between her breasts in fear of what I'd find if I looked at the small strand of cloth hanging on her delicate hips. If it was as sheer as her bra, I would be done for. The curves on her body made my mind spin faster than I could attempt to ignore them. Ryan slowly crawled her way up from the foot of the bed toward me, intertwining her legs with mine.

As I mustered up the strength of a fly to attempt pushing her off, she swung one leg over and straddled me—effectively ensuring I couldn't move. She held my hands and pushed them against the headboard with slight force. All the while, the drum of my heart competed with the lack of oxygen and the blood I could swear was draining out of my body.

Ryan leaned her head back and I found my eyes lingering on the candlelight bouncing off her skin. The glow travelled from the top of her neck down to her belly to her—holy fuck! I went to grab her shoulders to try and put a break to this before it went too far, but she only laughed and leaned in closer. I forgot all desire to stop her as the intoxicating scent of her delicious coconut shampoo disabled me. Holding my gaze, she adjusted her position. Automatically my hands skimmed the edges of her thighs and went up her back. My fingertips rubbed along either side of her hard spine.

That wasn't the only thing that was hard. Her lips parted slightly before trailing my neck, planting slow kisses along my jawline and then finally the side of my mouth. She playfully bit my lower lip . . . then the top . . . then gently pressed her full mouth on mine.

The kiss started out small. But then it grew bigger

and more intense. The range of feelings had me ready to explode, but I was doing my best to control myself so I stopped. "I thought you'd never . . .?"

"I haven't. That's why it's a gift," she said and pulled her head away from my shoulder.

"Ry, are you sure?"

She nodded before gasping in reaction to my fingers tracing the edge of her underwear toward the front. In response to my exploration, she arched away, giving me a fantastic view of her beautiful long neck. I raised my head and licked the trail of bare skin before I nibbled her chin with my teeth. I pulled her hair gently as she moaned my name, and said, "Now."

CHAPTER TWELVE

*B*EEP . . . *beep* . . . *beep* . . . *beep.*

I jumped out of my bed and looked around. "What the fuck?"

I sprinted to the bathroom to splash cold water on my face. When that didn't work, I turned on the shower and jumped in there with my pants still on. I had no business dreaming of her. None.

I paced around my apartment for a while before deciding to go for a run. I needed to seriously take my mind off that dream before going to work.

Dammit, Chris! It was his fault.

Nick sent me a text to let me know he and Ryan would be trying the amplified hypnosis today. After getting dressed, I hesitantly went to work to be there for Ry.

I ARRIVED AT the training center a little after nine and found Nick in one of the training rooms talking to Ryan. It was a relaxed atmosphere, specifically for hypnosis training. The walls were yellow, there was a three-piece sofa set in light blue facing a fake fireplace, and soft instrumental music was playing in the background. I assumed it was to make it a serene experience, but frankly it just made me sleepy.

"Okay, remember this might not work," Nick said.

"It's been years, though. Would that make a difference in their memory?" Ryan asked.

I looked at her. "Come on, Ry. Do you remember the first time you were told about being a Luminary?"

"Of course."

"Right," Nick said, "and that was years ago. Off the top of your head you might not remember all the details—in fact, you might just focus on emotional memory. But if I asked you what you or the person who talked to you were wearing, I bet it would come back to you."

Ryan thought about it. "I was wearing one of my mother's shirts and old sweat pants. Everything else was destroyed in the fire . . . along with her."

"Right. Not exactly where I wanted your memory to go, but what about Jenny? She's the one who found you and talked to you, right?"

"Yes." She closed her eyes.

I went around and put my hands on her shoulders, then rested my chin on her head. "And?" I encouraged

. . . right before moving away to get closer to Nick. The nearness to Ryan and her hair's coconutty scent brought back last night's dream with all its glorious details. I attempted to gulp but my throat was so dry I ended up coughing.

"You okay?" she asked.

I nodded and rubbed my clammy hands against my jeans. In trying to avoid looking her in the eye I ended up bumping into Nick.

"Watch where you're going, man." His eyes narrowed.

"Sorry, ah—yeah . . . sorry, Ryan, go ahead," I said, crossing my arms over my chest.

Ryan tilted her head in concentration. The lines between her eyebrows were deep as she creased them together before saying, "Jenny was wearing jeans and a light blue shirt. She had a coffee stain three buttons down. I remember because that's all I could focus on when she was talking to me."

"And that was four—? Five years ago?" Nick asked.

"Yes."

"So can you believe that Dr. Carson and his then-assistants would remember the big projects they were working on? No matter how long ago it was?"

"I didn't think about that," she said smiling. "Let's try it, then. I hope I can help you recover their memories."

I remained quiet until they were about to call the three scientists to come to the training room. "You don't really need me here, do you, Nick?"

"No, but I thought you wanted to support Ryan."

"Yes, it was your idea, Kev," Ryan said. "Come on, I'll feel better if you're here."

I looked around the room and then saw Nick studying me. "I have a potential lead I want to check out," I said.

Nick nodded. "I was gonna say, this has to be the first time you're passing up an experiment like this."

"Yeah, I'll let you handle it." I turned to Ryan. "Good luck . . . *dude*, you got this." I gave her a quick fist bump and sprinted out of the room.

I GOT TO the Org and went straight to her office to check up on Chris. They wouldn't know I lied about the lead, and if they asked I'd say it didn't pan out.

He looked up from his laptop when I walked in, and said, "Hey, man. Back so soon? How did it go?"

"I—ah, had something else to do." I took a seat on the chair next to his desk and grabbed one of his basketballs, spinning it in my hand. "We'll have to wait for them to fill us in."

Chris picked up a paperclip and proceeded to straighten it out. "Yeah, Ryan will tell us everything. She's good like that."

I frowned, thinking about what Annie said. "Yeah. You having fun with her?"

"Fun with her?"

"Yes. Working together without me watching over your every move."

Chris shrugged. "It's fine. I'm just ticked off. I asked to go in with you guys to see if I can learn anything from Nick but she said no."

I nodded. "The good news is Nick wants you to go meet him later to watch him work after Ryan is done."

"I wanted to see it all in action. It's not like one more person would ruin everything or something."

"She was nervous," I said, putting the ball back in its place.

"She had no problem with you going," he pointed out.

I raised my eyebrow. "Do you see me in there?"

"Whatever."

I looked at him closely and noticed he looked stressed. "You okay, man?"

"I kissed her," he blurted out.

"WHAT?"

"Last night. I don't know what I was thinking. I figured you had a girlfriend now—that it would be okay."

"What did she do?" While I dreamed of making love to Ryan, there Chris was, making out with her. My mouth was suddenly a desert.

Chris shook his head. "Nothing. She just left. Didn't say a word."

"Why did you kiss her? You know we're supposed to be protecting her from jerks like us, right? Not *be* the jerks?" I asked, noticing the laptop screen flickering.

"I know, I know."

I stood up and tried controlling my breathing. "What were you planning? Kiss her, sleep with her, and never work with her again?"

"No, I thought since we actually know each other well, it could be my shot at something real. I've always liked her."

"You said you didn't," I said, pointing my finger at him.

"I know what I said to you . . . but—"

"You don't disrespect my family. Ryan is family," I warned, shoving my hands in my pockets.

"I wouldn't, bro." After a while, he asked, "We good?"

I took a deep breath and nodded. "Just talk to her. Say sorry and then ask her out properly." It was fine. I was going to suggest a double date anyway. This was good. *It's good—it's their decision.*

Chris picked up a second paperclip and repeated the straightening action. "I know I have to. If it wasn't Ryan, I'd make her forget it and save myself the embarrassment."

"Don't hypnotize her, dude."

"Nah, but can you talk to her for me? Make sure she's not angry?"

"I'm not your wing man with her. I'll just make sure she doesn't close herself off from the team. If she friend-zone blocks you, let this go."

He nodded and I left. Once I got out of the office I

pulled out my cell phone, which I'd been gripping firmly the whole time. I didn't need to look at it to know it was busted. I just didn't want issues with my friends. The last thing we needed was drama between them. The dream had me riled up. That was all.

I focused on knowing I'd be hanging with Gabby, so that helped. I also made a mental note to look up how to stop myself from dreaming from now on. There must be something of the sort; I'd smoke sage or eat spinach if I had to.

I MADE MY way back to my office and worked on paperwork the rest of the morning. It was boring work but I needed to keep my mind occupied. The *bing* on my computer screen alerted me to a message. The digital envelope took over the whole screen and opened up with a message instructing me with my next assignment. I met with Derek, who was in the conference room with Jenny, and got the rest of the details.

Ryan was called out from working with Nick to assist me. We required a sensor, and we needed to be as discreet as possible if we were to roam the offices of the FBI. Ryan could help with both, and I could get us out of there if needed. Getting Pine in trouble was not in our best interest.

I'd snuck in to see Gabby before the mission. And thank goodness I was able to; it cleared up my state of mind. For the most part it also prevented my thoughts from straying back to the dream. The couple times I did think of Ryan naked, I repeated Gabby's name over and over in my head and it would pass.

Ryan parked the car, but before we got out, Pine tapped on my window. "Hey, what's going on?" I asked.

"They changed the meeting's location." He handed me a piece of paper. "Here's the address. The meeting is probably already in session."

"You're not coming?" Ryan asked.

"I can't. They knew someone would show up here and changed the time and place. If I show up with you two, they'll know it was me who tipped off the Org."

"But what if they see us?" Ryan asked.

Pine shook his head. "Don't worry, neither Lobo nor Oats know who you two are."

"You'd think they would meet somewhere more private," I said, reading the name of the restaurant.

"I have a feeling the person they're meeting is the one pulling the strings." Pine rubbed his chin. "Derek thinks it might be a rebel, in which case it makes sense they rather meet in public."

"Right. We'll fill you in later, then," I said.

"Please do." Pine tapped the top of the car. "Get going, and stay out of trouble, you two."

WE GOT TO the restaurant and took a seat at a table in the back corner. I wasn't exactly screaming 'rich client' with my jeans and gray sweater, but Ryan looked amazing, so she fit right in with the rest of the high-end people. She was dressed in black, in what she called a sweater dress, high boots, and a pretty hot leather jacket. Had I dressed more appropriately we might have gotten better seats. On the other hand, this allowed us to walk through the restaurant to where they intended to hide me in the corner.

We spotted New York's field office assistant director, Carl Oats, and its special agent in charge, Peter Lobo—Pine's direct upline. We couldn't hear them from where we were sitting, but we had a good view. Ryan's back was to them so she made a series of poses and I pretended to be taking pictures of her. I had some clear shots of the man they met. He reminded me of the man with the mustard stain who had been with Blondie a few months back. They could pass for brothers, I thought.

Ryan got up and walked closer to them pretending to look for the bathroom. With the big distance, her sensors wouldn't work. She said it was too wild with everyone else's emotions in the middle.

I watched her sway her hips as she maneuvered between the tables. Flashes of the white string hanging on them from the dream kept coming at me. I drank my water and hers and concentrated on paying attention to her . . . for her safety.

While the waiter refilled our glasses, I counted at

least five men following her every move; a few of them were even in female company. On her way back to our table, one man grabbed her hands and told her something. She motioned "no" with her head and smiled sweetly, freeing herself. He tried to grab her one more time, but she beat him to it. She pushed his pinky upward and had him gripping the table in pain with his free hand. His two friends just stared at Ryan, ignoring their friend's pain.

She leaned in closer to the man and, smiling, she said something else through her teeth. That was Dangerous Ryan at work. It was pretty hot, I had to admit. She reached our table and snapped me out of my thoughts.

"Let's go," she said, and put on her jacket.

I finished downing my water and followed suit. We didn't get a chance to eat since the food hadn't come yet, so I threw a couple bills on the table for their trouble and went after Ry.

"Why are we leaving? You already took care of that asshole," I asked, opening the door for her to get out.

"Yes, but I called attention to myself. It's best to leave. We already have the man's picture and I can confirm he's a Luminary rebel."

"Of course he is—"

"Hey, bitch!"

I turned to see the guy who'd grabbed Ryan following us. "Who are you calling bitch?" I asked walking to the man. I stared him down. He was my height and dressed nicely in a suit, but his face screamed "bully" from miles away.

"It's okay, Kevin, let's go." Ryan tried pulling me away.

The man looked at Ryan. "You dirty whore, you almost broke my fing—"

I punched him in his jaw and his head spun. I was too busy enjoying the satisfaction of his pain and didn't notice his two buddies next to him. The blow to my eye was a surprise, to say the least.

I raised my left elbow to block the next punch coming at me as my right fist connected with his rib. He was quick, though. He caught his balance immediately and used the momentum to sock me in the jaw. In full force I broke his nose with my head.

I went after the first guy who'd gotten up and was yelling some choice words at Ryan, but she beat me to it. She gave him a low side kick and made him join his buddy as he fell backward. The third friend was about to join in the fun when the restaurant's sign above us exploded. He retreated and went to help his friends while Ryan and I ran away from the scene.

My hands still buzzed but I made sure to send some glass shards on those idiots. I wanted to increase the chances of them being charged for destroying the sign.

I HAD TO hurry to catch up with Ryan as she slammed the car door and made a half-run back to my office.

"Asshole!" Ryan fumed.

"It's okay, Ry, I got him good," I said, rubbing my face.

"No, you're the asshole. I said to let it go. You made a scene and everyone in the restaurant got a good look at us. Even Oats and Lobo were staring. If they see us again they'll recognize us."

"Hey, you made your own little scene inside the restaurant."

"I did it quietly and you only noticed because you were watching my back." She tied her hair up in a bun. "I tried leaving before you escalated the problem, but I should have known better."

I flinched. "Look, I'm not going to let anyone disrespect you."

Her fists curled up into balls. "I can handle myself."

"A simple thank you would be good. I know you can take care of yourself. But why can't I be there for you once in a while?" I asked, leaning against my desk. "You always have the load of responsibilities on your shoulders. We agreed I'd be that one person you can break down to and be weak with if needed."

She walked back and forth. "Did I look like I needed your help?"

"Maybe I'm the one who needed to help you." I raised my chin. "I will stand by you anytime I have to, and you need to accept that."

She loosened her bun again and stared at me for a few minutes. "Fine, but you're the one who's going to tell Derek that Oats, Lobo, and the rebel made us."

"Fine."

"And thanks . . . for defending my honor," she said with a light laugh. Then came closer and touched the bruise on my face. "You look pretty messed up, dude."

"Glad you think it's funny," I grunted.

"Well, it is a little bit funny. It looks bad though—want me to call Jenny to heal it?"

"Don't worry about it, I'll go find her later if it feels worse." I rubbed it again. "All I know is *you'd* better defend *my* honor, too, if necessary."

"By that, you mean get you more chicks to nail?" Her eyes widened. "Crap, well, you know what I mean. Not anymore." She shrugged. "It was just a joke."

"Bad joke. It's different now that I have Gabby."

She squinted. "You two are getting really serious."

"I think so."

"And you didn't think you would ever fall in love," she said with half a smile. She sat at the edge of my desk next to me, facing the door.

"I didn't say *that*. I can care for someone without giving up my identity or losing myself."

"That's romantic." Ryan rolled her eyes, but kept her eyes to the door. "And here I was thinking you were falling for her."

I shook my head and moved to face her. "Nah, I don't know. I only know I *need* her. Like I breathe thoughts of her. Is that natural? Am I falling?"

"That's exactly how it starts."

I took a step back. "What would you know about that?"

"I guess nothing. But if you do fall for her, don't hold back because you're nervous of losing yourself. It wouldn't be fair to her or you."

"Well, I can show her." I smiled.

She tilted her head. "You still wouldn't tell her that you love her? If you do?"

"I don't like those three words, Ry. I'll probably only tell my wife that." I laughed. "And only on our wedding day!"

"So you plan on getting married!"

"Maybe." I shrugged. "If I keep feeling this way and if Gabby sticks around."

Ryan stared at her shoes for a few seconds. "Have you two discussed your future yet?"

"Well, we haven't made anything official, but I think we're both feeling the same connection."

"Don't go assuming anything, Kevin. Ask her, if you want her to be your girlfriend. Don't just let it happen; make sure she knows you care for her."

"Did I ask for advice?"

"Did I ask for you to defend my honor?" She stared at me. "No, but we always look out for each other. Trust me on this one. Don't just hope she reads your signs. Act on it."

"Okay. Hey, speaking of that, I wanted to ask you

for a favor."

"Go for it."

"I want to bring her over to my place tomorrow night, and I wondered if you would—"

"I'm not cleaning your apartment!"

I laughed. "I thought about asking, believe me! But no, I need your help with something more important than that, actually."

"What would you like me to cook for you two?" A smirk crossed her face.

"Are you sure you can't read my mind?" I asked.

"Pretty sure I can't. But I do know you, Kevin Pierce, and it's only a few things you ever need from me."

"I have no arguments since you're not wrong at the moment. Lasagna, please?"

"You got it. I'll prepare it and leave it in your oven. When you get home, follow the instructions I'll leave on your counter."

"Thanks, Ry. I owe you!"

"After what you did for me today, I think we'll call it even . . . but don't do it again!"

I smiled. "Okay."

"Now go fill Derek in so you can rush to Gabby. I can see you're anxious." She laughed and put on her beanie hat. She looked cute with her crooked tooth, and with the curls peeking out from under, framing her happy face. So innocent and sweet. How could I not punch that guy?

I imitated her and put on my own. "I am—but first, tell me how it went with you and Nick."

"Oh, right, sorry. After rushing to meet Pine and everything else, I forgot."

"I get it, but go on, woman!"

"So impatient." She smiled. "Okay, so Nick and I decided to ease the three of them into things. We worked on them for about an hour each, trying to get their minds to be opened and fighting off whatever hypnosis was done on them."

"Is it working?"

"Yes, Nick got in there and is breaking down the walls. Whatever that means," she said, rolling her eyes. "And he's confident that we'll get some answers next time. He said he's working in the background of their minds, so they don't know what's happening."

I reached over to fix a loose strand under her hat, and she flinched in reaction. "Relax, I'm not messing your hair up."

She stared at me. "Uh, yeah . . . you better not."

I shook my head. "But really, it's cool that you're able to help Nick this much."

"It really is! He's undoing the rebels' work and said it would have taken months to get this far if it wasn't for me."

"See? I told you it would work."

"I know! I'm so excited. Nick said it's like peeling off layers upon layers of hypnosis. We'll work with them tomorrow and Derek is coming along to ask questions. I have to be there by seven so I'd better get going now."

"Seven? Like in the morning?"

"Duh! We might get a lot of information from them. It's going to take time and we had to cut it short today."

"What are you going to do now? It's only five thirty."

"I'm going to the supermarket, or did you not need a lasagna for tomorrow?"

I frowned. "How's that gonna work for you?"

"I'm preparing it now . . . oh, you're right. You know what? Come by my place tomorrow and get it from the refrigerator. I'll tape the baking instructions on the top. You'll survive that part, I promise."

"I feel bad. I'll just pick up something, Ryan. Go rest and stuff."

"Don't worry about me. You know I always have your back. Now go to Derek! 'Bye."

"Laters, homie!"

DEREK JUST LISTENED to what I had to say, downloaded the pictures of the man, told me "good work" and let me go. He was so distracted, he didn't seem concerned that Ryan and I might get recognized in the future.

I left him and went home to change out of my blood-stained clothes before seeing Gabby. The guy's blood had splattered on my sweater when I broke his nose. I looked worse than I was, as does any eye bruise. At least the punching made me feel better about missing out on some training the past few days. It felt good. This Sunday I had to get back to it, though; I'd been slacking. *I'll have to remember to text Ryan for that.*

I was in a much better mood after my shower, and cupcakes seemed like a good idea. I stopped by the bakery and got some for Gabby and me to share after dinner, which would consist of fast food because I wanted her to appreciate the lasagna even more tomorrow.

Before going to her though, I thought a new toy for Milo and a couple cupcakes for Ryan would be a nice thank you for her slaving away in the kitchen. I swung by her place but she wasn't home yet. I left the toys in Milo's favorite spot and the cupcakes in Ryan's special dessert holder.

I gathered some ingredients from her fridge and made her one of her power green smoothies she loved drinking. Then I set coffee and left a note telling her about the smoothie and to press start when she was ready for coffee. After I was content, I left and went to the training center.

"WHAT HAPPENED TO you?" Gabby came running to me when she saw me.

"You should see the other guy." I laughed.

"Actually, I've seen you fight. I do feel bad for the other guy. My God, look at your face. It's all bruised up!"

"No biggie." I shrugged. "I'm hungry though; can we eat?"

We went to the roof and spread a sheet for our make-do picnic. Since I wanted to ask Derek for Gabby to spend the night and most of Saturday with me, I didn't want to push my luck. I was nice and kept her on the grounds. Or roof, in this case. It was close to sixty degrees, but it was windy so we dressed warm and had a couple blankets . . . plus there was always body heat.

"You fought a guy for Ryan?" Gabby stopped eating her burger as soon as I told her what happened.

"Yes, he was disrespectful."

"Well, I think you overreacted," she said. "Ryan had already put the guy in his place."

"It's the principle of the thing, dammit," I said, exasperated. "And you weren't there . . . the way he looked at her and called her names."

"I still say she could have defended herself again if she wanted to."

"Yes. Yes, she could, Gabby. But I don't regret it. I wouldn't allow anyone to talk like that to any of my girls."

Her eyes narrowed. "So you do consider Ryan to be your girl?"

"Not like that. Come on," I said, holding her hand. "She's on the list along with you. And you are right at the top."

"Who else is on this list?"

"Annie, even though she's the last one to need me—

Beth, Jenny, and Elisa. There. That's the list of the important women in my life."

She smiled. "And I'm at the top?"

"Well, we do happen to be on the roof, so I would say: literally."

"Funny guy."

"I know. But are you *really* jealous of my best friend?"

"A little bit. I mean, she's beautiful and . . . you're so in tune with each other."

This again. I took a deep breath. "You'll get to know her in time and we'll all be friends. Unless you were just planning to use me and leave me?"

"You're on to me!" she said, laughing and holding on to my hand. The warmth was so nice and relaxing. I suddenly realized she was right about Ryan holding her own when necessary. I didn't have to be there all the time. I had Gabby now.

We lay on the blankets trying to get a peek at the stars in between our city's pollution. I had my iPod connected to a portable speaker and we listened to music together as usual. She sang loud and passionately. I didn't have the heart to tell her how out of tune she was. It was just too adorable.

She stopped singing and asked, "So how should I dress tomorrow?"

"Well, we're going to be indoors. And alone. And hopefully you'll want to stay and . . . maybe go out for breakfast on Saturday?"

"Hmm, do you think I can use your phone for a couple of minutes?"

"Sure," I said, handing over my phone. "You know you can't—"

"Reach out to people I knew before all of this went down, got it. Don't worry, I'm just reaching out to my future friend, like you called her."

I watched her walk away while she called Ryan. She laughed a lot and seemed to have fun but she kept playing with her watch. Women. Why were they always so intimidated by one another? She walked back to me. "Everything cool?"

She smiled. "Yes. I needed a favor. She'll see me around six thirty in the morning. Goodness, I'm glad I can go back to sleep all day long if I wanted to or I would tell you I didn't like your friend."

"She has work to do at seven," I said, defending Ryan.

"I know, she told me. I can't imagine being in charge of such important things. I mean, she and I are both twenty-one. While I'm trying to decide what to do with my future, you guys put your lives at risk to help those in need. It's really cool. And you start, what? Really young?"

"Yeah, but we love it."

She sighed. "You are amazing. All of you."

"I think you're amazing."

"Oh jeez, it is tough to be locked up all day and still smile when I see you. Go ahead, keep telling me how no one can do it like I do."

I laughed. "Well, apart from this tough job you have going on, you did care for your mother and sister and went to school and taught self-defense to helpless women. Those are all amazing things to me."

"Yes, but you guys actually save lives," she said, shrugging.

"This is not a competition to see who's more amazing. I think you are wonderful and beautiful and more special than you know. That's all I wanted to say. This, what I do, is just part of the cards I've been handed. I decided to play the game. You and what you did, or probably still do for your mother, is by choice. You could have walked away anytime but you didn't."

"You could have, too."

"Nah, I love teleporting too much. Give up my power? Please. I thrive here."

"Well, Mr. Thriver, I have one more thing to ask of you."

"What's that?"

"Can you get Mom's prescription again? You know she's particular about her pharmacy."

I shook my head. "Sorry, I can't. Derek said our people would handle that from now on."

"I'll tell her." She nodded and played with her watch. I studied the action and thought I'd be nervous too, if I had to relay the message to Mrs. Ryder. That woman had an intense vibe.

"Hey." I frowned. "What are your parents going to

say tomorrow when I don't bring you back?"

"I'll tell them I'm going to Ryan's or something. Don't worry."

"I could talk to them, if you want."

"No, it's too weird. Mom doesn't care and Dad's mind is not really on me anyway. He keeps mumbling to himself and is living in his own scientific world. I think he's just too upset about Grace. I'll deal with them."

"All right."

CHAPTER THIRTEEN

AFTER RUNNING A few miles on Friday morning, I jogged to Ryan's place to pick up the lasagna before going home. This way I didn't have to worry about it later. I saw that her kitchen was a mess so I decided to clean up. She would laugh since I hired someone to come clean my own apartment. But I knew Ryan, and she must have been too exhausted for her to have left it like this. Besides, it was only in this condition because of me.

I washed the dishes and cleaned down the countertop before opening the refrigerator to get my lasagna. It was neatly packed in a bag with two pieces of paper stuck on the top. One was the baking instructions, and the other was a note. She thanked me for the cupcake, smoothie, and coffee that I'd left for her last night. I opened the bag to find a banana cream pie staring at me. Aww, Ry surprised me with dessert.

I would have said I owed her, but the small act of

smiling at the surprise made my face ache from the fight I'd had over her. Maybe we were even after all.

I made sure everything in her kitchen was in order and went home to shower and get ready for work. I had barely made it in when Derek called me to the conference room.

"You're late."

I looked at Derek. "Come on dude, I'm not that late. Plus, my morning didn't have any assignment scheduled."

"Kevin, I'm your boss. Calling me 'dude' is disrespectful."

"Sorry." I had to remember to be on his good side if I wanted him to agree for me to take Gabby away tonight . . . and tomorrow.

"Just watch it, at least when we're not in the privacy of my office. Some of the others already feel I play favorites with you because Annie and Nick are on the board with me."

"Well, you do." I shrugged.

"But must we shove it in their faces, Kevin?" Annie asked, closing the door behind her.

I smiled and asked, "Okay, what's going on?"

"I already told him about your plans, so that's set. You and Gabby are good for your overnight date," Annie said.

"Wait, how did you know?"

"Gabby. Well, Ryan had to get some toiletries to Gabby, but Derek called her in earlier than expected, so

Ryan asked me to take care of it, and—well, it's a whole chain thing now."

"Okay, you women are too confusing, but thanks for talking to the boss." I turned to Derek. "And thanks for agreeing."

"No problem. Before you sneak her out of here without me knowing, I'd rather consent to it."

"Cool."

"Now, on to business: you are going on surveillance . . ."

I HID BEHIND a commercial garbage container, waiting to see some movement. Nothing. I'd been there for almost forty minutes and hadn't heard a pin drop. I didn't see any cameras either. Nick was pretty sure that this intel was correct. Of course, it was intel that would have been more helpful five years ago—but they had no reason to have moved locations after the precautions they'd taken on everyone they left behind.

Thanks to Ryan, they retrieved the locations much faster than expected, but Nick was still working on Dr. Carson. Out of the three scientists who were brain-screwed, he was the one with the most information. Their memories were back and in full mode, and Nick had to hypnotize them to cooperate in case their memories returned with the state of mind that we were the enemies. Ryan's part was over and for now, it was all up to Nick to extract what we needed from them. She wasn't needed the whole day like she'd originally thought, so she was on this mission with me. Where was she? She should have been here by now.

Ryan had decided to go use her feminine charms and walk around to see if anyone would talk to her. Or, at the very least, to see if she sensed anyone or anything—but she hadn't returned. That was ten minutes ago. *Screw that.* I got up and walked onto the main road. The factory we had been sent to was out in Long Island, right smack on a main road, but the factory itself seemed lifeless. There were no signs of her so I walked around the building once, then doubled back in case we were following each other in circles . . . but nothing.

I went to the back and teleported on top of the building. I found one guy at the top; how did I miss him before? Well, he didn't see me, so one fast blow to his head took him out. I grabbed the receiver from his hand and listened in. *Crap!* They had Ryan inside. How is it that she hadn't sensed anyone?

There was one door at the corner of the roof. I went and listened to the other side. Silence. Good. I went to teleport in but found myself right where I stood. *What the hell?* I tried a couple of times but I still couldn't get in. They'd blocked me somehow. I had to get in there. They had Ryan.

Unsure what to do, I tried to pull from the big industrial lights that were on the roof. They were the type used in highways at night during construction. I frowned, realizing they were on during the day. It was odd, but hey, it wasn't my electric bill to pay. If I could melt the knob or electrocute it or whatever, I wouldn't make any suspicious noise. After a few minutes of attempting it, nothing happened. I actually felt weak, which only happened to me when I tried to teleport too many people without Annie or Ryan's help.

Okay, I had to think. I rested my hand on the knob and my wrist turned it by mistake. Oh! Well, I'm an idiot. It had been unlocked all along. That's what happened when I tried solving everything with my powers—Annie would have a good laugh at this one.

I went in slowly. I wasn't sure how many guards might be there and I didn't want to get caught before getting to Ryan. I tried teleporting again onto some big support beams below the roof but I didn't move one inch from where I stood. How in the world did they find a way to stop my powers? This was not a good thing. Lucky for me, Nick and Annie had always thought it was important for us to train without using our powers.

The stairs seemed to be unguarded. I went one level down and then through a doorway to a narrow passage. The passage wrapped around the inside like a rectangle and had a railing that was about four feet high. It had an opened center.

I noticed there were two sets of stairs going down.

The level I stood on consisted of offices. They each had big windows with no curtains, so I could see most were empty except for two of them. I took out a small mirror I kept just for these situations, and angled it to look below. Ah, crap. I scooched near to the closest railway and peeked my head to figure out a way to get there.

Right in the middle of the open space, Ryan was sitting with her hands and feet tied up. The area was surrounded by more of that industrial lighting; it was extremely bright. Couldn't they just use the ceiling lights and cover all grounds? Idiots. I counted about fifteen men surrounding her. This was going to be interesting. I went to meet them.

"Looks like I'm late," I said, walking down the stairs with hands up in the air. Without my powers I couldn't stop them from hurting either Ryan or myself. Their eyes and guns followed me with each step I took.

A man smoking a cigarette stood up from behind the rest of them. He had been hidden from view when I'd looked. We met at the bottom of the stairs, and he flicked his cigarette at me. "You must be her partner."

"Nope. I was just in the neighborhood and decided to pop in. Well, actually." I frowned and walked toward Ryan. "I couldn't pop in. Any idea why?"

She shook her head, and the man spoke. "So what's your special power, kid?"

"Kid? Me? Now, you're insulting me."

He turned to a man standing beside Ryan and snapped his fingers. The man slapped Ryan across the face twice. He then pulled her hair and forced her head backward so she stared straight at the ceiling.

I flinched.

"You get one more chance, *kid*. What is your power?"

"All right, look. Take it easy on the girl. She's only a sensor, okay? I'm the one you want."

"Because?"

I tried to get a better look at the men. I needed to make sure no one recognized me. For all I knew any of the other guys whose ass I'd kicked during the kidnapping could have been there. "Well, because I'm her senior. She's working under me. But to answer your original question, I have no power."

"Do you take me for a fool?" He snapped his finger, and Ryan got slapped a couple more times.

I clenched my jaw. "I don't know you, so I'm going with a 'no' for now. But I have no power . . . because somehow you've managed to disable it," I said, as he turned to look at the man next to Ryan again. "Apart from that, I can move objects with my mind." A variation of the truth, but easily proved if they turned off their barrier.

"And by objects, Kevin, I do hope you mean yourself. You see, I would hate to think you'd lie to me when your partner, Ryan there, has her life hanging by a string." He walked up to me. "A string controlled by your words."

"Well, you didn't let me finish. I can move objects with my mind, and I can also move myself and my partner"—I lifted my chin to Ryan—"from one location to another. This we call teleportation. Now can you ask him to back off her?"

"Very good." He nodded, and the man next to Ryan took a few steps back. "Now, my question is: how did you find this place?"

Knowing I was in danger didn't automatically make me mature. "We jumped in the car, took the Long Island Expressway all the way to Exit—no? That's not what you meant, got it. I'll tell you, but can I ask first why or how it is that my powers don't work here?"

"This is the only question you get to ask. We've developed a unique transmitter specifically designed to disable your powers. Now, how did you find us?"

"Well, I figured that much on my own, but I just wanted to know—"

"Answer my question or she suffers."

I nodded. "We found your mole."

The man laughed. "I very much doubt that. Last I heard, you only just found out you had one. How are interrogations going at the Org, by the way?"

I balled my fists. "I don't kno—"

"Last chance for honesty. Speak. How did you find us?"

"One of our agents cracked one of the scientists you left behind," I said.

"This agent, would it be Nick?"

I rolled my eyes. Nick's reputation followed me everywhere, apparently. "Yes."

He lit another cigarette. "I believe he tried this before with no success. What changed?"

Okay, these people knew too much. I hadn't believed we had a double agent before, but now I had no doubt. I had to make it a priority to find this person when I got back.

At the corner of my eyes, I saw that Ryan shook her head ever so slightly, so I said, "You know all about Nick, I assume?"

"We do." He nodded.

"Then you know he always finds a way. There's a risk when any hypnotizer pushes someone to their limit. After we found out we had a spy, he decided it was time to sacrifice your old people's brains if necessary. All he did was push harder than before."

"And you expect me to believe that?"

"Personally, I don't know how hypnosis works." I shrugged. "You'll have to ask Nick for more details."

"It's not the Org's way. You value lives above all and you wouldn't risk damaging someone's brain or changing their lives drastically." He took a puff and waited for me to talk.

"He will try to make the poor guy's mind right when he's done. If not, he'll give your guy a new identity and make him forget the rest. Sometimes sacrifices have to be made, and no one understands that better than Nick."

"Why did they only send you two?"

"Normally I would have been able to get us out of here on a moment's notice, and because Ryan was going to try and sense if there were any Luminaries in here. We just came to scope the place out."

The man turned and looked up at a woman who stared at us from the upper level. She gave him a nod and then talked into her cell phone. I checked on Ryan, who was staring at the woman with deep concentration. I turned back to look at the woman, and she looked familiar somehow; I guess that's what Ryan was trying to figure out. The woman continued talking on the phone, and turned her back to us. She was maybe in her mid-forties and seemed in good shape. Her wavy black hair fell a little below her shoulder, and she wore a skirt suit.

She hung up and looked at Ryan first, then me. "Take care of them."

That was never a good thing. I jumped and kicked the man who stood next to Ryan. I dragged her chair all the way to the back wall and stood in front of her. In one swoop I cut the string off her hands with my penknife. She took it to cut off the binding from her feet while I braced myself for a fight.

"Are you deluding yourself into thinking you have a chance? You and your little friend are done," the man said.

"I might die. I might not, but I'm taking down as many of you as I can with me."

"Good luck, kid." He laughed and flicked his cigarette.

I backed up closer to Ryan and created some distance from the men. "If you see an opening, you run."

"I'm not leaving you."

"Yes, you are." I turned to see the panic set in Ryan's eyes. "I won't let anything happen to you."

"It's not me I'm worried about," she mumbled.

"Call Andrew," I whispered hurriedly. "If we can get you a gun, shoot your way out of here. Aim for the glass door." She looked at me with trembling lips. "You got this, Ry."

I cocked my head to the side and pulled her to stand back to back with me, like Nick taught us. I motioned with my middle finger for my new dance partners to come. "I hope you can fight with those heels," I whispered.

"You have no idea what these babies can do," she said before the first set of men started walking in on us. "Three R," she said, and we took three steps to her right . . . which was closer to the door.

I waited for them to start throwing the first punches. In the meantime we took a few more steps to our intended destination.

Game time started: a left punch came my way, but I promptly blocked it and grabbed the guy's hand. I twisted it behind his back and sent him backward, knocking into the two who followed him. They fell on the floor. It wouldn't keep them down but it was a chance to run closer to the door. I pulled on her jacket and whispered, "Ten."

The rest came all at once. I punched, she kicked, I got a blow to the head, her cheek got a cut. We went at it for a bit before I saw the next set coming with knives. I looked up, noticing we had moved below the ceiling, right under the rails that blocked off the top passage halls. Ryan stooped and made a spin on the floor to knock two other guys off their feet. I saw a bigger guy coming to her side with a knife, and pulled her. "Jump and grab, Ryan."

I interlocked my hands and she bent one knee while placing her other foot in my hand. "Now," she yelled. I pushed off the floor and we both jumped, throwing her in the air. I didn't get a chance to see if she caught on the rail because the knife in my shoulder was a bit distracting. I pulled it out and kneed my attacker while throwing the knife at the man trying to grab Ryan's leg. She was hanging by one hand; the knife went straight into his wrist and he let go of her. She made a swing and held on with both hands, pulling herself sideways, one hand at a time, toward the door. All she needed was to drop when she got closer and run out.

My job was to keep them away from her.

I heard one guy say, "Shoot them."

"No. Boss said no guns," someone else yelled.

I frowned as another knife flew by my face and nicked my ear. I grabbed the guy by his shirt and sent his head through a glass table. The bottom floor seemed to be several offices like upstairs but these were all blocked in, no windows. While I was trying to scope out what I could use against these guys, a laser beam hit my shoulder. *What the hell?*

"The purple light, Kevin," Ryan screamed.

I used the heel of my palm to strike up a guy's nose, and thrust my other elbow into the throat of the one behind me. I held onto him to use as shield, and squinted to where Ryan pointed. I noticed some blue-violet lighting closer to the glass entrance. It was hard to see with the other bright light, but it bounced off the dark clothing of a guy who stood under it. He threw a laser beam at me. I dropped the guy I'd been holding and dove to the floor, rolling away.

Good. Now I knew I needed that light to teleport. But now they knew I knew. On cue, a group of them walked toward the front door.

Awesome. Just the perfect spot for them to block. I gritted my teeth.

I noticed Ryan had climbed all the way up and had one leg hooked on the middle rail, reaching out her hand in the air. I thought that was odd until I saw a hint of that violet light, but it was too far for her to reach. As I tried to calculate what to do next, another beam zoomed its way to me. I dodged it and went back to fighting. With the injury in my shoulder, these guys were breaking me down fast.

Just as I broke one guy's arm, I heard a whistle.

Looking up, I saw Ryan hooking her other leg on the rail and snapping her fingers, which signaled it was time to go. As she hung upside down, her arms reached out and I saw her finger pointing up, so I kicked the other guy in my way and ran, jumping up to catch her hands. She swung me up and I fell on the passageway. I helped

S.K. ANTHONY

her out and saw a dark room a couple feet ahead of us with more of the same purple-blue lighting. I ran with her inside, hoping that was our way out.

The woman who had given the kill order was standing inside by the window. That side of the room was completely dark but the glow of the fireball in her hands made it easy to see her face. We were already in the purple lighting; I tried reaching for Ryan to teleport out, but she stood by the door, staring, and shaking her head. She raised her hands and said, "Don't do this."

As the fireball came our way, I jumped in front of Ryan. It hit me on my stomach as I heard her scream, "Noooo!"

I was half unconscious and unable to think, yet I found myself at the Org before passing out.

CHAPTER FOURTEEN

AFTER JENNY HEALED my wounds, I left the infirmary and went to my office to change, since my shirt was burnt and was soaked in blood.

I found Ryan pacing back and forth. She ran and gave me a hug when she saw me. "Oh my God, you're okay!"

"You can let go now," I said after a minute. All my senses were on alert after just being healed, so her shampoo was overwhelming my nose.

"I was worried," she said and pulled back. "Oh, no, your shirt. Let me get you your spare." She stared at me, then got a T-shirt from the bottom drawer of my desk.

"What was that back there?" I asked, massaging my neck. "Who's that woman? You seemed to recognize her."

"I—I'm not sure. Oh my God, Kevin. I thought you were dead. I'm glad we got out so fast."

"Yeah, how *did* we get teleported? It wasn't me."

"No, I think I did it. I panicked and grabbed you. Then I tried to amplify you but you looked . . ." She shook her head. "Never mind, I freaked out 'cause they were coming in on us. I had the intense desire to get to the Org and it was so fast! It felt like we were on a foggy conveyor belt. Then I saw the infirmary, which I was looking for—I reached out, and it felt like everything was shimmering when I pulled and got us off."

"You channeled me!"

She nodded. "That left me dizzy, though. And high . . . like, I feel high and excited. How are you able to do that!? Like for real, feed my brain with the theories."

"Oh, now you wanna know? Before, you didn't care much; it was all about studying your own."

"Well, I actually experienced it." She nodded quickly. "It was so weird!"

I laughed. "Now that you've put the mechanics of it into use, you might understand what Andrew and I speculated."

"Hit me." She sat at the edge of my desk with eager eyes.

"The world is not really solid. It's just a bunch of electrons and protons swimming in a space-time foam. In the 'in-between' we can teleport. Some people call it the astral plane. Like you saw, it feels like we're on a mist-filled conveyor belt. Both Andrew and I see it like a movie screen with shimmering images passing by."

"So you're not the one moving?"

"No, in bending space I don't actually move. I look

for what I want and pull it toward me, so the real trick is getting off at the right spot. Andrew manipulates his portal differently, though. He walks through it and bends time to appear slow while he looks for his destination."

"Trippy."

I laughed. "Yes."

"But are we telling Derek I did it? I mean, he didn't want anyone out of the original group to know about transferring powers. I don't want to tell him after messing up the last mission. He'll just say I'm breaking all the rules. Please just say you did it."

"Yeah, whatever." I stretched my arms out. I always felt overly relaxed after being healed. The stretching helped my body feel normalized.

"I'm just glad I got you here in time for Jenny to heal you. It was so much blood—your stomach was—"

Her blue eyes filled with tears and I pulled her in. "Come here." I closed my eyes, taking in her hair scent and feeling my body react. *That stupid dream!* It needed to stop haunting me. Having just been healed didn't help matters either, the way it heightened my senses. I moved my arms up to embrace her shoulder, thinking it would help, but in response Ryan hugged my waist tighter.

"Am I interrupting?" Gabby said as she took in the scene in front of her. Ryan and I were hugging and I still hadn't put my shirt on. Yep, she looked pissed.

"Gabby!" Ryan said, pulling away. "Glad they brought you. I wasn't sure how long he'd be in the infirmary and thought he would like a visit from you."

"Andrew brought me along. He told me you sent for me," she said, giving Ryan a hard look. "Thanks for thinking of me while my boyfriend was dying. Least you could do since he was saving *your* life."

"Gabby, don't be like that," I said.

"How do you want me to be? She's clearly in love with you." She looked at Ryan. "Yesterday he beat a guy up for you, today you almost got him killed, and now I come in here to find him half naked hugging you? How am I supposed to feel?"

Ryan's eyes widened as all color fell from her face. "I'm sorry. I'll leave you two alone."

Gabby opened the door for Ryan to leave and slammed it behind her.

She turned to me. "And maybe you should put a shirt on or something."

I crossed my arms over my chest. "There was no need for you to be rude."

"Wasn't there? She didn't deny it."

"What?"

"That she's in love with you."

"For the last time, Gabby, please drop that. I don't do well with the controlling type."

Gabby stood there, staring. Her fists were in balls as she focused on breathing, and watching me put my shirt on.

She pinched the bridge of her nose, I assumed trying to center her anger. "I'm not usually controlling, but I can't deal with you two," she said, sitting down. "You risked your life for her! You could have died and I would never see you again. And then you're in here shirtless, all hot . . . and she's in your arms . . . I don't know. I freaked out on her . . . I'll apologize later."

I stooped and held her hands. "Look. I understand it's not easy, but Ryan is important to me. I hope you can accept that. Of course I risked my life for her; she's done the same for me countless of times. We're partners. That's what we do. And if it's not her, it would be someone else. My job is dangerous. You know firsthand—it's how I saved you."

"I know."

"And I hugged her because she was crying. I can't take it when your female species start with the tear-dropping. She feels bad because she froze for a second and that's what gave the woman time to throw the fireball at us. I jumped in front of her and got hit instead. It's normal to feel guilty about it."

"And the shirtless part?" she asked, playing with her watch.

"My shirt was burnt and full of blood so I couldn't wear that one anymore. Ryan was in here, upset, waiting for me when I came. I consoled her, that's all. I'm *your* boyfriend. There is no misunderstanding anywhere."

She bit her lips and held on to my hands. The warmth felt good as she squeezed. "Sorry. I know we haven't talked specifics about our relationship, but I was jealous, and have you seen yourself without a shirt? You forgive me, right?"

I laughed, feeling flattered. "Of course. I understand why you reacted this way." The warmth of her hands felt more intense. "I guess you're right. Ryan should know better."

"As long as we're okay."

"We are, and I think we can confirm that we're together in a relationship before we hang out tonight. That's if you still want to hang out."

"Yes, of course I do." She raised an eyebrow, smiling in triumph.

"Good." I hugged her. "Now, let's get out of here. I didn't realize it had gotten so late."

I called Derek to let him know I was leaving with Gabby and told him he'd have the report on Monday. We picked up her little overnight bag and I teleported us to my apartment.

We had a nice conversation as per our usual. It was great to see how the sadness in her eyes made less and less appearance as time passed. As she shared childhood stories of her and Grace, I realized her lack of tact at times was related to her being so closed off. And with her strange parents as role models, who could blame her?

I snuck a quick text to Ryan when I got a chance, to tell her I was sorry and I would call her soon. I also avoided telling Gabby our meal had been cooked by Ryan.

When we were done with dessert, Gabby practically pulled me off my chair. "Show me your bedroom."

"Okay," I said and made the short walk. As soon as

we entered, she turned to face me. She got on her tippy toes and wrapped her hand around my neck, pulling me to her. She was aggressive, which was different for me since I was usually the one in charge. We found ourselves in a desperate dance of exploring each other while trying to savor the moment.

I spun Gabby so her back rested on the door while I pressed up against her. I traced my tongue along her lips and then went on to give her a deep kiss; one hand tugged at her waist and the other caressed her thigh. I pulled her up in one motion and got her legs around me as I slowly licked and kissed the top of her breasts. Her head was now at my level so she leaned down to kiss my neck. I felt like I was ready to burst.

I pulled her hair back and rushed to the dresser on my left to sit her down. We knocked some things on the floor, but neither of us bothered to look at what they might be. She pulled at my shirt and managed to take it off very hastily. I was feeling thrown off by her show of force, but the feeling of warmth of her hands tracing my back overwhelmed me. Considering I couldn't wait any longer, I decided her ferociousness was an interesting change. I raised her dress and pulled it over her head. We barely managed to get everything off before I lost myself in her.

I ROLLED OUT of bed and enjoyed the smell of coffee in the air. Gabby was not next to me, so I quickly went to pull on my boxers and brushed my teeth before meeting her in my kitchen.

She was standing in my T-shirt, sipping on tea and watching the coffee pot as it finished brewing. I hugged her from behind. "Good morning, beautiful."

She set her cup down and turned, smiling. "Good morning."

I kissed her again and she pushed me away. "Drink your coffee. I don't know about you, but my energy is a bit low after last night."

"Oh, I think I can muster up some more if I must. If I die this morning, at least I will go happy."

"Shut up!" She laughed.

"You want to go to the diner downstairs and eat or want me to make you some hot dogs?" I asked.

"God, please, no! No more hot dogs."

We spent the day doing mindless things, naughty things, and dirty things before going to visit Nick and Annie. I wanted Gabby to meet Jack.

"Oh my gosh, the cuteness!" Gabby said, holding the crying baby.

"I know, and look what I got you, Jack." I took out a miniature black beanie hat I had squeezed into my pocket. "Now you match your uncle. Give me a tiny high five, little man." I touched my finger to his palm.

"Look at you. You really like babies, huh?" Gabby asked.

"I do. You?"

"I do. Hey!" She bit her lips and sat closer to me. "We just exchanged 'I dos.'"

"Oh no, li'l bro, Uncle Kev is not falling into this marriage epidemic. And don't you fall either, you hear me. Just because you're being raised by a married couple doesn't mean you have to follow their lifestyle. *No, you don't! No, you don't!*"

"Kevin!" Gabby looked at me wide-eyed for a few seconds. She then laughed, and said, "What are you telling the baby? Stop it!"

"What? This is guy talk."

She looked at Jack. "You don't have to listen to him, you little cutie pie."

"He totally looks like me, right?"

"Ha! You wish," Annie said, giving us each a glass and taking Jack away. "Enjoy this for me, will you, Gabby? I'm still breastfeeding and I miss my wine terribly. Oh no, he drooled all over your blouse. I'm sorry."

"No, its fine," Gabby said, wiping the drool off with the bib.

"Aww, look at that, babe. He just welcomed you into our bro-hood," I said.

"Better his drool than yours." She laughed.

Nick came from the kitchen with cookies in hand. "You can borrow one of Annie's tops if you want."

"Nah, it wasn't much. It's okay." Gabby grabbed a cookie and bit into it. "Wow, these are good!"

"Yeah, I love these suckers. I had to bribe Ryan into giving me a couple dozen," he said.

"Ryan made these?" Gabby stopped mid-bite.

"Yes, best thing that happens when she's upset. She starts baking. I kind of talked her into these cookies last night," Nick said, clearly proud of himself.

"Dude, you realize just because you convinced her to make these doesn't mean you get credit, right?" I asked.

"Whatever. Don't have any, then," Nick said, taking another cookie from the bowl and putting the whole thing in his mouth.

"Of course I'm having a couple." I closed my eyes as I enjoyed the first one. "Man, Ryan could tell me she poisoned her food and I'd still eat it."

"Yep," Nick agreed, and stuffed his mouth again.

"So is there anything Ryan can't do?" Gabby asked.

Annie came back with Jack and made eye contact with me, shaking her head 'no.' "She's a lovely member of our family, is all. And these boys use her for her talents, much like they do the rest of the women in their lives."

"We're not that bad!" I said, attempting to show some hurt in my eyes.

"No, you guys are not bad." She turned to Gabby. "They are worse than bad!"

I wasn't sure what that even meant. I left them talking and texted Derek to see if I could keep Gabby one more night, and was happy when he said yes. Then I tried calling Ryan, but she didn't pick up so I sent her a selfie with me making a sad face. She sent back a pic of her sticking her tongue out and said we'd talk during training tomorrow. She looked so goofy and adorable in it. I saved it as her profile picture on my sixth or seventh phone so far this year. I'd actually lost count. I just hoped Gabby wouldn't fret about it if she saw it.

Annie packed some leftovers for us to take home. "Best take this before he feeds you bread and beer, Gabby."

"I still might feed her that and keep this to myself," I said, grabbing the container.

"I'll see you at work, guys. Thanks for stopping by," Annie said.

I gave her and li'l bro a kiss on the forehead each and then left with Gabby.

SUNDAY WAS ANOTHER great day. This time Gabby and I did make it down to the diner and had a good breakfast. We went back home and had some fun practicing our fighting moves. She was really good— much better at blocking than on hitting with force, but I was impressed all the same.

Monday morning, I dropped her off at the training center. Her dad was already busy working in the lab and her mom was sound asleep. My phone buzzed as I kissed Gabby good-bye. It was a text from Ryan, reminding me I had a meeting with Derek and to see if I wanted coffee before I met with him.

I popped into my office as Ryan was walking in. She smiled. "Had a good time?"

"Yes. Thanks for the lasagna and pie. It was delicious. Oh, and the cookies you gave Nick were finger-licking good, too."

She nodded. "What did you do yesterday?"

"Spent the day with Gabby. You wouldn't believe how good a fighter she is. We had a nice session—oh shit! I was supposed to meet you again. I know I'm the one who asked you to meet me—it won't happen again, I promise."

She shook her head. "I wondered why you didn't at least text me . . . but you completely forgot."

"I didn't know she'd be able to stay another night, and we got so busy."

"Don't worry about it. I didn't wait *too* long this time." She rolled her eyes. "Only thirty minutes. I was really tired. After you didn't show by nine thirty, I just went back home and slept."

"Don't act all pissy; you could've texted me," I said.

"Right." She looked at me and forced a smile. "My fault. Let me go help Nick. Talk to you later," she said and walked away. With both coffees in her hand, nonetheless.

I didn't say it was her fault. *Whatever*. These women were too much to handle. Maybe Jenny could help me.

"WELL WHAT DO you expect?" Jenny placed both hands on her hips.

"I don't know!" I paced around the all-white infirmary room. She'd been rearranging supplies in the glass cabinet when I walked in.

She stopped what she was doing and stared me down. "You were supposed to apologize to Ryan for ditching her, not accuse her for not texting or calling you. And Gabby is threatened because Ryan is a wonderful and beautiful girl. If you haven't noticed that yet, then you have to open your eyes."

"Well, of course Ryan is cool. I know that. But I hope Gabby can accept Ryan as my best friend." I hopped to sit on the hospital bed.

"Gabby's inner turmoil is off the charts," Jenny said.

"She IS a little crazy, right?"

"No, give her a break. She's dealing with a lot . . . I can tell you: as a sensor, her emotions give *me* heartache. Plus, it's easy to feel insecure when you know your boyfriend's hot friend is in love with him." Jenny's eyes widened. "I mean, she thinks. *She thinks* that Ry is in love with you."

I stared at her as she twirled her hair. "Jenny? Is she?"

"You should talk to her," she said and started acting

busy.

"Well, that's not exactly a 'no,' Jen."

"I don't know, Kevin. She cares about you just like the rest of us."

"I've known you forever, Jen, and nothing like that gets past you. Ryan has feelings for me?" I hopped off the bed and went closer to her. "How long?"

"I'm not getting into this. If you want to know, ask her. My advice is to let it go and keep your friend." She slapped a palm to her forehead. "I don't know why I always open my big mouth."

"Oh, you want me to ignore this? I can't exactly un-know this, you know." I brushed my hair with my hands. *Shit. I hadn't noticed.* "I can't believe Ryan would—how could she do this to our friendship?"

"Excuse me? She didn't do anything to you. Better be careful with what you say if you do talk to her about it. I'll repeat: don't bring this up."

"I'll think about it. Can you help Ryan with transferring powers, though?"

"Transferring? Like *we* do?"

"Yes."

"She's not supposed to know about that, Kevin. Derek made it clear he didn't want anyone knowing it was possible t—"

"Yeah, yeah . . . transferring gave his dad the idea to kidnap Annie and use her as his personal battery, yada yada." I rolled my eyes. "But none of us are power-hungry maniacs. Regardless, Ryan's the one who channeled me and got us back here. I'd tried teaching her before but she never got the hang of it."

Jenny nodded. "She was under distress and desperate to save you; those emotions helped her."

"I figured you being a sensor . . . you could explain it to her, in secret? Please?" I begged.

"You want me to go behind my husband's back?"

"Err, yes?"

Her eyes narrowed. "Why?"

"I don't want him to pull the plug on it. But also Ry is freaked out he'll think she's breaking his rules again."

"Hmm, that's odd of her. I'll just talk to her and then decide. But right now I have to go try find our mole."

I frowned. "Wait, you're looking now?"

"Derek will fill you in."

"How odd you passed the interrogation," I joked.

"Ha! Now go before you're late. You know how he gets."

I LEFT HER and walked to Derek's office, where he greeted me with Pine and Chris.

"I hope you had a relaxing weekend with Gabby," Derek said.

"I did, thanks," I answered, taking a seat.

Derek tapped a pen on his desk. "Okay, first things first: no going out on any assignment on your own. Now that they can block our powers, it's too dangerous. So wherever you go, grab a partner."

I nodded. "Do we know anything about the block?"

"Very little for now. Based on Ryan's report—I'm still waiting on yours." He looked at me with creased brows. "They were aware we were looking into our people for a mole?"

"Yes," I said, and turned to study Pine.

Pine was the only person who knew and could actually share what he'd learned with Oats. Or with the rebels.

Pine smiled. "Great instinct, Kevin. I thought the same thing so I came on Saturday and told Derek my suspicions."

I frowned. "Which were?"

Derek took over. "Pine was afraid maybe he'd been compromised so he asked for Nick to check and see if his mind had been tampered with."

"Oh," I said looking at Pine. "And?"

Pine nodded. "I knew something wasn't right. Nick helped me remember. I went to see Oats a few weeks back and he had that man in his office."

"The one from the restaurant?" I asked.

"Yes. He introduced himself as Michael; I knew nothing else about him. Except that he hypnotized me to get intel from the Org. Nick already had me protected against information I previously knew, but on the new findings I couldn't help it."

"So are you in trouble with them now that you've been telling us what they've been up to?" I asked, shifting in my chair.

"No. I was asked to share what Derek was up to. None of my other actions were questioned."

"Right," Derek said. "So we know what little information Pine shared, and that can be controlled since it was nothing major. I also shared Michael's picture with Dr. Carson and he recognized him. Michael and his brother are the ones calling the shots with the rebels. He doesn't remember either of their names so he can't confirm if that is in fact the man's name."

"So much for that," I said.

Derek continued, "Even with this development, we're not in the clear. They knew some things that Pine wasn't aware of."

I frowned. "Like?"

"Pine didn't know we'd been interrogating our own people."

"Ah, so we still have a mole."

"Yes. And we've found no suspects so far. But now Jenny and Ryan will take over that search to see what they can sense. Chris is going to stay with Pine to protect him against any further hypnosis."

Pine and Chris got up to leave. I hadn't talked to Chris since he'd confessed he kissed Ryan. I thought avoiding the subject was best for now. Pine shook Derek's hand and turned to me. "Stay out of trouble."

I grinned, and said, "Always."

I SPENT THE rest of the week with Beth, gathering information and interviewing innocent bystanders throughout NY's boroughs. The rebels had been busy causing havoc, and we'd hoped to find a hint of their other locations. Or at least find a pattern that would help us see what they were after more clearly. Everything came back clean, except we knew they were leaving clues for us to know it was them making a mess for us.

Since Chris was already with Pine, I sent them to the people who'd seen more than they should have, and had him modify their memories. Having people go around talking about fireballs and electric waves was not something we needed. Derek was already losing his shit as far as I could tell.

And that's exactly what I thought they were up to: wearing Derek down with all the chaos they were creating. At least they had the decency to keep things to robberies and fights only, and not murdering people . . . for now anyway. I really wouldn't put it past them.

CHAPTER FIFTEEN

R YAN HAD SENT me pictures of the shoe
organizer that Saturday evening. I was smiling
and about to reply when Gabby jumped on my
lap.

"You're texting with Ryan? Why is she sending you a picture of her shoes?"

Ah, crap! "The organizer was a gift. She received it this morning and wanted to thank me for it," I said.

"Wait." She stared at me, unblinking. "A gift from *you*?"

I shrugged. "Yes."

"That looks expensive. Did you get it while we were together?"

"I ordered it a couple weeks ago." I gently pushed her off my lap to sit next to me, and looked her in the eye. "And whether we're together or not, I can still get my friends gifts, Gabby."

She finally blinked, and held my hand. "Of course.

But you can see your actions are confusing, right? You treat her like a girlfriend. Maybe you need to back off, give her some space. Tough love is sometimes the best."

"You're right," I said and put my phone away without replying to Ryan. The warmth of Gabby's hand felt nice. And strangely, I agreed. *Ryan did need space.* Part of me went back and forth thinking she'd be pissed I ignored her, but the other part was convinced this was best for her. I shrugged. That's what spaces and breaks were for anyway.

I SPENT THE rest of the week avoiding Ryan. In an odd way, I didn't know how to look at her. She even knew that I knew about her feelings so it was weird all around. On Tuesday when she visited Gabby to give her some magazines, Gabby decided to confront her.

Gabby told me they'd talked and that she was cool with Ryan even though she admitted to having feelings for me. But she would rather me not hanging out with Ry much. I didn't know how to act around Ryan now, so I listened to Gabby and ignored every call and text I received from Ry.

Ryan had asked me to please meet her at the bakery on Sunday morning to grab a coffee and catch up. I only went because I felt obligated. Well, that . . . and Gabby had no idea.

"You're late," she said.

"Sorry, I was—"

Ryan squinted. "Trying to decide if you should show up or not?"

I nodded. "Something like that."

"I thought Gabby understood. She . . . she doesn't want you to see me anymore?"

"No, it's me. I just feel uncomfortable deep down."

Ryan put her hands to her chest. "Ouch."

"Come on, not like that."

"Like how, then? You're going to have to get over this, you know. Nick and I made big progress with extracting information. He thought he could do it alone but he needed me all along. Even Annie couldn't help him." She smiled.

"You should be proud," I said.

"I am. I just—okay, so we now know how the rebels got together and teamed up. We also know that they were getting help from Derek's father."

"Weren't they part of his people?"

"We thought so! But it seems he had an agreement with them. At first they started out as thugs who stole and did their own thing. Then they joined with Lake Senior's Luminaries and became something bigger—with their own vision of control and who knows what else." She sipped her coffee. "The one thing Dr. Carson could tell us was to be on the lookout because they've been biding their time."

I frowned. "What are they waiting on?"

"Their children to grow up. This group has been going for years, and they've accumulated resources and have done far more intensive research than we've done at the Org because they don't care about their subjects dying. They have advanced formulas and some crazy gadgets. If we could take them down and get our hands on what they've discovered so far, then we'd be able to disable the rebel Luminaries who are on the run instead."

"Disable?"

She nodded. "Take their powers away. Like they're trying to do with us."

"You're excited about that? I don't know about you, but I didn't like being powerless."

"No, I know. It's just—I'm just glad we've been able to extract all this information from them."

"I thought they were after getting stronger too?"

"Yeah. But unlike what Dr. Ryder said, Dr. Carson thinks it was to make them stronger than we are, not stronger than they already are." She frowned. "I don't know; it's confusing. He's still getting pieces of memories back, so we might still find out more soon."

I looked at the time on my phone. "What about locations? Any new ones?"

"No more locations. This is the only one they knew of. Do you want me to order you coffee?"

"No, I'm good. And the mole?" I asked rubbing the back of my neck.

"Nothing on that, either. They don't know or weren't involved with that part of the operations that the rebels had in place. Jenny and I are still working on that."

"So they want to take down the Org, and then what?"

"Beats me." She shrugged. "Milo misses you, by the way."

"Take him to work. I'll play with him there."

She leaned in closer across the table. "Why are you like this? You're not . . . *you*. Ever since you got a girlfriend you've been so different."

I felt an unfamiliar anger toward Ryan, and found myself repeating some of Gabby's words. "Leave Gabby out of this. Maybe it's you who's jealous. You even got a makeover. Was it to impress me?"

She dropped her coffee. "What? Are you seriously saying this?"

"Maybe it's best if I go. I said I'd meet you for coffee, and I did."

"That's it?" she asked, and for the first time since I've known her, she ignored the mess on the table. "Kevin, is there nothing I can say? How long should I continue giving you space and allow you to treat me like I don't matter? We're friends, Kev."

I stood up. "What do you want from me? For now, that's it. I have to go meet Gabby; she's waiting for me."

I had to walk away. I was reacting with anger and didn't want to zap anyone by mistake. I just couldn't stand to keep seeing her looking at me with tears in her eyes. I couldn't deal with this kind of shit right now. The worst is that I knew I was being a coward but I couldn't help it. I needed more time to figure out how I could deal with the whole thing. Plus, I really felt like Gabby needed me.

I went to get Gabby to spend the rest of our day together. We were watching a movie when Derek called and asked me to pick up Ryan and meet him at the Org. I hung up with him and called Andrew to get Ry for me. After dropping off Gabby, I teleported straight into Derek's office. Dr. Carson, the scientist, was sitting in there, sweating. His long hair was tied in a ponytail and he kept adjusting his glasses over his nose.

"Hi, Dr. Carson," I said.

He shook his head. "Call me David."

I nodded while Derek asked, "Where is Ryan?"

"I'm here," she said, walking in with Andrew following behind.

"Okay, good," Derek said. "I asked you in because David here remembered one big detail. He called me right away after realizing this." Derek paced. "Those kids that they're waiting for to grow up? It's one or more of them that they sent into the Org to infiltrate."

"So younger Luminaries?" Ryan asked.

"Yes, so you and Jenny will be going around to the kids in training and to our newer operatives to see if you get anything from them."

"Okay," she said.

"And it goes without saying, but it would be best if we could get this mole or moles as soon as possible," Derek said. "I also want you, Kevin and Ryan, to take Marcus to the factory right now. He wants to look around to see if he can figure out how they did the blocking."

"Do we know if it's empty?" I asked.

"Yes. It's been empty since you two were there. We've had our people standing guard there and they have all been able to use their powers."

"Why don't we take someone else, though? Aren't they still after Marcus?" I asked.

"Yes, they are. But he's the only one who understands their work. He'll need help with some equipment in case he's able to run any tests. Just get out of there if something doesn't feel right."

"Sure," Ryan said.

"Actually, I can't," I said. "It's like conflict of interest or something. I'm dating his daughter. Andrew, can you go?"

"Yes, of course," Andrew answered.

I saw Ryan staring straight at Derek, avoiding me. I got up and left.

I WENT BACK to stay with Gabby and wait for her father to return. "He's going to be okay. Andrew and Ryan will take care of him."

"You should've gone with him to protect him!" she said.

"Gabby, I didn't want to go with Ryan. Okay?"

"I know. It's just this once."

"No. You're already jealous of her and I don't know how to act around her anymore. It would affect me, I think."

"I get it," she said, resting her head on my shoulder.

When they returned, Andrew brought Dr. Ryder to the training center and informed us that all traces of anything they'd used was wiped out or gone. Dr. Ryder didn't find anything.

I left Gabby alone with her dad and went home. I got a few texts from Ryan, one telling me Marcus had found nothing on their little outing. Another was to ask if I wanted to pick up any leftover baked ziti she had made. And the last was a picture of Milo destroying one of her throw pillows. I didn't respond.

THE NEXT DAY at work I didn't see Ryan but she left me a container with food on my desk at the end of the day. I would have hidden it from Gabby if she hadn't been with me when I found it. I felt torn. I didn't like feeling this way toward Ryan, but I was so sure it was the best way to handle it.

I waited until Friday afternoon to drop by with Gabby to leave the container back in Ryan's apartment. She was in her kitchen having a heated discussion on the phone with someone and was crying when we appeared in the living room. She didn't know we were there.

"I DON'T CARE! Call me pathetic all you want, I—" she said as she spun and saw us. "I have to go." She hung up.

"Hi," Gabby said.

"We brought this back," I said, raising her container for her to see.

She laughed *and* cried. "You know what? I am pathetic. Right, Kevin? You think so, don't you?"

"Me? No." I took a couple steps back. "What are you talking about?"

"No? Is it not pathetic to swallow my pride? To keep trying after you've treated me . . . like this?" She scrunched up her face. "So bad? Because I need you so much?"

I moved closer to her again. "No, Ry—"

"Can I just be honest for one second? As much as you've been an asshole to me, I've missed you so much. And what about me?" She came to stand in front of me. "I'm nothing to you. I was supposed to be your best friend, but in one second you've destroyed it all? You don't even try to pretend you care about me! You don't call me or text me or want to hang out anymore." She jabbed me in the chest. "Explain yourself."

I turned sideways to look at Gabby then back at Ryan . . . who was busy downing an almost-empty bottle of wine.

"You are not my girlfriend," I said.

"I never pretended to be." She put the empty bottle down and waved her finger in my face. *Man, she was drunk.* "I never made a move on you. I always respected you as my friend and you treated me like I'm nothing. Even before you knew how I felt. What the hell? You're so different now." She took another drink from the bottle, realized it was empty and threw it across the kitchen floor.

My eyes followed the bottle. "Uh—"

"You met Gabby and forgot about me. I'm so stupid. It's like I was never your friend. You couldn't even give me the courtesy and tell me not to waste my time all those times you left me hanging"—she pointed at Gabby—"to hang with her. I thought your word meant something to you. It clearly doesn't."

"I've always been your friend . . . it's just that now . . . I don't know how." I stared at my shoes because I didn't know how to explain myself to her while my girlfriend witnessed everything.

Gabby hadn't moved since we got there; she stood by the couch in silence. Part of me wanted to explain to Ryan that I was weirded out by a dream as well. She'd understand that. I knew she would. The rest . . . *I don't know.* Even I didn't understand it.

"Bullshit." She stabbed her finger in my chest repeatedly. "You don't want our friendship anymore."

"Of course I want to still be friends," I said with all honesty.

"Really? 'Cause the last time I checked, when someone really wants something they make it happen. I know it and you know it. Don't insult me with excuses. You and I? We are better than that. We *were* better than that."

Those words stung. "I care about you."

"Not enough. And now it's time to shut you out because while I offered you my friendship and stifled my heart in the process, you turned your back on me. And it hurts." She raised her chin. "I just hardly recognize you anymore."

I shook my head. "Ryan, you're drunk. We should talk about this another time."

"Right . . ." She went to get another bottle of wine. "'Cause you're not going to stand me up again? And I don't even care about that as much! You're so hung up on me loving you that you're not even realizing why I'm upset." She tried inserting the opener several times but kept failing. She handed me the bottle. "Open this for me."

I took it. "Ry, I—"

"You hurt me." She tilted her head, looking me in the eye. "You turning your back on our friendship is what hurts the most."

I opened the bottle and she pulled it out of my hand, taking a gulp. "It hurts more than the fact that you'll never feel the same for me romantically. I never expected you to, actually, but my loyalty and friendship? Those were yours."

"We can still—"

"I'm done now." She put the bottle down. "With you, I'm done. I just—I miss you. I miss my friend." Tears rolled down her cheeks. "But you shut me out completely. How could you shut me out like I was never anything to you?"

"Ry, that's not true," I said, dashing some looks at Gabby. She still hadn't moved. She just stared with wide-open eyes.

"Isn't it? And then you find out how I feel and you decide to crush my heart. You turned your back on me!" She wiped her face. "You . . . just cut me off! You just . . . cut me off," she said, hyperventilating over and over and repeating in between short breaths, "You just cut . . . *me* . . . OFF!"

I went to hold her and hugged her for a few minutes. "I'm sorry."

"You suck, Kevin. I want to hate you so bad. You treat me so rough! I couldn't . . . I can't."

"What do you want me to say? I don't know how to act now that I know how you feel!" I said.

"I tried my best to never let you see the truth, but now you know and I'm like the worst of germs to you."

"No! Of course you're not, Ryan." I pulled away from her and took a step back. Then I saw a picture. I picked it up and stared at the dark-haired woman. "This is your mother."

"Yes."

"But she's the woman that gave the order to kill us at the factory."

She closed her eyes. "I know."

I rubbed the back of my neck. "Ry, what's going on?"

Her lips trembled. "I'm the mole."

"WHAT?"

"I was . . . I'm not—not anymore. *Listen*, I have not given them any information, I don't know how they know anything."

"Ryan, what the fuck?"

She let her hands drop at her side. "Well, I was sent to spy but I met you and I've—well I've cared for you the entire time. Then I understood what the Org stood for and the work they do and I knew from back then I didn't want to be part of the rebels and I . . ." We stayed silent for what seemed like forever. "Say something!" she screamed.

"I have to report you," I said.

"No, please, Kevin. I—I'm not working with them. Listen to me," she said, crying. "Mom is mad because she knows you're the reason why I turned on them; that's why she ordered them to kill you. They were never going to hurt me. Look at me, Kevin. You KNOW me. I promise I'm not working for them."

I frowned. "She didn't die."

She shook her in slow motion. "No."

"So why didn't you ever mention it to me? Especially if you were never on their side? You pretended to be sad she was burnt alive and set up."

I held her shoulders, staring into her eyes. Hoping I'd see something I'd understand.

"I couldn't just bring it up." She stepped back and wrapped her arms around herself. "It's not easy to confess these things."

"I would have understood. Heck, I would have even kept your secret." I ran my hands through my hair. "You know that. You know everything about me."

She buried her face in her hands and cried. "I know. I

just—do what you have to do. We both know they'll lock me up or erase my memories. I know too much . . . I'm a liability."

"Kevin, think about this for a minute," Gabby interrupted. She came to stand next to me and held my hand. "Ryan is your friend. The person you know will be gone if they erase her memory. Is that what you want?"

"What the hell do you know about that? And why do you even care?" Ryan's eye narrowed as she looked at Gabby.

"I'm . . . I—I lived with Grace. And now with my mother, and she's not really gone, but her mind is bad enough that I know Kevin wouldn't want that for you. If he cares, I care." Gabby turned to me, squeezing my hand. "Tell her to go. She should leave New York, move away or something."

"No, I'm staying . . . I should stay."

"I think you should leave," Gabby told her.

Ryan pointed at Gabby, and said between clenched teeth, "I didn't ask YOU!"

Gabby's eyes widened and she left my side to go stand on the other side of the kitchen island. She seemed afraid of Ryan, taking gulps and fidgeting with her watch, but still said, "It's for the best."

"No, no, no." Ryan shook her head. "You'll have my back, right, Kev?" she asked between shallow, rapid breathing.

I leaned my back against the counter and thought about it for a few minutes. I truly felt Gabby was right about this. "Get your bags and leave, Ryan. It's the best I can do to prove I do care about you."

"I don't have to go anywhere, Kevin. I'll stay with you. I'll do what you want!"

"You don't understand. I don't want you here," I said through gritted teeth. I hated saying this to her, but I needed to protect her. I knew they'd follow protocol no matter who she was.

"But . . . I'll stay with you. I'll talk to Derek," she insisted.

Don't stay with me . . . Don't stay with me . . . I can't bear to see you become an empty shell if they erase who you are . . .

I gave her a hard stare. "Go. Just go, get out of my life. Get out of *this* life."

"Kevin . . . I'll never see you again . . ." She came closer and lifted my chin to look at her. "Is it really what you want?"

I gripped the counter so hard behind me, I was afraid I'd break it. "Yes."

She backed away. Between quick breaths she held on to her chest, and said, "I'll leave, then."

"Good."

"You're really okay with . . . watching me walk away?"

I looked at Gabby who nodded. My ears were drumming so hard it was difficult to hear myself when I said, "Gabby and I are leaving. In one hour I'm notifying Derek. You'd better be gone by then."

"'Bye . . . Kevin," Ryan said, her lips quivering.

I'd planned on just getting out of there, but my traitorous arms pulled her to me before I knew it. So there . . . in her kitchen: a sad mixture of pieces of wine bottle and tears witnessed the first time my heart broke. I gave her a kiss on her forehead and ran.

I crashed into Gabby and teleported to the Org. There, I waited the longest hour of my life.

Then I called my boss to turn in my best friend.

I WENT BACK with them and watched as they turned her place upside down while I fought hard to hold it together. I stood by her bed and stared at her shoes neatly displayed on their spinning stands.

It was okay, I convinced myself, though I didn't know if I did the right thing by the Org or by Ryan. Nick brought Milo to me and placed his hand on my shoulder. As un-bro-like as it was, I cried for her.

"Her collection is in there except for her favorite combat boots," I said, trying to regain composure. "I liked those boots. We had history together."

"I know, man." Nick patted my back. "I have to go

out there. Stay here with Gabby."

Gabby stared at me and didn't say a word. She collected everything I would need for Milo and came back to stand by my side. Ryan had left a note asking me to keep him. I would. Of course I would. Ryan was gone now.

"Do you want to drop me off so you can go spend some time alone?" Gabby asked.

"What? No. I need you with me."

"Even after this?"

"What does that mean?" I asked.

"Well, since coming into your life, you lost your first charge and now Ryan. I think I'm some kind of bad luck to you." She slumped her shoulders.

"You can never be my bad luck, Gabby. Grace was your sister, the first person whose life I couldn't save. Ryan . . . well, Ryan was a mole."

"Was, Kevin, *was*. I believed her when she said she turned her back on them. She was willing to stay and face the consequences. I think knowing that you would be by her side for that, as her friend, she knew it was the right thing to do. But then you said you didn't want her around you, so what else could she do?"

"You think I should have offered my support and asked her to stay?"

"I don't know. Look, I told you to let her go but I don't know how your boss would take this. If you think they would have erased her memory, then yes, I stand by the decision to let her go. If you think you could have helped to keep her memory and have her give you guys information in return, then I think it was a bad move. But in the end, we don't know if they would torture her for that information or if Derek would even listen to you. I don't know, I guess this is still better."

"You are rambling."

"I know, I'm sad to see her go." She played with her watch. "I know I was jealous of her, and I probably made everything worse, but she was always nice. And she cared for you."

"I'm such an—I don't know, I was mean to her." I wiped my eyes and tried to keep my cool.

"You were."

"Uh . . . thanks?"

"I can't sugarcoat it, Kevin. She was right, you did shut her out. All because you didn't know how to deal with someone you care about being in love with you."

"I didn't know how to face her!" I went to sit on the bed. "You were the one pushing and pulling me on how to treat her. You confuse me."

She sat next to me and grabbed my hand. "Relax, Kevin. She got herself into this. It's not your fault."

I repeated, "It's not my fault."

"No, now breathe." She nodded slowly. "You hurt her."

"I did hurt her," I said, looking away.

"Yes," Gabby said, squeezing my hand.

I pulled away to rub my face. "I treated her like all the girls I slept with then never called. She didn't deserve that. But now, this was the best I could do by her; I hope she knows that."

"If she can't see it now, she will eventually, Kevin. She's a smart girl and she knows you well. I'm sure time will help her understand why you acted like an idiot. You won't be able to fix it, but she'll understand."

My head spun to watch her. "What? Are you trying to make me feel worse? 'Cause I can drop you off and go home alone."

She pulled me closer and said, "Maybe you just need to go away again. Take a break. Come back when this is all over."

I genuinely felt this might be the best thing to do. Still, my instinct was to never avoid a problem, so I asked, "Why would I do that?"

"I don't want you getting hurt. And that is the truth. I know it goes against who you are, but I wish you'd listen. It's for your own good."

I frowned. "Gabby, you're acting odd—wait, what do you know?"

She kissed my hand and smiled. "I'm not acting odd, Kevin. It's been a long night. You're tired. We're good. Let's go home and sleep."

"Yes, we're good. Of course we are," I said, interlacing our warm fingers together and teleporting back to my place.

CHAPTER SIXTEEN

THE NEXT COUPLE weeks felt like I was walking on a cloud. A dark, humid cloud. I was surrounded by the sunshine that was Gabby, but I kept my sadness inside for the friend I'd lost. I hadn't heard anything from her. There were no traces. No news. Even Pine couldn't find her. This was good, I suppose, but I wished I knew something. Anything.

I knew what it was like to be alone out there. And I know she's older than I was back then, but to suddenly have no one, after having friends who were also your family, I couldn't imagine. If I were in her shoes, I think I'd find this to be worse punishment than losing my memory. At least the pain and loneliness wouldn't haunt me. I wasn't the one who was alone, and yet I felt like I'd lost one of the best parts of me.

I hadn't gone far away like Gabby suggested, but I did take time off from work. Gabby had been understanding and supportive. I couldn't ask for better. I just wished I had my friend back. A friend who wasn't a traitor to the Org and who wasn't in love with me. Annie was right, though. I had let Ryan go mainly because of her feelings. It was the cowardly thing to do. I saw an easy solution and I took it.

I hadn't stood by her, and I was afraid that in reality I was *her* traitor. Had I stuck it out—and Derek chose to erase my friend's memory, I could have teleported her and we'd be on the run together. But now she was alone . . . It was so easy to make up possible scenarios once the moment was gone.

"Earth to Kevin!"

"What? What?"

Annie put her hands on her waist. "I said go and get the baby! He's crying and I'm busy cooking for you people."

"What are you burning this time?" I asked as I picked up Jack from his playpen.

"Watch the attitude," she said, walking toward the kitchen. "So, back to work tomorrow?"

"Yes. I've taken enough time off."

"Good. Chris is back so you'll have him for what's next. Nick has some very interesting things to share with you two tomorrow."

I frowned. "What about Pine? Who's watching his back?"

"He's taking some personal time so Chris can assist you."

BETH, ANDREW, AND Elisa joined us for dinner, so we didn't talk about anything work-related. Elisa was into repeating everything she heard so it was best to keep her ears out of it. Nick came home right before dinner, looking exhausted. He'd been working through the weekends. Not just trying to find out more about the rebels, but also to find Ryan. Derek and Jenny couldn't make it.

"A little boost, honey?" Nick said giving Annie a kiss.

"Oh sure, use me for all I have," she said, and transferred some energy into him. In a matter of seconds the dark circles under his eyes disappeared and the paleness in his face was replaced by a pink hue.

"Don't be silly, Anniewee, I'm not using you. I love your kineticism as much as I love you."

"Sure you do."

"Always. Here you go." He smiled and handed her an origami rose.

"That shit is cool," I said. "I need to come up with my own little thing to give Gabby."

"Where is she? I thought you were going to bring her for family night," Nick said.

"Her mom was having an episode so she wanted to stay back with her."

Annie's eyes met Nick's. Beth and Andrew stopped eating and looked at Nick, also. He swallowed his bite and said, "I'm sorry to hear that."

"Do you guys think I'm an idiot or—"

"Or just a silly Uncle Kevin? Of course you are!" Beth said, touching Elisa's hands.

"You know what? Maybe I should go check up on Gabby, then."

Nick stood up. "Not a good idea, Kev. Avoid that place until tomorrow's meeting. Let's go to the kitchen."

I stood up and took my plate with me. Nick and Annie followed.

"What's going on guys?" I asked.

"We're not sure about Marcus, but Mrs. Ryder is a Luminary."

"No, she can't be. Gabby would know."

Nick placed his hand on my shoulder. "Kevin, I know this is hard."

"What are you saying? Is Gabby—?"

"No," Annie said. "All her blood work came back clear, but with both her parents possibly being rebels, she's stuck in the middle and even lost her sister because of them. Jenny didn't sense anything from her, and doesn't think she's aware."

"I have to be there for her," I said.

"Yes. She's going to need you, but we need you as well. We need you to bring the rebels down, including her parents, if they're both involved. It's the only way to avoid more casualties in the future, to make it right for Grace, and to find Ryan."

I DIDN'T SLEEP. I spent the night fighting the urge to go and get Gabby out of there. But I knew if I saw her parents I would want to confront them. In the past I would have done it regardless, but that's exactly why I've made so many mistakes. I act first and think later. Time away from Ryan had forced me to be my own voice of reason. I much preferred it when I could be annoyed at her for pointing these things out. I knew Gabby would be okay, though. And I knew with no doubt that she was innocent in all this. I just . . . *felt* it.

I MADE IT to the Org early and found Chris waiting outside Derek's office.

"Here." He gave me a cup of coffee. "Annie said you'd be back today. I know I haven't reached out. I really wanted to stop by to talk about Ryan, but Gabby's been with you the whole time."

"It's okay, man. Thanks for this," I said, raising my cup.

"I can't believe Ry was . . . I don't even know what to say."

I shrugged. "There's nothing to say."

We drank our coffee in silence and watched as Derek, Annie, and Nick walked in together.

"To my office," Derek said. He waited until we were all settled and began talking.

"KEVIN!" NICK YELLED from behind me. "Get back here. You have to follow orders."

I turned to look at my brother. "Seriously? This is my girlfriend you're talking about. I have to be the one to talk to her."

"No. We told you the plan; please stick to it."

"I can't do that."

"Kevin?" Annie came from behind and placed her hand on my shoulder. I looked down to meet her eyes. "Don't you trust me?" she asked.

"Of course I do, it's just . . ."

"Jenny and I will talk to her. You need to go with Chris. This is crucial."

I rubbed the back of my neck. "She'll hate me."

"She'll understand," Annie said. "If her father says he needs her out of it, he must know why. Nick is going to work on Marcus in the conference room now. As soon as we get him to release the address, you and Chris need to go and get him those files."

I nodded. "Fine. Come on, Chris."

"Yep," Chris said. He was standing, watching the

exchange, and just followed me when I called him. We went back to my office, where I had left Milo.

Chris looked at Milo and asked me, "You need time to cool off?"

"No." I sat down and looked at him.

He nodded and remained quiet.

I clenched my teeth. "Okay, let's focus. So we know that the Ryders were working with the rebels. At least Dr. Ryder was, until he ran away with his family, which explains why they were kidnapped after. That much he confessed. I wonder what scared him enough to grab his family and run . . . and why Mrs. Ryder is working with them even after that."

Chris nodded. "Right. And then we have to confirm that she was the one who tipped them off as to their whereabouts when they were at the safe house. She's really in deep with the rebels to go against her husband and allow her daughter to die. I never liked that woman."

"Could be her meds," I said. "Hang on—is she even on meds?"

He shook his head. "Don't think so, dude. Derek said she wasn't sick."

I looked at my computer. "But she had us fill her prescription for her."

"She must have something." Chris shrugged.

"I have to remind Derek to check on that. He's too stressed with the pressure from the government right now." A message appeared on my screen. "Ah, he just sent the address. Let's go check their old home."

Chris stood up. "I can't believe we hadn't thought of it before."

"Well, we wouldn't have," I said. "We've been operating under the assumption that they're all victims."

We drove to the address given to us in New Jersey. It took us a little over two hours but we needed to bring back all the files we could find, and without Ryan, I wouldn't be able to teleport everything back along with Chris. I would have asked Annie for a boost, but she had her own worries. Plus, we weren't allowed to go on missions by ourselves.

We walked in and, though we knew no one had been there in at least a couple of months, it didn't look like anyone had ever lived there. The house was scarce of furniture and looked like it served as a mini lab.

"Dr. Ryder sure spent time here; what about everyone else?"

"I don't know." I shrugged and went to look around. "I'll have to ask Gabby."

The refrigerator was empty, the few shelves and cabinets were empty, and the bedrooms upstairs didn't even have beds. On the first floor, where the one lab table sat, there was a futon with one pillow. No pictures, no clothes. "Even if the rebels found this place, I can't believe they would get rid of all the Ryders' possessions."

"It's strange," Chris agreed. "I'll go check the basement. You wanna call Derek?"

"Yes, I'll do that. You can go." I turned back to go to

the living room-slash-lab area and felt a blow to my head. I fell to the floor and heard Chris curse. My head was pounding, but I was conscious. I raised my eyes to find us surrounded by rebels. Someone grabbed me from behind and pulled me so I could stand. I turned and saw Chris had a gun pointed at his head.

"We meet again," a woman said, smiling. She walked until she stood right in front of me. "Hello, Kevin."

"You're Ryan's mom." My jaw tightened.

She stared me in the eye, and said, "Ryan, honey? Look who I found."

I turned my head so quick that the pain in my head increased. There she was. Ryan was behind the guy who held his gun to Chris's head. She walked toward me.

I felt a thousand pounds fall off my shoulders as I saw her alive and well. "Are you okay?" I asked.

"Yes," she answered softly. She wore my gray hoodie.

"You're working with them?"

She nodded. Her mother cut in, "She was never one of you, dear." I looked around and counted five men, plus Ryan and her mother. "Now, we need you to cooperate with us or we'll kill Chris."

"No, we're not doing anything you ask," Chris said to Ryan's mom. They brought him to stand next to me.

"Bring us Ryder," Ryan's mom told me. "And you can have him back alive."

"Don't let them touch," Ryan said. "If he makes

contact with Chris, they'll teleport."

Ryan's mother smiled. "Very well. Thanks, honey." She turned to the men who were holding us, and said, "Keep them separated."

I could have teleported the gun to me before they dragged Chris away. I would have had enough time to grab him and leave, but Ryan was here and I wanted a chance to talk to her. I gave her a hard glare and she didn't even look away. "Do what they want, Kevin. It's for the best."

I raised an eyebrow. "For who, Ryan?"

"For Gabby. Bring her to us."

"Wait, what?" I asked frowning.

"You thought we meant Dr. Ryder?" Ryan gave me a tight smile. "Oh, no. We need Gabriella Ryder."

"What for?"

Ryan's head tilted. "Come on, you really think I'm gonna answer that? I know your schemes; I know how you get information from your enemies. I'm not going to fall for your tricks."

"Is this some kind of revenge because I chose her over you—?"

Ryan walked up to me and slapped me so hard I thought my cheek would fall off. "Don't you dare make this about that. Your little girlfriend can't be trusted."

I noticed the lights flickering around us. "You'd know all about not being trustworthy, huh, Ry?"

"Someone turn off the lights. NOW!" she said.

While we waited for the task to be completed, Ryan

and I had a staring contest going. She won. The speckles dancing in those deep-sea blue eyes had melted all the needles digging into my bones.

"Just bring her to me," she said.

"No," I said, coming back to my senses.

I teleported the knives and needles from the lab table, and sent them directly to hit three of the men who were standing around. I got rid of the gun to Chris's head at the same time. In sync, Chris and I used our heads to hit the men holding us, and the fight started.

Chris got Ryan's mother, who was holding her own from what I could see, and I managed to knock out my guy easily. So now it was Ryan and me. The problem was that we knew each other too well, and we went on for a while, both of us escaping the other's blows. If only I could touch her, I'd send her to the Org.

She pulled some knives out of her new beige boots, and gave me a diabolical smile. "I got some new moves, Pierce."

"I see," I said, teleporting behind her. She saw it coming, though. She made a spin and almost cut me. "You bitch!" I said before her eyes went wide, and she threw one of her knives behind me. I turned and saw it hit one of her guys in his chest. He was holding a gun to me as he fell backward.

His buddy came running toward Ryan, calling her names. He threw a fireball at her and I jumped to push her out of the way. We both fell and I got a small hit on my arm, but I didn't have time to check it because one of the men I'd hit with a lab instrument managed to pin me down at the same time.

I hooked my left hand onto his wrist and used my right hand to grab behind the same elbow, trapping his arm to his chest. Then I threw him off balance by roughly jerking my hips forward, and taking advantage of his confusion, I turned over onto my knees to get on top. Once I regained control, I punched him in the face.

I turned to see the guy who'd thrown the fireball standing over Ryan. "I knew we couldn't trust you!" he said, and was about to hit her in the chest with the fire floating in his hand.

I ran toward him, but he saw me coming and threw a kick my way. I tried blocking it with my palm, but he was too fast and I ended up on the floor. I grabbed a gun that was next to where I fell and shot him a couple times until he dropped.

Ryan and I stood up and looked at each other. I was about to smile but she kneed me right where a man should never be hit. I fell to the floor again, but this time gripping my manhood. I winced and noticed Chris had Ryan's mother sitting on the chair next to the man he'd been fighting. He had them hypnotized.

"Chris," I called in between breaths.

As he walked toward me, we both stared at Ryan as she pulled out a few strands of my hair. It was so fast I didn't have time to react. I just grabbed Chris and teleported to the car.

"YOU OKAY, BRO?" he asked after we'd been driving for a few minutes.

I was still holding on to my groin. "Not really. She's a witch, that one!"

He shook his head. "She saved your life."

"And I saved hers. We've formed some bad habits."

"You think that's it?" Chris asked.

"I don't know. Yes. What is she planning with Gabby? And what the hell does she want with my hair?"

"Gabby? That's probably to make Dr. Ryder do what they want. Your hair? I don't know . . . because she's obsessed with you? Man, this is all kind of messed up." He turned to look at me. "Is that a tear?"

"I think I'm gonna lose my balls!"

"Hang on," Chris said, pulling over to a 7-Eleven. He went in and came back with a bag. "Here."

"What is this?" I asked as I opened the bag. "Ice. Yeah, thanks. We probably should never talk about this again, dude," I said, placing the bag on my crotch.

"What? That I bought ice for your balls?" Chris laughed, and then cleared his throat. "Yes, let's just— we'll keep that to ourselves. I'm not even sure it will help. The way I see it, it's better to be numb than in pain."

"She was vicious with that knee, though," I said.

"I saw her. She concentrated just like you taught her. So really, you should be proud of yourself. The more it hurts the more you know your training with her was perfect." Chris choked back a laugh.

"Keep that up, everyone will know you tended to me."

His eyes widened. "Nah, that's okay. We're good."

"Let's call Derek," I said, connecting the Bluetooth to the car. We told him what happened and waited for instructions.

"I'm glad you boys are all right. Come back here and I'll fill you in."

"No, man, come on," Chris said. "We were attacked, and we have a couple hours before we get back. Talk to us."

"They, the Ryders, have some kind of block. We tried to talk to them and they shut down. Marcus is playing along so his wife doesn't know he talked to us. And Gabriella refused to leave their side."

"Gabby didn't leave them?" I asked.

"No, she doesn't believe us. She keeps asking for you."

"I can teleport there," I offered.

"Stay with Chris. I thought we were done dealing with our mole, so I'm not sure how they knew you were going there. They might not be the only ones around. Just stay with Chris in case you're being followed and keep your eyes open," Derek said.

"No one's tailing us; we're paying attention," Chris said.

"Yes," I agreed. "So Gabby knows, then? That her mom is Luminary?"

"They 'fessed up. They are talking a little but she

won't leave them. We can't sense if they're lying and Nick isn't able to hypnotize them."

"What did they admit to?"

"Mrs. Ryder wasn't born a Luminary like the newer generation. My father and Dr. Lumin experimented on her. You two are aware that not everyone reacts well to the formula. She's one of them, but we don't know if she developed any power."

"You said there was a block?" I asked.

"Yes. David thinks they may know how to do the blocking after all and Marcus just didn't share that with us. There's a possibility they've been injected with it."

"Even Gabby?"

"Maybe—or maybe they modified her memory. We don't know enough. We would if we could get in all their heads, but like I said, they blocked us. She might not even know she was subjected to any of it. I have to go; I'll see you when you're back."

Chris disconnected the call and asked, "What are you thinking?"

"I'm thinking I have to get Gabby away from her mother. Mrs. Ryder already sacrificed one daughter; I don't want her harming my girlfriend."

Chris hesitated. "What if she's in on it?"

"How can you say that?"

"We have to think of all the options. I'm not saying I think she's working with them, but we have to be mentally prepared to deal with all possibilities. You're the one who always says that." His hands tightened on the wheel. "Would you say you're in love?"

"I don't know." I shrugged. "You know how I feel about love. But I can say that having feelings is confusing. I feel like I'm back and forth with needing her and acting like I'm someone else."

"Yeah, I noticed that too," Chris said, frowning. "She's—" He stopped abruptly. "Uh . . . nothing."

"What? You have to say it now," I insisted.

"There's something about her and you. I feel like she's controlling you, but that could just be women having a hold on us when we're dating."

"No way. She's not using me." I frowned. "We've had a connection from early on."

"You really like this girl?"

"Yes, I do. And she cares about me too," I said, feeling defensive. But his words still echoed in my head.

We were stuck in traffic, so Chris turned to look at me. "Right. So deep down, you know you'll be fine? Like it was meant to be? Without any doubt?"

I smiled. "Yes. Exactly. No doubt. I mean . . . she's amazing."

He turned back to the road. After a long while, he said, "*Amazing*. I think we might have another angle. I have to talk to Derek."

"What are you thinking? Don't be getting her in trouble, bro."

"I won't."

"So what was—?"

"I thought Ryan was amazing, before," he said,

distracting me.

I threw the bag of ice in the back seat. "Hey, did you have real feelings for Ryan?"

"Yeah, I told you before, but I never had a shot." He shook his head. "She only had eyes for you. Honestly, I thought you felt the same way about her, and that you were just dating around because you weren't ready to commit yet or were afraid to ruin the friendship."

I ran my hands through my hair. "I miss her."

"I do too."

"Why didn't you ever ask her out?"

"You. I didn't want to overstep. Plus, I knew how she felt so I didn't bother."

"I'll be right back," I said to Chris after an hour into the drive. We were at the rest stop getting some gasoline.

"Wait. No, man. Where are you going?"

"Back to the house. The rebels should be gone by now; they only went there to get us. Wait here for me."

"No, let's go together."

"If I find anything to bring here I won't be able to handle bringing you back. And don't call Derek to tell him I'm going in solo!"

"Nah, man. But let's stay on the phone the whole time . . . just in case."

I nodded. "If they're still there I'll come back. If I can't teleport, then you get Andrew to go there for me with backup. I think it's safe now, though." I took my cell phone and called him. "We'll stay connected the whole time."

"Hurry up," Chris said.

"Yep," I said and made my way behind the rest stop. When I reached the back of some big trees, I went back to the house. I decided to teleport in one of the upstairs bedrooms, since I thought those might remain empty. I doubted they would be anywhere but in the living room area. I walked slowly toward the stairs and listened for any noise. Nothing. I tried teleporting a few feet in front of me just to test that there weren't any blocks placed in the house and I was able to. "No power-blocks upstairs," I whispered to Chris.

"Be careful," he said.

I bent down and crawled my body at the top of the stairs to have a look. "No one's here. I'm checking out the bedrooms."

It was so cold and lonely. There was no way anyone had lived in this house in years. Spider webs were everywhere, the paint was chipping off the walls, and there was no sign of any girls ever being around here. I finished the two smaller bedrooms and walked down the hallway to what seemed to be the bigger bedroom. Same as the other ones: empty. The bathroom in the hallway didn't even have a shower. *What is this place?* And why was Derek so sure this was their home? Gabby *had* said they lived in Jersey, but wow.

I went downstairs and triple-checked that I was alone. Satisfied with the inspection, I collected the light bulbs from several sconces throughout the house. I roughly broke the bulbs and sprinkled the big shattered pieces in a trail outside the only room we hadn't been able to check out. If anyone returned, I'd hear them coming.

The room was right off the living room. Most likely, it was originally a closed-off dining room. I pushed open the door, and found what was now an office. I flipped the light switch and only a corner lamp came on. I had enough light to see, though. The room itself was bare and had no windows. There was a desk, a phone, and cables that must have connected to a computer at some point. "Bingo. There is an empty desk and an empty file cabinet. I guess we won't find what Marcus needs," I told Chris.

"Look around for any funny marks," he said.

"Yeah, I'm looking. Oh wait." I stooped down. "The file cabinet seems to have been moved back and forth; there are scratches on the floor." I pulled it away from the wall. "There's a safe here."

"Can you open it?" Chris asked.

"It's locked. Umm, let me try something. Hang on." I closed my eyes and placed my hand on the safe's door. I tried to pull from the electricity around me but couldn't. I was still feeling the pain inflicted on me from my earlier fight. This of course made me think of Ryan. I can't believe she was now with the rebels. I mean, her mom is part of them, but I expected better of her. As I thought of her, I felt the anger build up and I tried again. Normally, anger made me stupid when on a mission, but right now it was a big help.

The light wavered a little bit. I felt the sparks on my fingertips as they melted through the metal, making a small gap. Easy enough. I tried again and made a wider opening.

"What happened?" Chris asked. "Are you okay?"

"Yes, I just . . . I pushed my hand through the safe wall without opening it."

"How come you didn't teleport the contents to you?"

"I wanted to practice doing it a new way," I said.

"You walking through walls now?"

I shrugged, even though he couldn't see me. "Something like that."

"I guess that's not too different from teleporting," Chris said.

"Who knows?" I said and felt around. "There are some folders and a box in here." I grabbed everything and I pulled my hands out. I took a look and was happy to see no scratches. "Okay, I got some files and a few notebooks in a box. I'm coming back."

CHAPTER SEVENTEEN

W E WENT STRAIGHT to Derek's office once we got to the Org. He was on the phone but saw our expressions and said, "I'll have to call you back, Jen." He hung up and looked at me. "What happened?"

"They're liars," I said, through gritted teeth.

"Who?"

"The Ryders. Look at this." I threw the four folders on Derek's desk.

"What is this?"

"Their files. Dr. Ryder kept it in a safe," Chris answered.

Derek remained quiet while he read the files. "So neither Gabby nor Grace are her biological daughters."

"No, she's their stepmother. And look at Grace's file," I said.

"Grace's records show nothing out of the ordinary here," Derek said.

"No. Now look at Gabriella's. She's lied to me this whole time. She's a Luminary AND she's bipolar. She told me her sister was the one with the condition."

"She never asked for treatment on her condition." Derek looked up.

"That's probably why her behavior is all over the place. I knew that girl was craz—uh," Chris said. One look at me and he shut up.

Derek ignored him and said, "She's a blocker, and her birth mother was a Luminary. That's fascinating."

"Yes. So her dad knows exactly how it works, 'cause I'm sure he's studied her." I clenched my fist, and asked, "Did you see what else?"

Derek glanced at the file again. "She can influence with touch."

"I thought she did something of the sort because of Kevin's actions," Chris said, and then turned to me. "That's what I had figured out earlier in the car. You were just too sure of this girl. And too many of your decisions have been questionable. You haven't been you, bro."

I was fuming. "She made me screw it up with Ryan. I'm going to strangle her."

"Breathe, Kevin." Derek stood up as the light bulb above me exploded.

This time I'd felt the buzz coming from the tip of my fingers and heard the fizzing sound before the bulb burst, so I was prepared. In reacting quickly, I was able to suspend the shards midair above our heads. I twirled them slowly around the room before sending them crashing into the garbage can.

Chris went to the windows and opened the blinds to get some light into the now dark room. Derek's mouth hung open for a few seconds before getting back to the conversation at hand. "Look at me. Don't jump to conclusions. Talk to her first."

I rubbed the back of my neck. "You said her mother won't let her go and that they've been holding hands since they were confronted?"

"Yes," Derek answered.

"Gabriella is the power-blocker. So maybe that's why Mrs. Ryder is holding on to her. We need to separate them. You get the mother, I'll get the daughter."

WE WENT TO the conference room where the three Ryders huddled together. Jenny and Nick were sitting across from them. When Gabby saw me, she stood and ran to me. One look at my face and she stopped and said, "You know."

I nodded. Before I could say anything else, Jenny came and stood next to Gabby. "Do not blow up on her, Kevin! Listen to what she has to say."

"She's blocking your senses, Jen. You can't see the liar she is." I turned to Gabby, and asked, "Right, Gabriella?"

"Kevin," Derek said, "you can either leave with Gabby and Jenny or you can stay and listen to what her parents have to say."

"Gabriella, come sit next to me, dear," Mrs. Ryder said.

"No." Gabby shook her head. "You can't hurt me, and the—they don't know Daddy is helping the Org."

"My dear, when they find out you're no longer protecting me, they'll activate your daddy's kill chip. And trust me, they will find out. Now, what's it going to be?" Mrs. Ryder asked.

"Oh no, I do not think so," Dr. Ryder said. "I have, in fact, disabled my chip. They cannot get to me, Madelyn." He shook his head.

"Impossible," she said. "However . . . if you'd like to risk it, we'll all find out soon enough." She lifted her chin in challenge. "They know our every move."

"How is that?" Derek asked.

Mrs. Ryder smiled. "That's my secret, dear." She looked at her husband. "As for you, it would be a shame to see such a brilliant mind blown to pieces. You're a lunatic, but a genius, nonetheless."

"I can assure you I'm no longer in danger. No, no, no. I just needed my Gabby away." He moved his chair farther from his wife. "You already got my Gracie killed."

"Why didn't you two come to us before?" Nick asked, looking from Marcus to Gabby.

"Ah, good question. Yes, yes," Marcus said, repeatedly nodding his head in short, rapid motions. "Yesterday morning David and I succeeded in disabling my chip. My wife would not let go of my Gabby." He looked at each of us quickly, from one to the other and back to Nick, shaking his head *no* over and over. "I could not tell her."

"Dad, I didn't know. I would have—"

"Not to worry. We're free now. It's fortunate we have David at the facility. He worked directly with the chips so he knew just how to disable it," he said, looking around the room animatedly. This man's constant state of excitement was getting on my nerves.

He continued, "My temperature was lowered in a bath tub full of ice. Such a simple method, really. Anywho, with the right shot and with my vitals slowed, the kill chip automatically disabled itself." He beamed. "Practically dead, I was. Then David injected adrenaline into my heart and voilà. Simple. So simple, indeed."

The rest of us stared at him. I swear this man had lost his marbles.

Gabby's hand was over her mouth as she stared at Marcus, wide-eyed. "Daddy, that was too risky! What if you'd died? What would happen to me?"

"Nonsense," he said. "I was in capable hands. And we have excellent healers here. Had I passed, however, you would have gained your freedom. And now I am ready to talk. I just want my daughter safe. Whatever my wife's destiny, I do not care. She's manipulated us long enough."

"I will not speak," Mrs. Ryder said, and conjured up a fireball in her hand.

"This bitch," Gabby said through gritted teeth. "I'll stop her."

Before Gabby took her first step, Mrs. Ryder threw the fireball at her.

Gabby screamed and I saw her arm was hit. It happened so fast; my instinct was to protect everyone.

The crackling sound filled the room as I pushed what seemed like static rays into Mrs. Ryder. Someone pushed me to the ground and it all stopped. I tried moving, and noticed Nick was on top of me.

"Get a hold of yourself, Kevin," he said.

"I'm good, get off me."

I stood and saw both Jenny and Derek working on Madelyn to heal her. From the side, Dr. Ryder stood staring at me, blinking and nodding. "Yes, yes . . . interesting power, yes," he kept repeating.

Nick touched my arm. "Go to your office and cool down."

I nodded and made my way out.

I was in my office, downing water when Gabby peeked from the door. "Can I come in?"

"How's your arm?"

"It's fine. Jenny healed me."

"Good." I pointed to the chair opposite my desk. "Sit down. Let's talk."

She did as asked. "Okay."

"Tell me she was threatening you and your dad."

Tears welled up in her eyes. "Yes. I was afraid she'd have Dad's kill chip activated. And he was afraid she'd harm me."

"Why didn't you just influence her to leave you and your family alone?"

"I didn't learn about it until we were captured. Actually she took Grace and me there and then they forced Dad to work for them. Once I learned about the chip, I didn't try to do anything that would put him in danger."

I shook my head. "They need your dad; they really wouldn't have killed him."

"Maybe, but I didn't want to risk it. I was their biggest interest and I still had Grace to worry about. Then when you and Ryan showed up, they had already mentioned to the FBI they had three women kidnapped, so they sent Madelyn with us and we had to follow her instructions."

"Why were you their biggest interest?"

"My block. They studied me for months. Once they figured out how it worked, they kept Dad separated and were forcing him to develop a way to make it into a weapon of some sort. He'll have to explain it."

I nodded. "And the influencing?"

"While I was there, I learned I had it. I used it a few times on Madelyn, but when she realized what I was doing, she took it out on Grace. After Grace died, I was too scared they would harm Dad. Somehow they know every move we make."

I pointed my finger at her. "You used it on ME."

She looked down at her knees. "Yes."

"So none of it was real, you and me?" I asked.

"Of course it was." She placed her elbows on my desk and leaned closer. She said softly, "It still is."

"You expect me to believe that?" I asked, crossing my arms over my chest.

"I only influenced you with Ryan, I swear."

"I can't forgive that. And I can't trust anything I feel for you."

"I'm sorry, Kevin." She leaned back. "Umm, but maybe with time . . . maybe . . . maybe you'll see that I didn—"

"You could've at least told me about you being a Luminary," I said. "How is it your blood work didn't show you as one of us?"

"When I turn on the block, it shows me as ordinary. I don't know why. But I'm sorry I didn't tell you. I was scared for my dad."

"Actually, that I understand." I leaned forward. "But dammit, Gabriella! You made me get rid of Ryan!"

She burst out crying. "I'm so sorry. I was only trying to protect you. Madelyn knew about Ryan, and thought you were in the way. I tried to distance you two. I mean, I was jealous, too. But believe me, I just wanted to protect you."

I considered this. After a few minutes, I asked, "What about your condition? You made up a whole story about your sister?"

"I know, I'm sorry." She put her face in her hands. "I should have told you about me being the bipolar one, but

I was so embarrassed . . . about that . . . about the lie . . . I thought you wouldn't want to date me if you knew. And I really thought I had it under control."

I curled my fingers. "I would have seen it if you hadn't manipulated me."

She nodded. "Sometimes I did get really annoyed and I admit I might have influenced you, but then I tried fixing it as soon as I noticed."

"Did you know about Ryan?"

"No, I didn't know she was the mole. I just knew Madelyn didn't want you close to Ryan, so I had to do my part. She threatened to hurt you if I couldn't keep you out of the way."

I took a deep breath. "One more question: where exactly did you live?"

"In New Jersey, we have a condo in—"

"A condo?" I blinked. "Your dad sent us to a house."

"Did it have a lab? If it had a lab then it had to be our old house. When my real mother died, we moved, but he kept it. I can give you the condo's address if—"

"I'm not sure it's important anymore, but give it to Derek."

"Kevin, I'm so sorry," she said, with trembling lips.

"I need time to process this." I stood up, and left her in the office.

EVERYONE ELSE WAS still in the conference room when I got there. Madelyn was locked up in the prison downstairs after she was healed.

Marcus talked.

He admitted to being dishonest about the blocker because of the connection to Gabby. He needed us to know without putting his daughter in danger. He didn't know who the mole was and didn't want to take any chances, so he had Nick undo the modification on his memory. With Nick getting the address where Marcus kept their files, Marcus knew we'd understand once we found them. He knew if he was killed, his daughter would be under our protection.

The only thing he wanted was a better future for Gabby. Marcus knew the rebels were planning on eliminating as many of us as they possibly could, and he didn't want that for her. He went on to explain what we needed to know.

"The way it works is that Luminaries fall on the same frequency as ultraviolet lights. And perfect sense, it makes. Yes, yes, it does." He bounced in his chair. "We all know these lights mutate DNA, and that's what happened to you. Your individual DNA had to undergo specific mutations to become Luminaries, but you're also part of what made you. It's how you're able to control different frequencies from the electromagnetic spectrum." He stood and went to the other side of the room, pointing back to his now-empty chair. "On the opposite end of the spectrum we have infrared light. Gabby can project this, and when she does, it blocks the rest of you from using your powers."

"So they didn't need her blood for this formula?" Derek asked.

"No, but we did! We did need her! We needed to understand how it would work; both of these types of lights are invisible to the eye," he said, covering his eyes. "So we needed special equipment and a camera to capture what was happening. Now, it's just a matter of them finding the exact frequency number and you're shut off." He paced around the room. "Yes, yes, indeed. You must understand every aspect of it and—"

"So that's how they were able to block Kevin and Ryan at the factory?" Derek cut him off. I was happy he did. Dr. Ryder was too jumpy for my taste. It's no wonder his daughter had some issues herself.

"Indeed, yes."

"So is that the weapon they wanted so they could use it against us?" I asked.

"Ohhh, my boy. It's only one part. They did use her blood, too. It's why they kept me separated from her after we figured out the frequencies you work on." He shook his head, looking around the room and whispering, "They had me develop a formula with her blood that would wipe out your powers . . . *permanently*."

"So you succeeded with that," Derek said.

"No. No. I worked the formula best I could. Best I could! It makes sense in theory but something falls short. Before I could perfect it, the teleporter got me out," he said, pointing at me. "We were on our way to my home lab to get some formulas I'd stored but alas, I was saved.

I will continue working on it. I have all my notes and the files I need." He looked at Derek expectantly. "That is, if you approve?"

Derek nodded. "I do. But Gabriella has to consent to want to help. It's her blood, after all."

"Very well, yes. Yes, she'll cooperate." He clapped his hands. "She's curious about the possibility of not having powers. And now you know everything! Yes, indeed."

IT TOOK A while to adjust to everything I'd learned about Gabby. Two days after I found out the truth, I went to heal an injury I'd caused on my right hand. The whole situation had me so consumed with anger that I'd punched a wall so hard, I broke both the wall and my hand.

While gripping my battered hand with my bloody T-shirt, I walked in to the infirmary and found Gabby in Jenny's lap, curled up like a lost puppy. It reminded me of how lonely and sad she'd been after Grace's death. Her eyes were bloodshot and she'd refused to take both sleeping aids and her stabilizing medication. I couldn't help but talk to her and promise to give her a second chance if she'd follow her prescribed treatment.

Jenny healed my hand and helped me understand how Gabby had been honest in her motives. She assured me the medications would make a difference with Gabby. The improvement wasn't immediate, but I saw the gradual changes in her mood as days went by.

On her end, Gabby didn't want to be a Luminary, but she agreed to help us block the rebels if and when necessary. Derek didn't want her in the field, but he thought it best if she trained. He wanted her to practice focusing on specific targets so that not all of us would lose our abilities if she turned her block on during a fight.

She stayed over at my place a lot after it all went down. We weren't in the same place as before, but we tried to work it out. I still cared for her and I wanted to believe that my feelings for her were my own. Plus, she was so much sweeter when on her medications.

"I got us some breakfast," I said, walking into the apartment a week and a half later.

"Is Madelyn still not talking?" Gabby asked.

"No. She is still blocking Nick. I guess all that time with you in the same room gave her a lot of time to absorb your ability."

"How does that work again? I don't get the absorption aspect of it."

"Well, it's not something known or taught. Derek thinks it could be dangerous for other Luminaries to think they can just pull from the rest of our abilities. He doesn't want to give the rebels any more ideas than they already have, plus it really drains us when we do it."

"But you have Annie."

"Yes. It's still dangerous, though. It could be why your mo—Madelyn is always weak. She kept pulling from you so she wouldn't be caught." I shoved the bagel in her hand. "Now eat. You'll need your energy today."

She played with her watch. "I'm nervous."

"Don't be," I said. "You'll do fine. Training is actually fun."

"I just don't want to embarrass myself."

"That's the least of my worries. I wish you didn't have to learn this."

"I have to." She smiled.

I sighed. "I don't want to put your life at risk when we're ready to take the rebels down."

"Too bad it's not your decision, then. Look, I know you don't want me to get hurt. How do you think I feel every time you go on a mission? You almost always come back sporting some kind of new injury. I normally wouldn't think to date someone in this line of work."

"A Luminary?"

"No, I mean, anyone who puts his life in danger on a daily basis. Cops, firemen, military guys, none of that. You guys are heroes and I appreciate what you do for everyone; we need you. But I worry too much. I can't live my life worrying every single day if the person I'm with, or married to in the future, will come home or not."

I frowned. "But you're dating me."

"Yes." She smiled.

"How come you decided to give me a shot,

regardless of that, then? Because your memory was modified?"

"No, that didn't change. The thing is, even if I kept you around as just a friend, it wouldn't change the fact that I would still care and worry about you. So I figured if I'm going to worry anyway, I might as well go all in."

"I'm glad you did." I smiled. "I promise you that I don't plan on getting badly hurt. I'm not saying it won't happen, but I don't want it either."

"Good. But now I have to go to training. I can't believe I'm part of you super-people." She laughed. "Sure you don't want to come with me?"

"Nah, I'm taking my Sunday off. Derek wants you to concentrate without me anyway."

"Fine." She kissed me as I grabbed her hand and teleported her to the training center.

I sat down on the couch and was about to bite into my breakfast when I heard a soft knock on my door. Odd. I have a bell; the only person who ever . . . Ryan! I opened the door and sure enough, there she was.

"Hi, sorry to just show up. Can I come in?"

I stared her down, unable to move or even form a sentence. She took two slow steps toward me. When I didn't stop her she went inside and turned to face me.

We remained quiet for what seemed like hours, just eyeing each other. After a while I pulled out my phone and her shoulders slumped. I didn't even know where to start. "What are you doing here? You know I have to inform—"

"Please don't call anyone," she said, and reached out to lower my hand with the cellphone. "I saved your life. You owe me that much."

"I saved yours back. I think we're even."

"Please?" she said again.

It was hard not to still trust Ryan, so I nodded. "Ten minutes max."

"That's good enough," Ryan said and grabbed my hand.

I frowned. "What are you doing?"

"Relax, I just . . . I've missed you." She gasped as she saw Milo, and let go of my hand.

She ran to pick him up, and started scratching his belly. For a few minutes all we did was listen to the purring satisfaction coming from him.

I took a deep breath. "Are you really with them? Can't you come back to the Org? Talk to Derek?"

She shook her head. "No. My place is with the rebels now."

"You can't be serious."

"I am."

"Ryan . . . why?"

"I have to." She looked sad. "I have to do this, Kev. There are things happening and I'm just trying to figure it all out."

Lights started flickering as my anger built up. "Leave, Ry. Before I call Derek."

She nodded. "Sorry I came. I just wanted to make sure you were okay. And . . . look, I'm not sure you'll believe me but Gabby is a Luminary. You need to have Chris make her confess. She has the power to—"

"She already told me. She's in training as we speak."

"Oh, really?" She frowned. "I thought she was—"

"A traitor like you?" I asked.

Ryan forced a smile. "Yes. Well, it seems I'm the only horrible person around; soon nothing I say will matter anyway. One last good-bye hug?"

She didn't wait for me to answer; she leaned in and I automatically reciprocated. "What the hell?" I said as she pulled out an injection from my neck.

"Sorry, Kevin," she said and held me tight. "I had to."

"I can't . . . feel . . . my legs."

"Relax, don't try to move. It's going to be worse if you fight it."

"What did you do to me?" I tried to swing my arms but I could barely manage to keep my eyes open.

She carefully put me to lie on the couch. "You are paralyzed. But listen to me: Gabby is—"

That's the last I heard.

CHAPTER EIGHTEEN

MY EYES OPENED to a dark room. I got up, but I was dizzy. My skin ached. My head was threatening to burst. I was still in my living room. I dragged my feet and flipped the light switch. I looked at the time, almost seven thirty p.m. I tried to teleport to the Org but didn't move. I was still drugged up.

I put my hand in my pocket to get my phone; a note was stuck to it with Ryan's handwriting.

I'm sorry.

"What the hell?" I frowned and went to the kitchen to get some painkillers. I pulled my phone out and called Nick.

An hour later, I was in the Org in excruciating pain and losing my mind. I was crammed in Derek's office with him, Jenny, Madelyn, Nick, Annie, Andrew, Gabby and her dad. I yelled questions at Madelyn while she stared in silence with a smirk on her face. And Derek? He was quiet. He wasn't even helping me. With the anger rising in me I was afraid I would blow up his office. I stood up and kicked Madelyn's chair. She flinched, but still didn't say a word.

Jenny came up to me and held my arms. "You're in pain, I can sense it. Sit down for a minute."

"I don't need you to heal me. I can deal with my aches." I knocked her arms away. "Sorry, I'm not trying to take this out on you. But one of you better make her talk! She has to know what's happening to me." I pointed at Madelyn.

"Kevin," Jenny said. "You're in pain because your body . . . your genetic composition . . . is *changing*."

"What?"

"I think Ryan took away your powers," Jenny answered in a low voice.

"No, that's not possible. Look, I know I'm acting like a maniac, but you people need to focus on Gabby; they want her. Stop fussing over me. Ryan just came to warn me. It was nothing else. I know her. She just wanted to make sure I wouldn't turn her in; that's why she paralyzed me. I'm sure of it." *That had to be it.*

"Kevin, listen to me. I can't sense any Luminary power in you. She—"

"No she didn't, I can . . ." I looked at them. I tried teleporting and it didn't work. I tried pulling the electricity in Derek's office—God knows I was pissed off enough—nothing. "No, it's just the injection. Whatever it was, it's still affecting me."

"Let's run some blood tests and make sure," Jenny said.

I nodded and she opened the kit she had brought with her. I hadn't even noticed it before. She took my blood and on her way out, she stopped next to Gabby and her dad. She whispered something to Dr. Ryder, and he followed her outside.

Gabby sat in a corner, wide-eyed, staring at me.

When her dad came back, Derek spoke. "Dr. Ryder, they know about your daughter's blocking ability. Is that why they're still after her?" He was finally expressing the proper concern for Gabby's safety.

"They've already studied her. And if they now used the blocker on this young man I doubt they need Gabriella's blood. Unless—oh yes, yes, unless they need to reinforce it. He stared at the ceiling. "But they already made him—hmm . . . what would I call a teleporter who's stuck in one place?"

"Dad, this is not the time to name things," Gabby said. "You need to help him!"

Dr. Ryder raised a finger to his head. I never knew when he talked to us or when he talked to himself. "Ah-ha! Static. If you can't teleport any longer, then you're static." He paced around, talking to himself. "And he was experiencing electricity pull . . . right, right, how ironic he experiences both."

I stood up. "Is this amusing to you?"

"I'm sorry, young man. I was just considering the powers you once had and the irony of your current situation."

"Are we sure it isn't just a temporary side effect, Marcus?" Derek asked.

"I do not believe so. No, I do not." Dr. Ryder turned to me. "Your friend did this? If she took your Luminary power away, the formula had to be designed for you. I failed in finding a general formula. And it's almost impossible to make it work unless it's targeted to a specific person. Ah-ha!" He held his head.

"Marcus?" Derek asked.

"They must have found the element I was missing and need more supplies . . . her blood!" He turned to look at Gabby. "They're still attempting to make the formula, indeed, yes, yes. That's why they're still after her."

"Are you still working on your counteracting serum?" Derek asked.

"I'm trying to come up with something, yes." He pointed to me. "But that wouldn't help him. I wonder if we re-inject this young man with the original formula . . . if his body might resorb it?"

"Yes, let's try that," I said, standing up.

"Oh no, no, no. I do not think so. We can't just yet," he answered. "We need to give your body enough time to finish processing all the change that just happened." He shook his head. "We don't want to make anything worse. I must check your blood test. Yes! It will show me everything I need . . . and then I can come up with a plan."

"Okay," I said.

He placed his hand on my shoulder. "Don't worry, young man, we'll make you right again."

Derek nodded. "Thank you, Marcus."

Jenny came back and gave Derek a small pen-like box. "You can use this now."

He turned to me. "We will fix it, Kevin. Now let's deal with the problem at hand." He stood and went to Madelyn. "Start talking."

"No. There's nothing you can do that will make me talk," she said.

"Actually, I can," he said, and opened the box and took out an injection. "Hold her down."

"What is that? What are you doing?" she asked as Nick kept her still. Derek gave her the injection on her arm and we sat down to wait.

"Take her back to her cell. We'll question her in a few hours," he told Nick.

"What did you give me?" Madelyn asked.

"The debilitating formula. In a couple of hours, you won't be able to block Nick from hypnotizing you anymore. We'll get all the information we need from you."

She smirked. "If that's true, you would have given this to me before."

"We would have, but for our records and knowledge, we wanted to see how long it would take naturally for you to weaken. Now, we're just pressed for time." He looked at Nick. "Lock her up."

Nick took Madelyn. Andrew took Dr. Ryder and

Gabby back to their dorms. Derek stayed where he was. And I sat there, trying to teleport. Over and over.

The realization of what they were saying had finally hit me. I looked at Derek. "What do you think is going to happen?"

"You heard Dr. Ryder. He thinks we can inject you back with the Luminary formula that we received in-womb and it should work. It should still be in your genes."

I looked around the room. "But he's not sure."

Derek walked over to me and placed his hand on my shoulder. "I'm sorry this happened to you."

"This didn't just happen! Ryan did this to me. I can't believe I let her in. I should've taken her out right then and there." I pushed my head in my hands. "Now I can't help you guys anymore."

"Why can't you help?" Annie spoke this time.

I shrugged. "I'm useless now."

"But you are still one of the best fighters we have. You can take on the bunch of them if we needed you to. And when we find them, don't you think Gabby will block everyone to make it an even fight? You got this, Kevin."

I frowned and pulled out Ryan's note. "I don't understand." I kept reading *'I'm sorry'* repeatedly as if it held a clue.

Annie took the note and stared at it. "Hmm, we have to stop thinking of her as an ally. Taking your powers away is unforgivable."

"And I didn't sense anything from her," Jenny said. "She knew how to hide it well. I could bet my life that she genuinely cared for us. Derek, what do we do with her when we take them down?"

"Bring her back. I need to talk to her myself." He looked at me. "Kevin, why don't you go rest? You look exhausted. We'll wake you when Madelyn is ready to be interrogated."

"Yeah. I'll be in my office," I said and walked out.

Chris was sitting right outside. "You okay, bro?"

I shook my head. "I need to go lie down for a bit. My whole body feels like it's buried somewhere in Alaska."

"Jenny is in there, right? Have her take it away."

"I'm drowsy. When I get up, I'll have her try to heal me. Otherwise I'll go to that woman's cell and beat the shit out of her."

"Go. I'll get you when it's time," Chris said.

I WOKE UP to the sunlight blinding me. Chris was there, opening the blinds. "Rise and shine, buttercup!"

"Why is there sun in my face? What happened last night? You were supposed to wake me up," I said, jumping off my couch and getting lightheaded in the process.

"How are you feeling?"

"Better, but pissed."

Chris nodded and gave me a bottle of water. "We tried to wake you, man, but you wouldn't budge. You broke out in a fever and sweated like crazy. I would go take a shower if I were you. But first drink your water; Jenny said you'd be dehydrated."

I was thirsty. I finished the bottle and went for a second one. After I gulped it down, I asked Chris, "I wouldn't wake? I feel better now."

"Yes, Jenny healed you as much as she could. The injection thing was still working on you and she couldn't do anything about that. She healed your exhaustion and fever and made you peaceful enough to sleep."

"I didn't want to sleep! I wanted to be there when Nick interrogated that woman!"

"We know, dude. You were just in no condition for that. Go down to the gym, take a shower, brush your teeth. You need it." He scrunched up his nose. "I'll go bring you something to eat and an extra-large coffee."

"Did she talk? What did she say?"

"Don't know. They didn't tell me anything. I was on babysitting duty with you."

"What is this that I taste?" I said, realizing for the first time the metal-like taste in my mouth.

"Dunno, bro. You had some foaming moments there. You looked a bit rabid. After you puked, you went right back to sleep. The best we could do was wipe your face. Not your best moment," he said, shaking his head.

"Not really feeling the jokes right now." I grabbed some extra clothes I kept in my office and left.

On my way down, I noticed maintenance guys working on our lighting. *Derek and his checkups.* I shook my head and went to clean myself. Even I had to admit I smelled funky.

After I got dressed and got out of the locker room, I saw Chris waiting for me outside. He handed me a cup and a brown bag.

"It's just a buttered bagel, nothing too strong. Jenny said that should do the trick," he said.

"Thanks." I grabbed it, realizing for the first time how hungry I was. I devoured the food as we walked out of the gym area to go meet Derek.

Chris turned to me. "Did you try to—"

"Yes. I can no longer teleport."

"I'm sorry."

I nodded as we went into Derek's office. I didn't even knock. "What did we find out?" I demanded.

"According to Madelyn, who worked formulas in her own notebooks, she'd figured out the permanent blocker worked when targeted to a person's specific DNA."

"What do you mean? Worked formulas?" I frowned.

"She's also a scientist," Derek said. "She targeted Marcus so she could get him to work for the rebels. They were partners and worked together for years. After the rebels showed interest in Gabriella, he refused to keep working for them so she kidnapped the girls. She wasn't aware they'd figure out how to skip the DNA requirement for the blocker, though. So she can't explain how the shot worked for you."

"Ryan pulled out a piece of Kevin's hair when we were ambushed at the Ryders' house," Chris said.

"Then that exactly is how she did it," Derek said. "Right now, Marcus is studying both his and Madelyn's notes on how to make the blocker work without targeted DNA."

"Good. Let's have our own blocker ready," I said.

"Yes, it would be good to have on hand, but our priority is to find a way to counteract it. As it is, your blood work from last night and this morning show no trace of anything Luminary. Your results are compatible to those of ordinary people."

"So what does that mean for me? Are you going to kick me out of the Org after we're done dealing with the rebels?"

"Of course not," Derek said.

"Come on, I was only here because I could teleport and because I'm Nick's brother. I cause more trouble than you need."

Derek stood up and came to sit on his desk opposite me. "You're part of the family and you still have the knowledge and skill we need in our agents. You heard what Annie said last night. We still need you."

"But—"

"And to make things clear: you're here because of your own value, not your brother's. In twenty-four hours, we're going to do some extensive experiments on you. That's if you're willing."

I looked up fast. "To return my power?"

"Yes. Marcus believes it's enough time for that formula to be flushed completely out of your system. We didn't find any trace of it in this morning's test, but you were in bad shape. It's best to give it time in case you experience any other changes."

"So what's the plan?" I asked, hopeful.

"Tomorrow he's going to start trying to reboot your system, so to speak. Annie is going to be with you to give you energy. It might help speed up the process, and Jenny will assist to help you manage any discomfort."

"So it's going to be painful."

"Probably." Derek nodded.

"What else do we know?"

"Madelyn gave up their location. Beth and Andrew are on surveillance as we speak. They've confirmed that there are suspicious activities there. Jenny will go with Annie on the next shift. We want to make sure she can sense if they are Luminaries." He patted my back and went back around his desk. "We'll know more soon."

"I want to go with the team when they bring the rebels down," I said.

"No. We need you to get better."

"I am better."

He thought about it. "Maybe you *should* come; Gabby is part of the operation. We've been training her just for this. When we attack, she needs to help us."

"I don't understand," Chris said. "Don't they already have blockers? I mean, when you were at the factory, neither Kevin nor Ryan could use their powers. So why do we need Gabby? Chances are when we get there they'll turn their blockers on."

Derek nodded. "Yes, but based on what happened at that factory with Kevin and Ryan, we know they have special lights in designated areas. We have to be vigilant for when they try to use it against us." He turned to me. "You said it was difficult to see when it was in the bright light, Kevin?"

"Yes. You can see it, but the other lighting is too bright. We'd have to know where to look."

"Okay," he said. "We'll get Gabby to one of those sections and have her block everyone. Someone has to keep her safe and in the right spot. We'll be on even grounds that way. Oh, that might be a problem, Kevin."

"What?"

"If you don't show signs of your powers back soon, we'll have to put off the experiments for later. It's more important to understand their movements and strike in a couple of days. We don't want to give them time to know we're about to attack."

"What do we do now?" I asked.

"Now, we learn about the rebels." Derek handed me a small black stick. "This has files and profiles. Madelyn had them in a chip hidden in one of her notebooks. It's all been transferred to this flash drive. Take it home and read in between resting. Chris, make sure he *does* rest!"

"Okay, let's go learn what powers they have and what to expect," I said to Chris. He drove us back to my apartment and we got to work.

Around four o'clock, Chris said, "I have Milo, in case you wondered."

I looked up. "I forgot about Milo; where is ı.

"You've been totally screwed with, bro. It's understandable. Shit, I left him at the Org, though. He probably ruining the carpet. Don't you ever cut its nails.

"It was on my to-do list yesterday." I shrugged. "Let's go back for him and stop by to see Gabby a bit. She is meeting with Derek this afternoon."

CHAPTER NINETEEN

TRAFFIC WAS HEAVY, so what normally would have been a fifteen-minute drive turned out to be over forty minutes. We walked into the Org and found everything to be quiet. Too quiet for this time in the afternoon. There should still be people running around and making noises. The gym area was empty and the cafeteria locked down. We went to the second level and even that floor was in total silence.

"Something's going on," Chris whispered.

"Yeah, let's go see Derek. He's probably running a meeting . . . can't believe no one called us—" I felt something behind my head.

"Put your hands up. Both of you."

The tip of a gun dug deeper into my neck. I lifted my hands and turned slowly to see who held my life in their hands. "Blondie!" I said, and looked at Chris. His hands were up too. Nothing was holding him back except the gun to my head.

"Hello, Pierce," Blondie said.

"You know my name now?"

"Walk. We're going upstairs to your conference room," she said, pushing me forward.

On our way there, I noticed that a lot of our coworkers—all strong Luminaries—were frozen in place. Literally. It was Monday, so most of the active agents who weren't currently out on assignment were there. At least forty of my people were displayed on the first floor like some freaks in a museum . . . and they looked . . . *fluorescent?* The lighting in their offices had a bright yellow tint to them. What was that about? I could see they had all been caught off guard when they got hit with whatever it was that hit them. I prayed they were at least breathing. I'd never heard of this Luminary power before, but I guess I'm not surprised someone out there had the ability to turn us into human mannequins. And, of course, it had to be one of the bad guys.

We got up to the third floor and I immediately turned to look into the conference room. I was relieved to see that at least the few Luminaries in there were moving. Only a handful of rebels roamed the downstairs level, which I guess was understandable since everyone there was frozen. But there were rebels everywhere upstairs. I had no idea they had this many; I couldn't even count. Through the windows, I could see the strongest Luminaries packed into the room. They were the target, I believed, and by the fierce look in Annie's eyes when she saw me, I knew they weren't going to let the rebels bring down the house without a fight. *Good.*

Blondie pulled us to the side to allow the rebels to pass. We stood by the wall in between the stairs and the elevator. There was too much hustle. The rebels were taking boxes out of the elevator and blocking us while they worked.

I got a peek inside one of the boxes and saw . . . bulbs? "What are those?" I asked her.

"Special lighting. Didn't you guys have maintenance recently?" She smirked. "You should really pay attention to who you hire."

I thought about the yellow tint and guessed that's what made them all . . . *paralyzed.* My eye caught Ryan walking around with them and I felt the anger burning. She had done the same thing to me. Did this mean they were all losing their powers too? But I remember being able to move, and the way they were stuck in place . . . no, it had to be different.

"Did you know Ryan was one of you when we first met?"

Blondie shook her head. "No, I was surprised when I found out."

"She brought you here?"

"You and I both know she couldn't talk. You are all programmed to keep this place a secret, so we had to get more creative. And actually, we have you to thank for finding the Org," she said, smiling.

"Me?"

"Yes. Pick up any prescriptions lately?"

"Shit," I said, realizing. "A special pharmacy. So it had a tracker?"

"A tracker and a transmitter. You brought Madelyn to have a meeting once?"

I nodded.

She continued, "Right. She left a special pill in one of the plants in your conference room. We've been listening to most of your conversations. Too bad she couldn't get to his office." She shrugged. "No matter. If it wasn't for the fact he was doing maintenance and explained his routine when he apologized for meeting her in the conference room instead of his office, we wouldn't have come up with our lights and with this plan."

"That's how you knew when and where to ambush us," I said. My eyes followed Ryan around. I pointed to her. "Did *she* give you other information on us too?"

"We tried getting her to talk. No amount of hypnosis we used seemed to work on her. It's a good thing she saw her mother again and remembered what she was fighting for."

"And what is that?" I asked.

"We want to become you."

I frowned. "What the hell does that mean?"

"Our freedom. We don't want to be controlled by Lake like the rest of you; we're going to control him instead. Once the rest of you are eliminated, we'll be working for Oats."

"Seems like you're already working for him," I said.

"We have an understanding. He needs Lake's face to

continue the agreement with the Org. So he'll have that, we'll have the official Luminary jobs, and we'll allow them to experiment on us." She looked me in the eye. "For good compensation, of course."

"You're okay with being a lab rat?"

She shrugged. "It won't be me. We have our scientists who'll work with them and we'll take over your up-and-coming Luminaries. The right ones will be trained to work with us, the rest will be used for experiments."

"What do they want with the experiments? What's the end goal?"

"I don't know and I don't care."

"I'll give it to you guys, Blondie. You're good. So you must know where the trainees are," I asked hoping she'd take the bait.

"No, but we will."

"How's that?" I asked.

"I don't know. They don't tell me everything."

I thought about it for a couple minutes. "You know, I missed you during my last adventures with your people. How come you weren't there?"

She smiled. "I'm sure you did. The bosses like to keep us compartmentalized into groups. In case any one faction gets taken down, then we still have backup. And if we're captured, we only know a small part of their plans. They don't take chances."

I laughed. "And you say we're the ones being controlled?"

"We're still free to do as we want when we're not

doing work for the group . . . which, by the way, pays really good money. Plus, we can go and come and no one hypnotizes us for secrecy's sake." She rolled her eyes. "Who cares if the world knows about us? We can take all of them stupid humans on."

"And what is up with the Ryders?"

"They've played their parts." She stared me in the eye. "We've had the upper hand this whole time with Madelyn getting on the inside. Your girlfriend? We still have plans for her; in fact, she's around here somewhere. Why don't I take you to her?"

I tensed as I followed her. The boxes that were being taken from the elevators were already being dispersed. Most of them had been taken to the conference area, where the rebels began changing those bulbs. Chris, who had been quiet this whole time, touched my arm and pointed to some industrial-sized lighting. These again. With all the commotion I hadn't noticed that the place was brighter than usual. Several of them were on, shining on every surface on this level, but everyone was still moving, unlike downstairs. If we were going to make a move it had to be now. I was ready to start the party, but first I had to get to the rest of my friends.

We went into the conference area and I noticed our chairs were piled on top of each other toward the back wall. Gabby was sitting on the floor with Jenny. Milo was on her lap. They seemed okay. Beth was at home today with Elisa and Jack so I knew she was safe. The rest of my family was here. Nick, Andrew, and Annie were standing and they were on edge . . . while Derek stood by the corner of the table looking at his wife. Two rebels were each pointing a gun at his head. I knew this was the reason they were all being so compliant.

Blondie pushed us in and stopped Ryan's mother by the door. She asked, "What's taking so long?"

"There are too many bulbs to change. It's taking time. Then we have to finish up the last part. The connection is giving him problems." She pointed to a man on the table with a laptop that had cables attached to the wires in the ceiling. She looked at Blondie. "Relax, they can't use their powers."

"Yes, but neither can we."

"Well, we need to shine it on them and only them, so we need to light that area specifically." She pointed to the middle of the room. "You don't want it to get you too, do you?"

Blondie didn't respond. She rolled her eyes and walked in to rush the guys with the bulbs. "I said it from the beginning. We needed something less complicated than these lights."

Ryan's mother clenched her jaw. "Maybe if you hadn't lost us the blocker girl we could've figured it out. Instead we had to work on this lighting."

"Why didn't we just use those in the portable lamps to start?"

"If we did, we'd all be paralyzed. We need to keep them from using their powers, but we need to be able to move too, so this is the only solution."

I went to Annie. "What's the plan? Is Gabby going to block everyone?"

"No need. Those lights are already doing that."

I looked at the industrial lights. "Those lights were at the other building when Ryan and I couldn't use our powers."

Annie nodded. "What I don't know is where everyone else is. This place should be packed with—"

"They're all frozen downstairs. Those yellow bulbs"—I pointed to the guys almost finishing the installation—"have a paralyzing effect. They're installing them in here so their group won't be affected when they're turned on. I just don't understand why the trouble; they can simply shoot us if they wanted. We have to make a move now."

"Yes, we do. '*V' up front.*" She pulled me closer to Derek, gave a nod to Jenny and Gabby, and screamed, "NOW!"

At that, I picked Annie up by the waist, her legs formed a 'V', and she kicked each one of the rebels by either side of Derek on their head. They went down but wouldn't stay there for long.

The fight broke out.

I couldn't keep up much with all that was going on, but I went after one of the industrial lightings. I knew we needed to take those down to get away—there were too many rebels for us to take on, and Andrew was our hope since I could no longer teleport. I wasn't sure what we would do with the rest of our friends downstairs, though.

I kept an eye on Gabby and saw she was fighting alongside Chris. They seemed to be doing well—I trusted him with her. I was still distracted, though, and didn't see the chair coming my way. It hit my ribs and since I was still weak and in pain from Ryan's injection, I dropped to my knees. I stayed there for a second before another kick hit me on the other side. I looked up and saw Ryan coming my way from outside the conference room, then noticed the guy kicking me falling unconscious. I felt hands picking me up.

"I got you, babe," Gabby said at my side, helping me stand.

I got up and remembered the lights. Before Ryan got into the room, I reached one and punched it. As soon as that happened, I saw Nick was blasted out with something and fell a couple feet from me. Some kind of gas was sprayed into the room, and it cut out our oxygen immediately. I had a hard time breathing. I couldn't even see Annie or the rest with the smoke, but I knew Gabby was right behind me, coughing.

Someone caught me in a headlock as I tried to feed my lungs some air. I stepped with as much force as I could gather onto the guy's foot and grabbed the arm squeezing my neck at the same time. I pulled forward and spun, and as he was losing his balance I kicked him in the knee and he fell backward onto Blondie.

She shoved him out of the way, and said, "Remember these?" She had red electric waves dancing in her arms and aimed them at me. "You'll die this time."

Before I could react, Ryan jumped in front to block me with her body.

"Stop," Ryan screamed as she tried to push Blondie away.

Blondie didn't stop, though. "You know I never liked you." She had the waves going so hard that Ryan's body was shaking uncontrollably as she fell.

Chris knocked Blondie down at the same time and I ran to Ryan. She opened her eyes slowly and looked at me. "When the time comes, don't move," she whispered.

"What?" I asked helping her up.

"You'll know. Don't move." She managed to stand and pushed me out of the way before Blondie sent more red waves at us. She hit Ryan in the head.

I tried pulling her away but I was electrocuted as soon as I touched her, and dropped to my knees. Ryan's body convulsed for a few seconds before she fell a second time.

Blondie looked at her hands and turned to look at Gabby, who'd joined Chris to take over the fight with her. She'd blocked them.

I held on to Ryan again. Her head was scorched and bloody . . . she couldn't be dying. She couldn't.

Her eyes opened. "I . . . I . . . my head—"

"Shhhhh, don't talk, Ryan. Save your energy," I said, sitting on the floor. I pulled off my beanie hat and put it on her while she looked at me. Her head was still hot as I rested it on my lap. "You'll be okay." I held on to her hands and didn't let go for dear life.

"I'm ss . . . sorrry, Kev. I . . . I messed up," she said as her eyes were fading out.

"Hang on, Ry. Hang on, I need you." I kissed her hand.

"I love you," she whispered.

I leaned and gave her a soft kiss on her lips. "I love you too, Ryan."

"You've never said that . . . to anyone," she said with a weak smile.

"It was never a matter of life and death before." I pressed her hands to my heart.

"Not the same. Ga . . . Gabby is in danger. Hide her—"

"Shhhh." I kissed her forehead. I felt her barely fighting to breathe. "You got this, Ry." I tried to give her a smile, but failed. My tears were traitors.

I was hardly aware that Chris and Gabby were still fighting around me. I had eyes only for Ryan.

"You have to . . . stay *frozen*," she said, panting. "Like the others."

"What?"

"It's the only fighting chance I could give you. Don't . . . *move*," Ryan said, and her eyes closed.

I lost it.

I got up and grabbed one of the rebels who'd been fighting Jenny—by his head, no less—and smashed it on the wall. I went after Blondie, but before I got to her, Ryan's mother yelled, "It's time!"

I turned and noticed that somehow they had managed

to trap all of us back into the wall where Gabby had been at first. This time though, a yellow light shone down and I stared at Ryan's body by Gabby's feet. Then I noticed that Annie and Nick were staring straight ahead and not moving. I looked at Derek, Jenny, Andrew, and Gabby . . . they were all the same. They stared straight ahead. Frozen.

"They're all paralyzed now," the man with the laptop said.

But I can move. What the hell? Luckily, no one was looking at me . . .

Oh!

Don't move . . . That's what Ryan had meant. I didn't move. No one else could defend themselves if I did, so I closed my eyes and followed Ryan's instructions.

"I need someone to get all of Lake's files and computer with us. We need the location to their training facility. And you! Come and help me! Get her body out of here," Ryan's mother said.

"It's no use. She's dead," someone answered.

"Take her, or so help me God—" That was the last I heard from Ryan's mother.

At the corner of my eye, I saw Ryan's body being pulled away from Gabby's feet. I couldn't turn my head to see what else was happening. I closed my eyes again— keeping them open would just cause me to blink. I kept seeing my family in my mind . . . they were all paralyzed now . . . and Ryan was gone.

I concentrated hard not to lose it.

After a while, I decided to risk it and peeked through every so often; it was quiet after all. I tried to nudge whoever was next to me. Nothing. I was hoping they were pretending also.

"What's that yellow light?" someone asked.

"It paralyzes those freaks."

"And us?"

"It wouldn't do anything. That's why they asked us to get the computers and files for them. If we had their powers and got too close to the light, we would be paralyzed too."

It hit me: Ryan had known of this plan. She knew I would need to not be a Luminary to get out of this.

"What are they doing with them?"

"I couldn't find any files, and all the laptops and computers seemed destroyed."

"Let's take them anyway. It's up to them to deal with it."

They were gone for what seemed an eternity. When I heard them come back, one of them said, "That one might already be gone. He's sitting in a pile of blood; let's take a look at him."

I couldn't look down or around; Jenny and Annie were blocking my full view. I barely opened my lids so I could see who the men were checking. Their backs were to me and they were blocking . . . Nick? Chris? They were both in the area the men were checking. I did notice the pool of blood on the floor, though.

"Yeah, I think he's dead. He has a knife in his back."

"Take the body out. If he's still alive, he would be out of his paralysis once he's in better lighting."

"What's the point? The place is rigged to explode; they're all going to blow up anyway."

"But they wanted their deaths to look like an accident from the explosion." I heard some shuffling. "Wait, this is the guy they want us to take to the van. What should I do? Take the knife out and take him, or we leave him here?"

"We only have fifteen minutes. Hurry up and let's do our job. Get the girl and the man. Let them deal with the knife or his body. That's not our problem."

"Do we still inject him to sleep? I already got the girl."

"No, he looks like he's already dead."

I peeked and caught sight of a wheelchair moving, I closed my eyes again when I heard one of the men moving closer. He made some noise and then all that was left was my heart pumping in my ears. The silence around me lasted a bit. I cracked my eyes open and moved my head slightly. I did this a couple more times until I was convinced we had been left alone. I scrambled up and grabbed a fluorescent Andrew who was next to me. I pulled him out of the yellow light, he started to open his eyes and move slowly. I couldn't break all the bulbs. There were too many; it was easier to get them out of the conference room. I hurried up and pushed Nick out, since he was right by the edge. I then got the girls out, and Chris last.

It took a few seconds before they all came to full control of their bodies and minds. While they were coming to themselves I went and knocked over a few of the industrial lights that would block our powers. One of them was still shining right where everyone stood, though.

"What the hell happened?" Annie asked as she held on to Chris, who was still wobbly.

I looked at her. "You were all frozen; you couldn't move."

I broke the remaining light and turned to Andrew. "Listen, this is hard, but tell me you can get us out of here."

"I can try," he said.

"No, Andrew, you need to get us out right now. This place is going to blow up any second."

"How do you know?" Annie asked, still trying to open her eyes fully.

"No time for that. Andrew?"

He nodded and opened up his portal. The swirling of mist starting from his hand widened into a space big enough for him to pass through. I pushed them all through the opening and went back to get Jenny.

She was looking around for Derek. "They stabbed him," she said. "The last thing I saw was Derek getting stabbed."

"Come on, Jenny. There's nothing we can do. They took him and Gabby."

Jenny didn't move but she didn't stop me when I pushed her through the opening either. I saw Milo hiding behind a plant; I ran to get him, and jumped into the portal. The explosion went off as I made it through behind them.

We got out on the roof of the building across the street not ten seconds later, only to witness all our friends dying in that blast. The building was in flames and slowly sank down as people all over gathered around.

"What . . .?" Annie asked.

"They killed everyone—"

"I can see that! What happened to Derek? Where is Gabby?"

"We were in there for a long time. I didn't move because I was waiting for a chance to get you guys out of the light. They have plans for them," I said, avoiding Jenny. She wasn't moving; she was almost the same as when she'd been frozen.

"Why didn't you stop them?" Nick asked.

"I couldn't do anything. I had to wait if I wanted all of you out of there alive. It was the best shot we had. They still had guns and you couldn't move. If I'd done something rash, they would've killed you, too."

Annie frowned. "You were aware the whole time?"

"Yes."

She gasped. "That's why she did it!"

"Yes."

"Who? What?" Chris mumbled.

"Ryan. I think she took my powers away because she

knew this part of the plan. She knew we'd be captured, that's why she told me not to move . . . she helped us."

Annie and Andrew were still staring at the building. The sound of fire trucks and police siren was getting louder as they approached the scene.

Nick's arms were wrapped around Jenny tightly as he said, "Let's get out of here. Andrew, take us to my place then go and get Beth. We'll need to stick together."

CHAPTER TWENTY

JENNY CURLED UP on the couch. Not knowing if Derek survived the wound was worse than knowing he was kidnapped. She was convinced he was dead without her there to heal him. It would have been so much better if she'd cry, but no. Jenny just stared. She didn't move. She didn't talk. She did nothing.

I knew just how she felt.

Annie asked, "Are you okay? We'll get her back, you know."

I turned to look at her. "How? She's dead."

"What? I thought you said they took her," Beth said.

"They took Gabby." My heart clenched. "Ryan is dead."

"What happened? You didn't tell us before," Nick said. Andrew left Beth's side and went to sit with Jenny.

"Ryan got in the way of an electric wave that was directed at me. It hit her in the head," I said, trying to ignore the pain in my chest. I didn't know what to do.

With tears in her eyes, Annie came and hugged me. "Kevin, I'm so sorry."

"Me too," I said, and she pulled back. I stared at my flashlight then looked around to see everyone in really bad shape. "How are you guys feeling? Any lasting effect from the lights?"

"Just weak," Chris said, rubbing his head.

Andrew nodded. "And disoriented."

"Annie, boost them up," I said.

"Right. I wasn't thinking." She got up and motioned for all of them to go to her. They held on and she poured her blue light into them. She went to Jenny, who was still sitting, and did the same to her. Jenny didn't even blink. It was like nothing had been done to her.

WE LEFT CHRIS to watch over Jenny and the kids while we went to our training center. We weren't sure if it was still standing or if anything had happened to all the young Luminaries staying there. Nick assured us that Derek did not keep the location on hand, nor did he have our personal files on any computer that wasn't fried. As soon as they knew they'd been compromised, Derek had set off the newly installed chips on all our laptops and computers. All motherboards had been melted, so we felt safe . . . for the most part.

"But if he's alive and they use hypnosis, he'll tell them. I mean, how else did they plan to control him?" I asked.

Nick nodded. "They might succeed with getting him to do what they want, but they won't get information out of him. I'm the one who actually knows everything."

I frowned. "What do you mean?"

"A few weeks ago, he had me remove any information that would put the rest of us in jeopardy from his mind. I used Ryan's help, so there's no way they'll ever peel off all those layers of blocks I added. He felt it was best, especially after learning we had spies."

"So you're the only one who knows?"

"Yes, we still have to deal with legal aspects, bills, and many details. I took over that responsibility so I'm the only one with the address. No one else has contact with our attorneys."

"What if something happened to you?" I asked, crossing my arms over my chest.

"It would go to the right person. If we don't contact our attorneys after a certain amount of time, they'll know what to do."

"But what if you're captured? It's so dangerous for any of us to have any information."

He smiled. "I'm the strongest hypnotizer around, remember? I'd use it on them before they could use it on me. I can work on multiple people at once. And so far no one has been able to successfully hypnotize me."

I grunted. Of course the ever-great Nick Logan couldn't be turned against us. I rubbed my face to snap out of it. "Still . . . after the day we've had, it's better to take extra precautions."

"I agree," he said. "We also need to talk to the doctors, Marcus and David, one more time."

Andrew took us close enough where we could watch over the building and make sure that no rebels were in sight. Once we were satisfied, we all went in from different points and agreed to meet up at the lab. We were wearing Bluetooth earpieces to communicate with each other in case we needed help or if something was happening. Annie and Nick went in first; Andrew had left them on the roof after leaving Beth and me to find different lower-level entries. He was to use his own portal to go to the first floor to check it out.

I didn't really want to be here. I wanted to be pissed off and brood in my pissyness. I wanted to curse the world out. I wanted Jenny to heal me. I wanted to console her. I wanted Ryan back. I wanted Gabby back. But I had to do this. I had to be strong for them. It was my only chance at saving Gabby and avenging everyone else.

I went to the back and before I popped open one of the basement windows, Annie spoke into the Bluetooth, "You guys can just come in, everything is clear."

I shrugged and went back to the front entrance. I waited for Beth to catch up to me and we went in. We walked down to the basement and met Andrew and Annie in the lab where Dr. Ryder was busy at work. A few minutes later, Nick joined us with David.

"So Madelyn is dead?"

"Marcus," Annie answered, "we are not sure. She was in one of the cells when the Org exploded, but it's possible they released her before that."

He walked rapidly back and forth. "And they have my daughter?"

"Yes. If you know anything else, now is the time to talk. We have to go get her," Nick said.

Marcus stopped walking and stared at Nick. "We already knew they found a way to replicate her power and use it in the lighting. But . . . but now, they have my Gabby." He shook his head. "No, no, no. You must get her back. This is dangerous. They want to kill you all."

"No," I said. "As far as they know, we're already dead. But they do plan on experimenting on Luminaries and possibly creating more. If someone gets out of control, they need Gabby to help them. They won't kill her. "

"But they have the lighting for that," Nick said.

"Either way, she's good to have around. If something happens to the lighting, she can block for them."

"Yes, Kevin," Annie said, "but they also wanted a universal formula to remove powers permanently, remember? They need her for that. Not everyone in training will join them and not everyone was at the Org." She frowned. "If too many stand against them, it might take too long to personalize each formula . . . in which case they'll use Gabby."

I shook my head. "Nothing stops them from doing the same thing they did to us. Wipe them out in one shot and start from scratch."

"We know Oats and Lobo are involved. They

wouldn't want to explain so many cleanups to their higher-ups. I should get to Pine," Nick said. "He might know something. But for now we need to know how to defend ourselves from their blocking."

David cut in, "We believe we figured out the counteractive agent. It should prevent Luminaries from losing their powers under the lights."

"Would it work under the paralyzing lights also? Or with Gabby?" I asked.

"I'm afraid not." David adjusted his glasses. "There's no way to replicate her powers one hundred percent. We tested it while she was here, but it only worked when she wasn't too close to the subject. In theory, it should work the same as under the lights since it's a weaker version of Gabriella's powers."

"And the paralyzing agent?" I asked.

"Well, we don't know how they managed that," David said. "You'll need someone to destroy the lights if you're all paralyzed."

"Ah-ha! Yes, yes," Marcus said, and slapped me on my back. "He's right here. He doesn't freeze!"

"Unless we make him a Luminary again," David pointed out.

"Yes, yes. Unless we restore his powers." Marcus frowned. "Then that is a terrible plan, indeed."

"There are other strategies," Nick said. "A couple of us could wait outside and listen in with an earpiece. Just help Kevin for now; we'll figure out the rest."

Marcus nodded. "I will continue my work on

restoring your powers, young man. David will work on the . . . ah-ha! Good name, yes: counterblocker. It's all settled now."

IT WAS ALL so surreal. Everything was in chaos, the Org was gone, the rebels had won, and our friends were dead. Most Luminaries were wiped out, because of a stupid light . . . created with the help of my girlfriend's genetics. I wasn't sure what I wanted most: have my powers back or continue being normal so I could save them again from being paralyzed. It was all just as well anyway. One way or another the rebels would pay.

"Okay, that's all fine. We can get Kevin fixed, but how do we even find the rebels? Everything is destroyed," Beth said.

"Not everything." I shook my head. "I have some files at home, including their location and Derek's plan of attack."

Nick looked at me. "Even if your laptop wasn't connected to our intranet, there's a chance it's not in working condition. Derek wouldn't leave something like this up to chance."

"No," I said, "but the laptop's screen was giving me a headache. I was still weak and drowsy from the shot Ryan gave me, so I printed most of it."

"Kevin, that's against policy."

"I know, Nick, but aren't you glad I don't always follow rules? We have what we need. Let it go, man."

He shook his head. "Right. Well, let's get prepared. Andrew, get us to Kevin's apartment."

We picked up everything we needed and went back to Nick and Annie's.

THAT NIGHT, WE didn't do much. We mourned our dead. We ate. And we slept. The next day we were once again all business. No one bothered us. Even the authorities didn't have contact information for us. Heck, they didn't even know we existed. The FBI knew about us but weren't aware of our location, much less individual information. The few who knew were hypnotized and couldn't talk about us even if they wanted to.

We learned a lot from the rebels' individual files. Unfortunately, matching their pictures with their powers during a big fight might prove impossible. But that might not matter if we were all blocked. We had Gabby, who could block everyone. They had their lights. Well . . . technically, they had Gabby, too. But we also had the possibility of David and Marcus coming up with something that would help us avoid the blockers.

"I SHOULD BE the one to get him," Nick said, pulling my arm.

I fixed the hoodie over my head and put on my sunglasses. "Relax, we can't have anyone know you're not dead. Now that you're the only one with critical information, we need you hidden. If Derek is alive he might have cracked and shared that much."

He nodded. "Hurry up."

I got out of my car and left Nick in the passenger seat, fidgeting with his phone. Once in the café, I watched Pine get his coffee while talking on his phone. As soon as he hung up, I took off my sunglasses and bumped into him.

"Hey watch where you—Kevin! What are you—I thought you were dead." He looked around the café.

"Not exactly. And I'm not exactly staying out of trouble, either."

"I can see that." He gave me a faint smile. "Are we being watched?"

"I don't think so. Follow me, and get in the car," I said, shielding my eyes with the sunglasses again.

I walked out and didn't look back. I slid into the driver's seat and few seconds later, I heard Pine get into the back seat. I drove off.

PINE HAD NOT been hypnotized further, as he'd done everything they asked of him. Nick double-checked and confirmed it was true. Pine wanted to make sure he had his full control, so he'd just complied with all requests.

"I had to rule it as a gas leak explosion. We were able to identify some of the bodies, but I was shocked when none of your names came up." Pine looked at us. "We just figured you were part of the unidentified group of bodies."

"We?" Nick asked.

"Lobo and me," Pine answered.

I frowned. "Hey, isn't he in on the deal with Oats?"

"I don't think so. He questioned Oats on his plans. Him and Derek—hey, Derek doesn't seem himself, by the way."

Jenny jumped out of her seat. "He's alive?"

"Yes, but he's not himself. He's in really bad shape, and Lobo noticed, so he questioned Oats on all the new changes. Oats brushed him off . . . so now Lobo and I are trying to investigate what he's up to."

"Did you fill him in?" Nick asked.

"Yes." Pine nodded. "I felt I could trust him. He said he vaguely remembers getting to the restaurant that day, but is aware he signed over all contracts with the Org over to Oats. He just couldn't explain why he'd do that since it was his and my job to handle Luminaries."

"Did he confront Oats?" I asked.

"No. We're playing it out for now. He was looking into finding out who Derek's contact was at the CIA, but hasn't found anything. He thought we'd get some outside help, but everything you Luminaries do is classified."

Nick nodded. "I'm not sure who that was, either. I

think Derek cut off all communications after his father died. He felt it was safer to work with one agency alone."

"I was afraid of that," Pine said. "We'll just have to bust Oats and fix this issue internally. We don't need a big mess on our hands. Too much commotion and you're all going to be in danger."

"I agree," Nick said.

"So what's your plan and how can I help?" Pine asked.

THE TRAINING CENTER had become our new Org location. Our group was very small now, so a big space was not needed. We used an empty classroom and kept our plans there.

We didn't share any of the happenings with everyone. Only the training instructors and scientists were aware of the horrible hit we'd taken, but the young trainees were kept uninvolved. The rest of the surviving Luminaries who hadn't been at the Org that day were told to stay in hiding for a few more weeks. Even when we planned to attack, they were to stay back.

In case we all died, we needed them to watch over the young Luminaries and protect them. We needed the rebels to think they'd won.

All legal and financial paperwork had been taken care of. Derek had Jenny, Nick and Annie as owners, and they were leaving their own set of backups. Not that Jenny was actively involved in any of the planning. She was still not talking to anyone. She only helped with Jack and Elisa, and basically lived on the Logans' couch.

Two days later I was told they were ready to begin experiments. I was instructed not to eat or drink anything past nine p.m. so I was a bit dehydrated and, frankly, quite cranky. Neither Annie nor Beth had arrived yet, but the team of scientists were hard at work. They explained that they would put me under to make it easier and that they would wake me after a few rounds of injections. Then I would be allowed to eat something and to move. At midnight—six hours after the last injection— they would test my blood to see if the experiment had made any difference.

They were aggressive. They used a highly concentrated formula, ten times the normal dose, because they felt as a former Luminary it would shock my system right back into gear. If I had absolutely no reaction, then they would try again after the attack with a prolonged and ongoing treatment—the attack, of course, being the one we were planning in a few days, on the rebels. We didn't think any of these plans had happened in the conference room, so they wouldn't have heard—plus they thought we were dead. Even so, we didn't want to take too long in case they moved.

MY EYES OPENED to Annie pacing around the room. I went to sit up but realized I was strapped down on the bed and I had a bag of IV fluids attached to my left arm. "Guys?"

"He's awake!" Annie yelped and came to my side. "Hey, handsome."

"Whhhhhattt happened?" I asked.

"We tried several times," Marcus said. "But each time we injected you with the formula you would crash. Yes, indeed. Yes." He nodded repeatedly. "When we tried dripping it slowly in with the IV, your heart failed."

I looked up at the IV bag I had now. "Is that what it's doing now?"

"I'm afraid not. You were throwing up blood, young man."

David cut in, fixing his glasses on his nose. "Your brother and sister-in-law gave the go ahead to try a few different ways of getting the formula into you, as they thought you would want that, but each time your body rejected it."

"So it didn't work . . ."

"No, it did not," David said. "You're dehydrated. Mrs. Lake here took care of your other symptoms."

I turned to see Jenny sitting in the corner. She was still giving a blank look, but the fact that she was here and that she'd healed me meant a lot.

"I still feel nauseous."

Marcus nodded. "We medicated you to sleep it off. Now that you're awake, you can be fully healed, yes,

yes." He turned to Jenny. "Go ahead, dear."

Both Jenny and Annie came to stand next to me. Jenny healed me, and David pulled out the IV tube from my arm. I felt like myself again in a matter of seconds. "So what now? We'll have to try again after we rescue Gabby and Derek?"

"Sorry, Kevin," David said. "Your body is rejecting anything Luminary. We thought Nick could donate some blood to you to speed up the process. But you had the same reaction . . . even though you're the same blood type. He's Luminary and you are not."

"Ah-ha! It would seem the formula was developed to ensure your powers never come back," Marcus said excitedly. "I must study it. Perhaps I could tweak it."

I ignored him. "No, but there has to be a way. It's part of who I am. I can't not be one of you anymore. Maybe another power?"

"No can do." Marcus, not one to be tactful, said, "On a positive note, when we get my daughter back, you two can live a normal life out of this Organization. It would be good for her, yes, yes. If her boyfriend is normal like her, then she'll be happy."

I wanted to strangle him, but instead I choked down my words and focused on my anger. "We will get her out, but I'm still working for the Org, even if it's just paperwork."

"Yes, he's not going anywhere," Annie said and looked at Marcus. "Kevin's relationship with your daughter has nothing to do with his job. Powers or not, he fights for and *with* us."

"Well, not *fight*. How can I play a hero with no powers?" I asked.

Annie held my hand. "Anyone can be a hero. They just have to have the right motivation. And the rebels have taken more than their share of what belongs to you, Kev."

"Aren't you worried he'll put all of you in danger?" Marcus asked.

"No, I'd worry if he wasn't there." Annie smiled. "But you should rest, Marcus. You've had a few rough nights yourself. We'll get your daughter back."

"Don't forget the rest of you could use my new development. It might still work since you're Luminaries," Marcus said, and walked out of the room.

"What's he talking about?" I asked Annie.

"Well, for the initial thirty minutes it seemed that you were changing back to Luminary and they took your blood. But then you crashed. While David tended to you, Marcus studied your sample and combined it with the counterblocker." Annie rolled her eyes. "Gosh, I'm talking like him now. Listen to me."

"So what happened when he combined it?"

"He thinks with your active genes and the blocker combined, it might keep us protected against both the powers and the paralyzing lights. He said based on the information on Madelyn's notes, it only works with the Luminary genes, which . . . you no longer have . . . umm, he thinks once he blocks the blocker, neither should work."

"So you'll be protected against both lights?"

"Yes." She nodded. "And I know this sounds wrong, but your experiment wasn't a waste after all."

I felt gloomy. It wouldn't affect me either way. I was no longer one of them so I had nothing to say.

"I got you a slice of pizza if you're hungry," Chris said from behind Annie, attempting to change the topic.

"Yes, thanks." I looked at my friends. They surrounded me and stood by me; I needed them. "Where is Nick?"

"He's with Andrew, staking out the house. Beth is home with Elisa and Jack," Annie said. "I'll call him if you want to talk to him. I already filled him in. He wanted to be here, but we switched. I've been boosting you back up, so it was important for me to be here, but I realize you probably need your brother more right now. Hang on—"

"No, it's okay, Annie. I just wanted to know where he was," I said, biting into my pizza.

"I'm so sorry, Kevin. Everything that happened and now no hope—I can't even imagine."

"Don't worry about it. I'll be fine. You taught me to fight, and I'll do you proud. I just have to run up the miles on my car now, that's all."

"Speaking of, I'll drive you home," Chris said.

"Sounds good."

CHAPTER TWENTY-ONE

W E SPENT ONE more day getting everything ready. We were able to get a lot of necessary weapons from the storage unit in the training center. We always kept a decent amount of supplies there for hands-on training with our younger Luminaries. We had a large arsenal: we carried Taser guns, real guns, knives, and bad attitude. Usually we didn't use these, except for the attitude, but chances were high that the block would be on and we weren't a hundred percent sure the counterblocker would work. For us to depend solely on our abilities would put us at a huge disadvantage. It's not like there were many of us, but at least we had the element of surprise on our side.

Jenny joined the team this time. They had her husband, and for her this was war. She hadn't been on the field in a long time but she kept herself in decent shape. Heck, she'd held her own at the Org during the fight and had come out with only a few scratches.

Annie didn't want her to go. She said Jenny might be too emotionally unstable and upset, but Jenny didn't take no for an answer. She pointed out that we were all suffering and we were all pissed and specifically said I was less qualified to go than she. That stung, but I understood.

Nighttime was the best time, we decided. According to our surveillance, the regular guards were mainly off duty, so we expected to deal with mostly rebels. At two o'clock on a quiet Saturday dawn, we broke into yet another building. It made me wonder about what Blondie had said about keeping them separated. I knew we wouldn't take them all out, but I kept this to myself. Bringing down the morale before a big fight would be stupid. I had to bank on the fact we'd already compromised a few other of their locations. Pine informed us that even the club had been shut down.

The house was a large blue split-level ranch with an attached double garage connected on the right side. It faced a major avenue, but the front yard was big with lots of trees that covered any direct view to the house. It had the entrance door and the two garage doors on the front, and one door with access to the garage in the back. According to the house plan Pine got for us, it should open to the living room. The kitchen and another two rooms were on this floor and the top level had five bedrooms. However they managed their sleeping arrangement, I was sure we didn't have all the rebels here. It was a decent size, sure, but I knew there had to be at least one more location, plus some probably had their own places.

There were four guards standing outside. Two on the flat garage roof watching the back, and two on the ground by the entrance. We planned on using the back door, which currently was blocked by a truck. I watched from the binoculars as Andrew and Nick went behind the guards on the roof, guns in hand. While Andrew held one of them down, Nick worked his magic and had the guard hypnotized and working for us. He did the same to the other one and gave us the signal to follow. Chris and I snuck up on the two guards in the front; I did the same as Andrew with the guards and Chris hypnotized them.

Chris left me to go meet up with Pine across the street and I went to the back to meet the rest. Annie used her insane strength and lifted the truck to slowly place it down a few feet from its original location—enough for us to walk through and get in from the back. The door was locked, but Nick used his beam and melted the knob off. We went in silently and took out two other guards who were standing there.

The garage opened up onto the living room with a couple step-ups; the light was on and shining brightly. We avoided that light and stayed close to the walls. There was no décor to worry about, as it was fairly scarce. Some scattered stools and that was it.

From what Jenny could sense, Gabby and Derek were being kept in the basement on the northeast side. We made our way in that direction but stayed together.

We wanted them secured by our side before we attacked the rest. We already had four of their own men hypnotized and on our side, so when the time came, they would fight with us.

We found no one on our way, which wasn't that strange since most of them should have been asleep by now. There was no door to the basement; just a set of stairs that led down. Beth did her cheetah thing and jumped down, landing as silently as a pin dropping. She crouched and motioned us to follow. The light was dim there and we saw no cameras anywhere, so we moved forward again. A few spots on the left were filled with boxes. There was more space in the basement than there should have been. I assumed they did their own alterations to make it this roomy.

The plan was to stick together. So we walked past the boxes and saw a couple beds on the back wall. Gabby and Derek were sleeping in them. As soon as we got close to them, the alarm went off and two gates fell from the ceiling. boxing us in the corner.

Gabby ran into my arms. "Baby, are you okay?" I asked.

"I'm fine. But now they have all of you, Kevin. I wish you hadn't come."

"We couldn't leave you here," Annie said. "And we have unfinished business with these murderers."

Jenny and Derek were hugging when we heard footsteps from the stairs.

Ryan's mother walked in and her eyes widened when

she saw us. "I shouldn't be surprised you survived. You're the best of the Org, after all."

A few other rebels followed her and stood by her side as she made a phone call. "You'll want to see this." She took a picture with her phone and I assumed sent it to whomever she was talking to. "Yes, they're not going anywhere."

She hung up and went back upstairs, leaving the other rebels to watch over us. I kept my eyes on the guard, but I paid attention to what Derek was saying behind me. He was whispering, so I didn't catch everything.

"So you pulled from Gabby, thank God," Jenny said to him.

"Yes," he said. "They had a healer in the van who helped me. When I woke up, I saw Gabby asleep so I pulled some of her blocking. They haven't been able to hypnotize me. I was worried I would give in soon though, with this new lighting."

"They kept trying?" Jenny asked him.

"Not really. I made them believe I was being controlled when they had me meet with Oats and Lobo once. I fed everyone false information when they questioned me the first few days. But it was only a matter of time before they tried for more."

While Nick filled him in on what had happened on our end, I talked to Gabby. She assured me they hadn't done anything to her except take her blood daily. She looked okay. The dark roots were growing out and the blonde hair looked almost white under the lighting. It washed out her gray eyes. Other than that, she looked rested.

Approximately twenty minutes later, Chris said in our earpiece, "There's a lot of rebels coming your way. Are you sure you don't want me in there?"

"No, stay in position," Nick answered.

Right then, the man with the mustard stain, Michael's brother, walked in, and said, "How nice of you to join us."

"You again." I felt my anger rise. "I should've killed you when I had the chance."

"I'd invite you to teleport out of the bars, my friend, but by now you're aware of what our special lighting can do." He gave me a smug look.

We were positive they didn't know about Ryan taking my powers away, so I ignored his question. Ryan must have meddled with the formulas when no one was around. It was a good thing she loved learning about it, even if she hadn't pursued it further. Two other men walked in with Ryan's mother. Oats and Michael.

I turned to Gabby and whispered, "Remember what we told you?" She nodded in response. "Good. Wait for Annie's signal." I really prayed their shots to block the blocker worked.

It did.

Annie jumped and gave the gate one of her super kicks. It snapped off the ceiling and went flying in the rebels' direction. She took a couple of them out with it.

"How? Uh—" Ryan's mother looked scared.

"You didn't think we'd come unprepared, did you? Your lights can no longer affect us," Annie said, while rebels came running down the stairs.

Annie went to punch Ryan's mom, but she was knocked over the head by one of the other guys. I tried pulling Gabby with me so we could stick together, but a girl came from behind me and tried to strangle me with a rope. Gabby was pulled back by her hair at the same time and I lost track of her. I knew she'd fight, so I didn't worry. I tried to pull the rope off my neck but this girl was strong. Out of the corner of my eyes I saw the guys in suits were running toward the stairs.

I leaned forward and then swung my head back. I hit the girl in her face and got out of the hold. Her hands were stained from the blood gushing from her nose. I took one more swing and punched her. She was out.

I noticed the gang holding their own, even though the rebel-to-Luminary ratio was about seven to one. They'd sure come back prepared. But we had the upper hand since my guys could use their powers under the industrial lights, while the rebels were blocked. So was Gabby, actually, since she hadn't received the counterblock shot.

I caught up with the three men before they got to the stairs. There was so much commotion and they were clearly not trying to fight. I used the Taser on Oats and Michael's brother, but Michael ran up the stairs.

I was about to follow him when I heard Ryan's

mother scream, "Turn the lights off. We need our powers!"

That was exactly what I needed them to do. I let Michael go and yelled into the earpiece for Pine and Chris to get him.

I then went after Gabby and helped her get rid of the guy she was fighting. He'd manage to pin her to the wall when I gave him a roundhouse kick to his temple. She jumped over him and reached my hand. There was so much chaos, but we were able to maneuver between the fights. I recognized several of the rebels I'd fought with before. Both 'Stache-dude and Cigarette Guy were holding their own. Annie, who'd been busy knocking most of them out, turned and made her way to them. That was their end.

I continued looking around and saw two guys running to the opposite wall from where our group was busy fighting. They were closer to the stairs by where the boxes were stacked. I saw them run toward a panel on the corner. I knew we should have stuck closer to the group but that was my chance.

I pulled Gabby and we went after them. The ceiling lights stayed on, but as soon as the industrial ones were out, fireballs were flying everywhere. I dodged a few and still had Gabby at my heels. We reached the guys halfway on their way back and were about to fight them when one of them shot electrical sparks at me. It was just like the ones I killed Simon with. "Now, Gabby."

She nodded and immediately all of the powers died

down. Back to good ol'-fashioned fighting once more. "It's insulting for you to attack me with my own powers," I said to Spark Guy; never mind I didn't have it anymore. He swung and I caught a blow on my jaw. I stepped to the side, and bumped into another guy who kicked my ribs.

I leaned over, wincing. As soon as he got closer, I jumped, grabbing his head, and pulled it down into my chest next to my armpit. I reached around his head with one arm and slid my forearm under his throat. I locked my hands together, putting pressure on his neck and cut off his air supply. It was just enough to render him unconscious.

"Get the bitch! She's blocking us!" someone said. I turned to look at Gabby as I felt a sharp pain in my stomach. Spark Guy grinned when I saw what he'd done. He left me and ran toward his friend as I pulled a knife out.

I hesitated for a second too long. Between him and his partner, they slammed Gabby into the wall.

Power fighting started again.

Spark Guy's partner left to go help his buddies whose numbers were dropping, and he turned to me. He held his hands out and the crackling sparks flew out to me; he held me in place, my body combusting. I felt like I'd been thrown into a furnace made up exclusively of knives on fire. I don't know how long that went on but it was long enough for him to frown and stop. He was weak.

"You should have died by now," he said.

I couldn't even talk. I staggered to him and he tried to punch me but I launched myself at him. He moved in time and I fell to the floor. He came at me again—sparks in hand. I pulled my gun out and I shot him.

I looked over at Gabby who was trying to stand, but I couldn't help her. I went back to the panel and didn't know which switch was which. There were four total, not color coded, not numbered, nothing. The panel was enclosed in a large glass box, to be opened with a key. I turned to see that only Jenny, Nick, and Annie were left standing. I saw Beth holding a bleeding Andrew. Chris was lying on the floor. I had no idea when he'd joined us, but more rebels were running down the stairs.

I threw my body into the glass, shards sticking into me—I flipped all the switches.

They froze.

Everyone but my guys were frozen in place.

Gabby and Derek, who hadn't received the shot, were frozen as well. "Guys? A little help with her?" I said and pointed to Gabby.

Annie grabbed her and pulled her to the bottom of the stairs, where Nick had already taken Chris, and Beth was on her way with Andrew.

Jenny was closer to me, trying to lift Derek. I put pressure on my wound and went to help her. "Here, let's pull him to this wall; the light won't hit him. Go and get Annie."

I sat him right under the panel and he unfroze. It took

him a few seconds to get back to his senses. He looked at the scene in front of him and then turned to me. "Good job, Kevin. Let's get Pine. He has a large number of arrests here."

As he said that, I heard some shuffling on my left. Behind the boxes and shielded from the light, Blondie peeked out. "I don't think so," she said.

She threw her red waves at Derek. His eyes bulged and his head snapped back a couple times into the wall before I jumped and blocked him with my body. Once again I was being electrocuted. I was facing Derek and noticed he was shaking too. Shit. I didn't notice him holding me before. He tried to push me away and I tried getting his hand away from me. By the time I managed to break contact, it was too late. His eyes were lifeless.

But I was still alive?

I spun and stared at Blondie. Her shocks had a hundred thousand needles digging into my skin as my bones kept buzzing. A loud humming sound came from the walls and took over anything else that was going on. This made Blondie stop and look around. There were sparks above her from some loose wiring.

"You have killed enough of my people," I said, and watched the wire wrapped around her in a matter of seconds.

The lighting flickered in the large basement as sparks crawled up the surrounding walls. I saw Blondie's body burn as I picked up Derek's body and handed him to Annie, who was behind me, watching.

We ran back to the others.

The lighting wavered back and forth, so some of the rebels were able to move in between flickers. Nick grabbed hold of one. "Where are you going?"

"He's going kill us all. Let me go man, I can't fight you."

"You don't deserve to go," Nick said.

"Look, take me with you. I'll tell you what I know, but we gotta get outta here, man."

Nick nodded.

Andrew, though weak, had already opened the portal. Oats, Michael's brother, and the rest were inside. They waited on us.

Smoke started coming out the walls, steaming almost. I was still fuming as pieces of debris flew all around us, but I saw Ryan's mother. "Wait, Annie, let's take her, too."

Nick handed me the rebel and went to get Ryan's mother as Annie walked in the portal, carrying Derek's body. Nick caught up with us and Andrew closed the portal.

Before we could take another breath it opened and we all fell.

CHAPTER
TWENTY-TWO

I WOKE UP in a hospital.

Two nurses were talking in my room. One of them was reading my chart and the other one was fixing my blanket. ". . . so that Alexa girl? Her toes were moving. I think she's going to come out of the coma soon—oh! Mr. Pierce, you're awake."

"How long have I been here?" I managed to ask. I felt achy but couldn't really pinpoint any pain.

"You came in yesterday around five in the morning. You and your friends were in an accident. Do you remember?"

"No. Can I see them?" I asked.

"Sure, let me see if I can find your brother. He was outside somewhere," she said, and walked out.

A few minutes later Annie came in. "Kev! You're okay."

"Drugged up, but okay, yes." I tried to sit up. "What happened?"

"We got into the portal but Andrew had lost too much blood. He lost control of it and we fell out, from pretty high onto the street. I didn't know where we were; I saw a gas station and ran to them to call 9-1-1."

"Is everyone . . . how is everyone?"

"Alive," Nick said, walking into the room and closing the door. "Gabby is fine; she's with Chris. I didn't want to leave him alone. I'll switch with her in a few minutes so you can see her. Andrew got injured pretty badly with some fireballs. Beth is with him."

I flinched in discomfort. "And Jenny?"

"Jenny is . . . well, she's okay physically . . . but you'll see for yourself . . . with Derek's death, well, she's worse than before."

I nodded. "I tried saving him . . . but I killed him instead. She electrocuted Derek thr—through me."

"There was nothing you could've done," Nick said.

"What happened? Where are Oats and the others we captured?"

He looked at Annie. I noticed a long cut on her neck. Almost a match to the scar on his face. "Yeah, umm, Pine has Oats and Joseph, both facing charges for conspiracy and murder. And we have Paddie in custody back at the training center."

"Who?"

"Joseph is a thug who worked for them. A regular person, no powers. And Paddie is Ryan's mother."

"Oh." I was thoughtful for a few minutes. "What happened to Michael's brother and Michael?"

Nick and Annie looked at each other. She held my hand. "They're . . . free."

"What do you mean they're free? How's that possible?" I frowned.

"Well, we have evidence against Oats. There are money trails and other documents he was careless with. Even Joseph is cooperating and is serving as witness against Oats. But we have nothing on those two."

"So Oats is done?"

Nick nodded. "Yes. Lobo made a good case against him."

"But why couldn't they keep the brothers in custody until we gathered evidence? Joseph can be a witness against them too," I said.

"He can't. I assume Michael hypnotized everyone who worked for him. But there really is no evidence. Plus there's the matter of . . ." he turned to look at Annie.

"Just tell him," she said.

He took a deep breath. "They are the legal face of the Org now."

"What?"

"They had everything legalized and set up with Oats."

"But Oats is in jail now. They can't believe that's valid," I said, agitated.

"No, but Derek signed it over. They have him on video shaking hands with the brothers and signing all the documents."

I shook my head. "But he didn't say anything."

"There was no time," Annie said. "We can't go fighting for the Org right now. We have the training center. We need to focus on them. We'll figure something out with Pine and Lobo. They know the truth and they'll help keep our identities hidden. If not for that, I'm not sure we could have brought any of you to the hospital."

"But we're already protected," I said, frowning.

"We are to some extent, but don't forget they had that bug at the Org for months. They knew some of our full names. Nothing stops them from going after us except they think we're dead. In the meantime, Pine will be alerted if there are any searches on us in any database. At least, everything we own is under different aliases, and well hidden."

"So how are we supposed to get by? Is he giving us new legal identities though?"

"Sort of," Annie said. "We have backup bank accounts and other things in place to stay under the radar for a while. We'll figure things out as we go."

I nodded. "Hey, and what happened at the house?"

They looked at each other. Nick placed a hand on the side of my bed, and said, "Pine took care of that . . . *explosion*. He pinned it on Oats, and I may have made Oats confess to killing everyone."

I smiled. "Good. Won't they question why?"

"Sure." Nick shrugged. "He hated Luminaries. It's all going to stay hush anyway. He now has two massive murder explosions under his belt. We have to wait a while before Pine can fill us in. There is a lot going on in his department at the moment."

Annie looked at me. "But that was fitting, right? We killed their people the same way they killed ours?"

"What are you talking about? That bitch sparked the house with her electric waves."

Her eyes widened. "Umm, that was *you*."

"How could it be? I don't have my—" I tried teleporting. Nothing. "Nope, I don't have my powers."

Annie smiled. "Marcus believes between the experiments you went through right before we attacked the rebels, and all the electric shocks you received, that your powers were given a jump start. He said it might take time, but you do have a slight trace of it again."

I sat up. "He tested me?"

"Yes."

I felt hopeful. Finally a little light at the end of the tunnel. "When am I getting out of here?"

"Probably tomorrow. Let me get back to Chris and Jenny," Nick said. "I'll send in Gabby."

"No, wait! Not right now. Tell Gabby I'll see her tomorrow." Nick nodded in response and I turned to Annie. "What's going on with Jenny?"

"She's more determined than ever to keep our work going. Nick and I, we thought it better to let it go and free ourselves from the government, but Jenny is also in charge and unless she agrees with us, we can't close it down."

"Well, I agree with her. You can't close it down.

What would happen to all the young Luminaries out there? To us?"

"I thought we would still help them. Give them an education with the money from the insurance . . . I mean, I don't know. This all happened too fast."

"Since when do you turn your nose up on action, Ms. Kinetic?"

"I have Jack to think about now. I don't want him to grow up without his parents; you and I both know how that is. I mean, we're free now; why not take advantage?"

"WHAT? Are you out of your mind? We can't leave those brothers in charge. Who knows what they're up to? Both Luminaries and ordinaries are in danger. If we don't stop them, who will?"

"We'll talk later. You look sleepy and it's now midnight."

"I am," I admitted.

Annie gave me a kiss on my forehead and left.

THE WARMTH OF the sun felt nice on my arms as I opened my eyes. I squinted and saw Gabby pulling the blind to block the light. She noticed I was awake and came over to give me an awkward hug. I was still lying down so it was a weird position to really reach over.

"I was so worried when I saw how hurt you were."

"I'm okay, Gabby. I'm sorry I allowed the rebels to take you from the Org . . . before it blew up. I was aware of my—"

"I know. Annie filled me in. It was the smart thing to do; otherwise we would all be dead."

"But I went back for you," I said trying to smile.

"You did. I can't believe everyone is dead."

I nodded. "Yeah. And we would have been too if . . ."

"If Ryan hadn't been on our side. What she did was a big sacrifice on her part," Gabby said and stared at me. "I know it can't be easy to lose her."

I tried to ignore the knot in my throat. "She's gone. Derek is gone. Everyone else is gone. Nothing is easy."

"But Ryan was . . ." She looked away and played with her watch.

"Gabby? You know what happened when she died . . . I didn't know what else to do."

"No, I know." She sat on the bed next to me. "Kevin, I understand. I'm not upset about it. I would expect nothing else from you. It's just what she said."

"What?"

"You've never told anyone else you love them. It's true, isn't it?"

I nodded. "It's not something I throw around lightly." I held her hands. "Gabby, I'm sorry if that bothers you."

"It's . . . fine." She stared at me.

I rubbed my neck. "Really? 'Cause you are giving me that look."

"What look?"

"The one that screams 'I wanna marry you, have a

couple of pets, and have our daughters take gymnastic class.'"

"I'm not gonna force gymnastics on them unless they want to." She smiled. "No, listen. I'd rather you tell me when you mean it, anyway."

"Gabby . . ." I stared at her for a while. "There's always going to be some doubt inside me about my feelings for you."

She looked down at her hands, and whispered, "I know."

"You manipulated me. And I was okay when you explained it was for my safety. But I can't give you what you need. I know that now."

"I saw the way you held her." Tears rolled down her cheeks. "I wanted to maybe still try, but I know it—it will always haunt me."

"What will?"

"That look in *your* eyes," she said, wiping her face. "I can wait forever, but I know that day will never come when I'm on the receiving end of it."

I frowned. "I'm not sure what you mean, but this is still best for us. I'm sorry."

She smiled. "You didn't even know, did you?"

"What?"

"That you loved her."

"I—" I swallowed hard, noticing Annie by the door. "Ryan is gone."

"And I'm sorry you lost her. I'm so sorry for the role I played in your last few months together. I hope one day you'll forgive me." She squeezed my hand. No warmth this time. "Take care, Kevin."

"Where are you going?"

"To the training center with my dad."

She walked away and Annie came closer. "You really didn't know?"

I shook my head. "Did you?"

"I think we all knew," Annie said, and brushed my hair with her fingers.

"You could've told me, you know. I wish she'd known."

"She did. It was clear to everyone but you."

I frowned. I really wished they'd share my feelings with me. "How?"

"You used to kiss her on her forehead." She smiled. "And you still look confused. The only people you do that to is Jack, Ryan, me, and even Nick once."

I shook my head. "No, I didn't."

"Five years ago, when you thought he was dead. While Derek healed him, you kissed his forehead and said 'I love you.' Since then it's been your way of saying it."

"Oh, come on." I sat up. "I've never said that."

"But we know. Plus, you were always lazy except for when it came to Ryan."

"What is that supposed to mean?" I asked, frowning.

"Whenever you wanted to do something for anyone, you'd get help. You'd hire people. You'd even get her help. But not for Ryan. For her, you'd buy things, make things yourself—like design a shoe closet. You'd even get up extra early to make her happy. We all knew how much you hated leaving your bed so early on Sundays."

"I really did." I nodded.

"You did everything for her."

"Not these past months, though. I was such a jerk."

"Gabby had a hand in that. Look at me, Kevin." She placed both hands on each side of my face. "She knew you loved her. Maybe not romantically, but she knew you cared. Now mourn guilt-free or she'll come and haunt you. You know it's what she'd want."

"I miss her so much."

Annie held me for a while. And we cried together. We cried because there was so much loss. There were so many depending on us now, and we needed strength for them.

She cried for fear of the future for her son. I cried for Ryan.

CHAPTER TWENTY-THREE

I LOOKED AROUND the cemetery. Saying good-bye to Derek and the rest of our friends made everything real. Chris was badly injured and was in a wheelchair, but that wouldn't last long. He just didn't want to miss the service. Beth's arm was in a cast, and Annie sported a long scar on her neck. I now called her and Nick 'the scarred couple.'

Gabby and I were okay. We weren't sure if we would make great friends, but we got along. No one dared to ask Jenny for healing, for she was worse off than the rest of us. She'd shut herself off at the death of her husband. She channeled that anger and was determined more than ever to bring down the brothers. We had no idea who they were. Like us, their identities had been protected. I didn't know what was happening with my powers. I hadn't experienced anything else with the electricity pull and hadn't been able to teleport. Marcus insisted I'd been fully restored, based on my blood work.

But I felt nothing.

WE STOOD THERE, staring at the spot where Derek had just been buried. I missed him; we all did. The priest had said we now had a place to visit and talk to him. I'd like to think he was looking down on us and offering his wise opinion from above. Yeah, I'd like to think that. I'm pretty sure he would give us signs if he could.

I also hoped that Ryan was looking down on me. I missed her most of all. Deep down I didn't want my powers anymore, to honor her in a way. It represented the emptiness I felt without her. Now that I didn't have to concentrate on a mission, or on getting my powers back, the feeling of devastation overpowered me. I was crushed. I needed her back and there was nothing I could do to right my wrongs. Her body had been taken care of by the rebels, so there was not even a headstone where I could sit and talk to her. Or bring her a picnic basket and eat both our shares of Gray's Papaya goodies.

I wished so many things. None of which would ever come true.

If only I'd been brave enough to look into my heart earlier . . . if only she'd been able to see herself through my eyes at least once . . . if only I could bring her back . . . if only I could hold her . . . if only . . .

I blew it. My real chance at love. I'd lost my sweet Ryan. But she'd be proud because I finally understood love. I finally understood what it was to see your soul in

another person's eyes. All I had to do was close mine and
see hers . . . because my soul was as lifeless as she was.

I SIGHED AND wrapped Jenny up in my arms.

Nick had gotten a lot of information from Paddie,
Ryan's mom. Paddie . . . I'd never even thought to ask
Ryan what her mom's name was. I was a bad friend.

There was yet another layer of rebels. Paddie's
bosses, whose names she'd never known, had their own
agenda with the Org. We did manage to ruin a big part of
their plans by taking Oats out of the equation. But
according to Pine, they didn't know we were alive. They
assumed we'd died a second time so they were carrying
on with their new group of Luminaries.

This gave us the upper hand for now.

Annie came and stood next to me. "Nick and I are in.
We won't let them get away with this."

"Good," I said.

"I can't wait to destroy the rebels."

I thought about it. "Actually you wouldn't want to do
that."

She frowned. "Why wouldn't I?"

I smiled. "Because, Anniewee, *we* . . . are the new
rebels."

CHAPTER
TWENTY-FOUR

Alexa

DARKNESS.
     Light.
     Pain.

"I think Alexa kicked her coma's butt," a woman said. I could vaguely make out the words.

"You've been saying that about every coma patient." Another woman laughed.

"But she's looking at us."

The second woman's head spun and they both stared at me. "We have to let them know."

I winced in pain. Where was I?

A man wearing a white coat came into the room. "Hello, Alexa. Do you know where you are?"

I tried to shake my head, but the whole room spun.

"You're in the hospital, dear."

"What happened?" I asked.

"We were hoping you could tell us. What's the last thing you remember?"

I stared at the ceiling, trying to think. "I don't know."

He came closer and listened to my heart, checked my eyes and blood pressure. He wrote something on his chart, put his pen in his pocket, and placed his hand on my shoulder. "You had some severe injuries when you came in. We're not sure what happened to you, but your blood tests have all been . . . interestingly inconclusive. Is there anyone we can call? Any family members?"

I looked at my hands. "I don't know."

"It's okay, Alexa. You can rest for now. We'll figure everything out later."

"Is that my name?"

He pulled his pen out again. "Don't you remember who you are?"

"No."

He wrote something down, then said, "I was hoping you were just disoriented, but it looks like amnesia. Now, look at me." I did. "We'll help you. For now, just think about your name. Maybe something will come back to you."

"Alexa," I said, trying to connect it to my brain. Nothing.

"Yes. You were dropped off at the hospital with a note. It said your name was—let me get it."

He opened the top drawer to my right and pulled out a piece of paper from a black knit cap. He placed it in my hand and walked out of the room.

I unfolded the piece of paper and whispered, "Alexa . . . *Ryan.*"

⬐THE LUMINARY
⬐ORGANIZATION

THIS AGREEMENT is made and entered into as of 09/01/2010 by and between THE LUMINARY ORGANIZATION (the "Disclosing Party" or "The Org") and Alexa Ryan (the "Recipient" or "Receiving Party").

The Recipient hereto desires and agrees to be an employee (a "Luminary Agent") of the Disclosing Party in connection with this Luminary Agreement. Both Parties hereto agree as follows:

Acknowledgement

The Receiving Party herein understands that he/she **has been genetically altered**, while in womb. **These alterations to his/her DNA have consequently gifted him/her with supernatural powers.** The Receiving Party acknowledges that the specific power he/she may display is yet to be determined. He/she agrees to work closely with The Org to help control, study, and develop these powers.

The Receiving Party herein understands that he/she **will be hypnotized in order to keep all confidential**

information protected. He/she will not be able to disclose to a non-Luminary information about his/her powers, or the location of The Org. The Receiving Party acknowledges he/she still has free will, and this action is to ensure the safety of all Luminaries alike.

Obligation

The Receiving Party herein agrees to **make use of these powers solely for the purpose of serving and protecting innocents.** Any deviation—including joining the rebellion group—will deem the Receiving Party a traitor, both to The Org and the United States of America. If determined to be a traitor, he/she will be treated as a national enemy.

Confidential Information

For all intents and purposes of this Agreement, "Confidential Information" shall mean and include any data or information that is deemed proprietary to the Disclosing Party. **All knowledge or information, including the Receiving Party's personal powers, are considered trade secrets.**

Remedial Action

If the Receiving Party is found to be a traitor or decides to terminate this Agreement with The Org,

he/she will be stripped of his/her memories. The amount of memory modification will be determined by The Luminary Organization. If the Receiving Party has been found to be involved in criminal activities, he/she will accordingly be punished under the laws of the United States of America.

Paragraph headings used in this Agreement are for reference only and shall not be used or relied upon in the interpretation of this Agreement.

IN WITNESS WHEREOF, the Parties hereto have executed this Agreement as of the date first written above.

By:

Derek Lake
President of The Luminary Organization

By:

Alexa Ryan
Luminary Agent

ACKNOWLEDGMENTS

IF YOU ARE me (and I am) you wouldn't pass on the opportunity to thank all the amazing people who've offered immense support in your journey to fulfilling your dreams. So here I am humbly saying thank you. Without you this book wouldn't be what it is. So if it sucks, then I also blame you.

To Natalia and Noah, I love you guys to pieces. Even though chances are high I would have finished writing this sooner without your sweet (and constant) interruptions, I wouldn't trade those moments for the world. Life would simply be too boring. Your hugs and kisses always make my days brighter and for that, I thank you.

To Jeff, your relentless support of this crazy dream—even when you're not sure if your wife's still around—keeps me motivated. For hanging in there and always believing in me and in everything I do; for making this possible along with so many other wonderful and incredible things that make up our love, thank you.

To my parents, you've taught me to fight for my dreams, so here I am. Look closely and you'll find yourselves in the book. You made me so I "made" you right back with my magic powers. You're welcome . . . and thank you.

To *Lynda, Lynda, bo-bynda banana-fana fo-fynda fee-fi-mo-mynda, Lynda!* (Dietz, in case you forgot your last name), I think the song says it all, really. Having a slightly strange friend who's also my rock in this journey, a natural Coffee Chatter, and a magnificent backhaver is pretty much perfection. I mean, it's like *me* times two so, really, what's not to love? Thank you.

To Debra Ann Miller, your encouragement, no matter the time and distance, mean the world to me. Thank you.

To Raymond Esposito, your words of wisdom, endless support, and (most importantly) coffee lover-ism makes you a great source of inspiration. Taking advantage of your researching skills and knowledge is always fun. Thank you.

To Sarah Beta Reader, your wonderful content editing skills totally drove me crazy. In the best of ways . . . *I think*. Thank you.

To JOYce and Tim, your support in this journey and in so many other things in life makes my heart swell. You're out of this world amazing, you crazy lovebirds! Thank you.

To Brandon Ax, the insight and constant cheerleading of my critique partner is always priceless . . . never mind the times I wanted to sweetly choke you.

For that, your backhaving, and for being my friend, thank you.

Special thanks to:

Regina Wamba of Mae I Design for the beautiful cover design, and Julie Titus for the wonderful interior formatting. Also, Tammy Theriault and Cheryl Esposito for being amazing beta readers! Last but not least, thanks to Jenny, Anali, Tariq, Zaira, Danny, Amanda, John, Josh, Hannah, Laura Wells, Bee Mitchell, and Shanny Seewald—without you this book would not be possible.

ABOUT THE
AUTHOR

S. K. ANTHONY is a writer, a reader and a make-stuff-upper who lives in New York with her husband and toddler twins. She is a wine connoisseur, which just really means she knows she loves it, and a caffeine addict. When she isn't busy with her family, she finds herself being transported into the world of imagination. Well, either that or running away from spiders . . . she is convinced they are out to get her!

www.skanthony.com

24583233R00242

Made in the USA
Middletown, DE
30 September 2015